THAT'S

WHERE

YOU

WERE,

THEN

ALSO BY JUDITH POND:

An Early Day

Dance of Death

Lovers and Other Monsters

A Shape of Breath

The Signs of No

THAT'S WHERE YOU WERE, THEN

JUDITH POND

STORIES

Freehand Books gratefully acknowledges the financial support for its publishing program provided by the Canada Council for the Arts and the Alberta Media Fund, and by the Government of Canada through the Canada Book Fund.

This book is available in print and Global Certified Accessible™ EPUB formats.

Freehand Books is located in Moh'kinsstis, Calgary, Alberta, within Treaty 7 territory, and on the traditional territories of the Siksika, the Kainai, and the Piikani, as well as the Iyarhe Nakoda and Tsuut'ina nations.

FREEHAND BOOKS
freehand-books.com

Canada | Canada Council for the Arts | Conseil des Arts du Canada | Alberta Government

MIX
Paper
FSC® C100212
FSC www.fsc.org

LIBRARY AND ARCHIVES CANADA CATALOGUING IN PUBLICATION
Title: That's where you were, then : stories / Judith Pond.
Names: Pond, Judith, author
Identifiers:
Canadiana (print) 20250229633
Canadiana (ebook) 20250229722
ISBN 9781990601972 (softcover)
ISBN 9781997534020 (EPUB)
ISBN 9781997534037 (PDF)
Subjects: LCGFT: Short stories.
Classification: LCC PS8581.O46 T43 2025 | DDC C813/.54—dc23

Edited by Naomi K. Lewis
Design by Natalie Olsen
Cover image © Heritage Images/Alamy
Author photo by Gerald Mills
Printed and bound in Canada

FIRST PRINTING

FOR MY MOTHER

There is this strangeness of a life story having no shape — or more accurately, nothing but its present — until it has its ending; and then suddenly the whole trajectory is visible.

JAMES WOOD, *How Fiction Works*

CONTENTS

TUPPERWARE

Here is Jenny. She lives down the dirt road in a house full of headaches, rude noises, and resealable containers. Everywhere you look, there's Tupperware Stack 'N Serves, Tupperware Whip 'N Chills, Tupperware Spin 'N Saves. Tupperware is everywhere!

Here is Jenny's little brother, Sonny. So cute. Too bad he's fat as a toad and his tongue hangs out.

Here's Mum; she's going to have a baby. Mum's actual name is Dorie, but it should be "Worry." Always going on about chores and being poor, and how she turned around and there he was (she means Dad), gone again, and how the milkman's late, and how it's bad when children don't eat what's been put on their plate. Doesn't Dorie know Swiss chard tastes like butt? And why is she always saying, "Be sure your sins will find you out?"

Sonny is naughty enough for two brothers, with his jiggly tummy round as a striped pudding, his short thick legs, his squinty eyes and goofy ears, despite which he can figure out absolutely anything faster than you can say *leave it alone!* His stubby fingers are always into Jenny's stuff, but when she complains, all Dorie says, in her same tired old way, is, "He has to live too." Then she goes, "And after all, Sonny might not have as long to live as you do."

That old song! All about how Sonny is "special," so you're supposed to be extra patient with him. If that's true, how come Dorie isn't extra patient with him? Though Jenny sometimes secretly pities her mother where Sonny is concerned. Nothing is safe from him, no door or latch or lock is equal to him; no Tupperware, however resealable, will ever contain him. Probably the whole world won't contain him.

Still, Jenny is an optimist. She needs to be. Other little girls have Mary Janes and crinolines and Play-Doh and sidewalk chalk; they go to birthday parties, ride around in nice cars driven by flesh-and-blood fathers, and get Pop-Tarts in their school lunch. Jenny doesn't need Pop-Tarts or a nice car, and she doesn't need a smelly old flesh-and-blood pop, either; she has her Heavenly Father, whose suffering eyes look right at *her*, whose posture is perfect, and who has promised to love her forever. Also, "for we know not the day nor the hour," He could turn up pretty much any time.

Mindful of Him, who could turn up pretty much any time, Jenny wears her best pedal-pushers while digging a backyard toad hole with her favourite green teaspoon. Already the toad hole is deep enough for Jenny herself to crawl into. The hole will be home to Buster, the bullfrog she is trying to convert into a sand toad by dumping dirt on it, a trick she calls the Resurrection. Her Heavenly Father helps her in this. He helps her in all things. When He hurries up and rises from the dead, He will take her to live with Him in Glory, which is somewhere near the United States border.

Day after day as she deepens the hole, she lulls her Sonny-rumpled temper by thinking about moving to Glory, and by lecturing Buster about bread and trespasses. "For Thine is the kingdom," she advises the frog matter-of-factly, "the power and the Glory, forever and ever, amen." She gives it a gentle shove: "You got that?"

Buster moves a bit, then quits. Its eyes are clouded, exhausted, like the sky. It doesn't seem to care about Glory.

Here are Jenny's fears.

That grackles will come clawing down the kitchen chimney on winter afternoons, sooty and dazed; that small, terrible men will climb out of her dresser drawers at bedtime, and stare at her with their small, terrible eyes; that her breakfast egg will be runny; that one of these days she will want some lunch, and there won't be any.

Awfullest of all: that something bad might happen to Sonny.

Thanks to her fears, Jenny is a careful child. She avoids the kitchen on cold days, remembers at all times to keep her dresser drawers closed, and prays at bedtime for unrunny eggs. Still, she often wakes up at night clutching a small, damp clump of blankets, thinking it's Sonny, and knowing she must not put the Sunny-clump down. As always when this happens, she longs to lie back and go to sleep again – she is so tired! – but she can't put the blankets down, something terrible will happen if she puts them down. How long does she stay this way, sitting up, clutching the blankets, longing for sleep? Sometimes she wakens in the morning, still upright, her neck painfully cricked and the back of her head numb as a slab of Dorie's frozen laundry against the hard headboard, the knot of quilts still clutched in her hands.

Jenny attends church every Sunday, sometimes with Dorie, always with Sonny. Today Dorie is having one of her headaches, so Jenny and Sonny must wait nicely on the front step and not get their good clothes dirty, until old Mr. and Mrs. Button in their green Volkswagen come rattling along the road, to collect them.

Already Sonny's bored. He lolls in the doorway beside Dorie's big belly, amused and golden, his merry eyes twinkling, wide spitty mouth grinning like a trick-or-treat pumpkin, stubby fingers twitching mischief.

"Hi Jenny," he grins, then makes his favourite pig-snorting sound just before Dorie sighs, "I need to go lie down. You're a big girl now; you'll be fine."

Jenny is as mad as she can be. "But he's so bad when you're not with him. He keeps me from talking to my Heavenly Father!"

"You and your Heavenly Father." Dorie touches Sonny's wicked white-blonde curls. "He'll be all right, just let 'im know who's boss." She glances back at the kitchen clock. "They'll be along any minute."

Jenny scowls. "Going outdoors."

"Don't you dirty those nice clean . . ." Dorie's voice trails behind her.

"Headaches, headaches," hums Jenny, running back to the toad hole to give the doomed frog an extra dose of sand. "Around here, everybody's always got some headaches!"

Taking dumb Sonny to church: now, *there's* a headache!

Jenny considers the frog's dim eyes and gummy skin, pats it almost fondly with the backside of her spoon, then shoves it quick down the hole. "See you later, alligator."

From the house, Dorie hollers, "They're here, the Buttons are here!"

Jenny gives Sonny a brisk twist of his squishy starfish hand. "You better be a good boy," she warns him. "Are you going to be a good boy at church today?"

"Yunh," grins Sonny. Then he does that thing where he flops back his head, and giggles at the upside-down sky.

Here is the church, here is the steeple, open the doors and see the real people, the comfortable farmers and the high-school teachers and the well-dressed mothers whose good little girls come to church in dainty white gloves, and get walked to their pews by dads who drive them in nice, perfect cars.

Jenny and Sonny follow old Mr. and Mrs. Button through the church's tall, varnished doors, past the high-school teachers and the upholstered mothers with their mannerly daughters who sit white-gloved in obedient rows, still as pearls. It's a hot July morning with flies buzzing and lilies expiring under panes of stained light. In her winter jumper, her dark hair porridge-bowl barbered, Jenny feels cross as an owl. But she maintains an expression of intense concentration, worn to remind the farmers and the teachers and the pearl-still daughters that she was born into the wrong family; that really, she is just the same as they are — and for all anyone knows, she could even be better.

To demonstrate this, she stands very straight and holds her chin high as she follows Mr. and Mrs. Button up the aisle toward the crucified Christ. But as she feared he might be, Sonny is dawdling. "Hurry it up!" she sideways hisses to her brother, who as usual has his own ideas about how to get where he's going.

"Love you," he retorts loudly and pleasantly. "Love *you*."

"Shh!"

"Jenny love Sonny?"

Sweat starts to tickle Jenny's scalp, to mist her upper lip.

"Jenny love Sonny," he sings not quite under his breath, "Jen-*nee* love Sun-*nee!*" His squishy fingers drum cheerfully on his striped chest, wave magnanimously at the silent congregation, the tall, handsome minister in his black vest.

Here comes the choir, hymning its way up the aisle. "All people that on earth do dwell," sigh the dry old ladies and the thin old men, shuffling and sniffling toward the altar as the two settle in, Sonny smiling and swinging his short legs briskly in front of him, Jenny doing her best to appear not to know him.

Here is the palely handsome minister with his lily-white hands, telling all about the miracle of the resurrection. "Christ was dead. Christ is risen. Christ will come again."

Christ sure better come again. Jenny is fervent in this. Kneeling before her bed at night, reciting her prayers, she sees Him descending on His pink cloud, purple robes swirling around His wounded feet, His beautiful sad face tilted downward as He scans planet earth in search of her, Jenny, His beloved. Jenny knows neither the day nor the hour, but she's pretty darn sure it is only a matter of time before her Heavenly Father comes like a thief in the night. When He finally shows up, Jenny's going to have a mansion in that bright land just over the hilltop, where there won't be Tupperware, or a messy kitchen down a dirt road, or a Sonny making pig sounds.

"O Lord of all our needs and wants," intones the choir as Sonny gets busy with his pants.

"What are you *doing?*" Jenny hisses through clenched jaws.

"Haf' go pee." A twinkle in his canny eyes.

"Shh! You can wait till Sunday school!"

"Haf' pee *now!*" An snort followed by a loud giggle.

“Soon,” Jenny whispers wretchedly, “after communion.” Beyond the church’s open vestry door, a cicada razors the hot air, and she can feel more sweat pooling under her Peter Pan collar.

“Pee *now*,” announces Sonny with more volume and an authoritative, head-nodding look around the room. For emphasis he gives the pew in front of them a smart rap with his plump knuckles, startling old Mrs. Brown so that the sunken cords in the back of her neck flush pink and stand out reproachfully under her wig.

“Pee *pee!*” Sonny chortles.

Jenny turns white as the lilies, still as the dried flies on the windowsills.

“Love you Jen-*nee*,” sing-songs Sonny pleasantly, the twinkle in his eye blossoming into an affable grin, which is further embellished by an astonishingly quick full-length appearance and retraction of his long spitty tongue. “Love *you*,” he crows with another business-like rap on the back of poor Mrs. Brown’s pew.

What can Jenny do? “Love you too,” she whispers miserably, “Jenny-loves-you-too.”

Oh, but she hates him, right in church, at the wounded feet of the crucified Christ, she hate, hate, hates him.

Though, in their own special way, they do love each other, these two. Sometimes they will play for hours in Jenny’s room at bedtime, Jenny arranging Sonny’s golden hair, straightening his trousers, smoothing his dribbled-on collars. She even gives him lessons in manners. “Stand up straight. Tuck in your tongue. Put it *in!* Got it?” Surely if she pats and sorts and smartens him enough, she will convert him into a good boy, make him, finally, calm and contained, fit to be taken out and seen. Then she'll be greeted the way the other children are received when they enter the church or the playground. Won't she be welcomed and exclaimed over, then. Maybe she'll even get a friend!

And there's another nighttime game Jenny and Sonny play, after Dorie's weary footsteps have creaked down the stairs, after the story and the chores, the brushing of teeth and the saying of prayers.

The game is that Jenny is in her bed all alone, hiding from the "wee folk," the terrible little men who live in her bottom drawer. Then, suddenly, Sonny is there! He shimmers in her door like her Heavenly Father, the remains of the evening light still caught in his fine, bright hair. Jenny says nothing. She doesn't have to say anything. Her eyes welcome Sonny as though seeing him for the very first time, as though he had never done a fart in church or stolen her crayons, as though he had not been born funny. At these special times, Sonny is her dear creature, her small golden man! Seeing him there in her door, she is filled with languid welcome. Come, her eyes say to him, and Sonny comes to her. When she touches him, it is with hands of forgiveness and healing, hands filled with radiance, with knowledge and with light. Jenny touches, Jenny strokes, Jenny kisses until the spirit fills them both, the two of them breathing in unison, moving in unison, as silently they witness the rising of his wondrous stem, the slow opening of its delicate petals, the miraculous presence of its dewy purple bloom. This is their secret, and theirs alone: the nightly miracle of the resurrection.

And no one is ever going to know.

Jenny is especially fond of communion. While other children look forward to being released for Sunday school, to colouring and cutting, to singing "God Sees the Little Sparrow Fall," Jenny longs to kneel at the burnished rail, to feel God's blood wash away her crossness and her worry, to look up and see her Heavenly Father, who loves her forever, and who will come again in Glory.

"The gifts of God for the people of God," murmurs the minister, his lily-like hands raising the dry host. This is the sign for the comfortable farmers and the white-gloved daughters to make their way to the altar, to renounce their omission and commission, to partake of the body and blood of the Lamb.

Row by pew the aisles drain, the supplicants in their summer polka dots and whitened shoes moving docilely toward the altar.

"This is my body . . ."

Jenny looks beside, behind. Where is Sonny?

". . . broken for you."

How did he get away? Instead of standing beside her like a good little boy, Sonny is hellbent for the font, dimpled arms smartly swinging, short legs nimble and quick as a nursery-rhyme Jack, round golden face dappled by an inward smile, as though enjoying a private joke.

Jenny looks up at her Heavenly Father, who is draped, as usual, over His useless cross, hands cruelly nailed, divine eyes closed. "Help," she breathes. "Dear God, make him stop."

But God is dead, and Sonny's just getting started. Quick as a wink, he's in the chancel. Cruising past the astounded choir, he knocks briskly on a pulpit here, salutes a pillar there, just to make sure everyone's awake and ready for his next trick.

Jenny feels sick.

"Jen-nee," calls Sonny softly from his new position behind

the rail where the shocked communicants kneel. "Oh Jen-nee, Jenny-come-see, come see Sonny's pee pee!"

And there it is in his fat little hand, the familiar stem with its terrible bloom. "Jenny come play with Sonny's nice pee pee! Jenny see it? Hee!"

Sonny with all the light gone out of him. In her mind, Jenny sees this. Sees him stopped and stilled, never to be resurrected. "Heavenly Father, wake up please," she prays as a sidesman grabs her bare-bummed brother from behind, hefts him under one arm, and carts him out the chancel door. "Wake up and make it be over."

But Heavenly Father must be all tired out from getting crucified; under His crown of thorns, He bleeds on, dead as a mackerel.

Here is the house down the dirt road. Here are the hollow cement-block steps, the pocked and dented aluminum door, the world-without-end Tupperware. But—Jenny peers into the dim interior—where is their mother? She is where mothers go in the afternoon, off to lie down with her headache, upstairs, over to the neighbour's for tea and squares, out to the corner store, to buy Kraft Dinner.

Out.

No need to go in, then. Jenny starts for the backyard to check on the toad hole, that excellent container.

"Sonny come too?"

Here is Sonny.

Here is Jenny.

And here is what she does.

PUFFBALLS

1

“What in the world is that smell? What in the world . . . ?”

Every spring Dorie asks this question, always with the same half-sour, half-sorrowful expression: it’s the look she wears when anyone belches or swears — the orphaned gaze of a person who, through no fault of her own, has stumbled into the life of an inferior stranger, the stare of a reader who’s been tricked into spending her precious time studying the wrong chapter. Which in a way, she has been. How could she have guessed when she married him, that her banjo-picking husband would one day manage to get on the TV, and then decide he liked cameras and road trips and raggedy-ass bands better than his family?

“It’s Rosie,” Jenny reports, boredly pointing at her baby sister, “she pooped herself again.” Jenny pinches closed her nose. “And by the way, Sonny just ate a fly.”

Jenny has no patience with her mother’s dumb question. After all, Dorie knows as well as Jenny does that the smell comes from Van der Eckes’, and that it’s Mr. Van der Ecke burning kittens down behind the Shit Pile, his annual fireworks in acknowledgement of the season.

Dorie upends her chin in the Van der Eckes' direction. "To think we have to stand for that foolishness every year . . ."

The two families are neighbours in the happenstance way country people tend to be, the Van der Eckes' farmhouse and rickety outbuildings being located across the dirt road and up a bit from Dorie's. Though, the only neighbourliness that goes on between their households is conducted by Jenny and Anneli, who is a year older, mean as a goat, has bad breath, and according to Dorie, suffers from "seriously neglected teeth."

Jenny is allowed to play with her only "because there's no one else." Dorie has numerous reasons for her disapproval, all relating to the personal – never to the national – peculiarities of the Van der Eckes. "I'm not saying anything about them being Dutch, I'm not saying that," she might observe from her post at the kitchen window. "Those people are known for their thrift. *She'd* make soup out of the wrapper a chicken came in." It is useless to remind her that Mrs. Van der Ecke (her name is Ortrud) kills her own chickens for soup, and that they come covered, not in wrappers, but in blood-bedraggled feathers, which must be plucked.

Well then?

They swear. This is bountifully clear from the sort of talk Jenny comes home with. "She thinks she's funny, but she's snot." "Arsehole." "Ant fucker." "Nosey poker." "Bastard." "What's a bastard?"

"It's a big bird, and don't you ever let me catch you saying that around here."

"Why?"

"Because we don't talk that way in this house, that's why."

"My dad does."

"Your dad's not here."

"Why not? Why isn't my dad —"

"Did you clean the mud off your boots like I told you?"

It is true that the Van der Eckes take their swearing seriously. Every one of them — Anneli is the pampered youngest of eight — refers to the large manure heap behind the barn, for example, as the Shit Pile. Unlike Dorie, Jenny acknowledges the rotting mound as a real and dignified geographical location, to which she makes sober and copious reference at home, determined to legitimize its vile presence, its filthy function, and most of all its glorious name.

"Where were you all morning? I could've used you here to mind the little ones. Rose was into everything, and you know's well's I do, Sonny's about as helpful as a hurricane. But if I ever catch you trying to put him in that toad hole of yours again . . ."

"Over at Anneli's."

"What?"

"That's where I was."

"Doing what? Though I'm afraid to ask."

"Digging dew worms in the Shit Pile, we found a whole bunch of those great-big-huge ones that fall all over when you grab 'em, and you can see their guts right through their skin." Jenny crosses her eyes and dangles her tongue out the corner of her mouth, to show the worms' sightless writhing. An unshakeable belief of hers at this time: if she can distract Dorie with enough shocking description, she might be able to trick her into just once recognizing the Shit Pile's proper name. It is her true, secret, and deepest dream to one day hear her mother say simply, "Oh. Okay, that's where you were, then."

Worse, perhaps, than the swearing, is what Dorie refers to as *butchering the English language*, of which the Van der

Eckes have their own eloquent version, potently laced with anglicized Dutch expletives only those in the know could possibly penetrate. Jenny speaks it fluently, and with a studied nonchalance:

Where is the scissor? (The lovely lack of a concluding "s".)

I want to wear the blue trouser, not the green one. (*Trouser*, not boring old pants.)

After the stove. (Said to a dog in disgrace.)

Now comes the monkey out of the sleeve. (Noted when someone's true character is revealed.) (Her favourite.)

You smarten up, *ence* (Van der Ecke for "or else") I'll send you home. (Not her favourite.)

Far from a form of butchering, the Van der Eckian lopping of plurals and plain, literal rendering of Dutch idioms into English seems to Jenny a kind of exquisite linguistic economy, subtle, mellow, elite, and it pains her when at home she says, "Make the light out" (turn it off) or "I've got a nose full" (I'm fed up), and receives only a chore — Dorie is famous for assigning chores for moments of maternal confusion or offspring behaviour — to do in return.

The list of small but real offences committed daily by the Van der Eckes seems inexhaustible, so that scarcely a mealtime passes without some grave observation from Dorie.

"Those dogs of theirs shouldn't be allowed to run loose. They chased the milk truck clear to the end of the road today and scared poor old Mr. Holt half to death. He's getting on, you know, but they wouldn't any more tie those things up than . . . I've got a mind to call the dog catcher." (Dorie knows how to make her daughter squirm. Jenny's relationship with Anneli, an uneven power struggle in which she is on nearly all fronts the weaker, would not survive such an insult. Suppose Dorie did call the dog catcher, and Anneli found out who the culprit was?)

"I see our neighbours've bought a new car. Good-looking vehicle. Must be wonderful to have eight kids and still be able to afford a brand-new station wagon . . ."

(It isn't *brand* new, they bought it second-hand from the Dutch mechanic Mr. Van der Ecke works for, that he knew in the old country, but what's the use?)

"Wasn't that Isa I saw downtown with a boy last night? Nine o'clock on a Friday night and her sitting around on the monument with one of those Corkum boys. I'd like to know what her mother thinks about . . ."

Then there are the offences that Jenny herself, in her triumphing of life across the road, reveals:

That the neighbouring goats are allowed to run about loose, and that one was let die of constipation.

That Mr. Van der Ecke washes his head with hand soap in the kitchen sink every night before dinner and places his teeth beside his plate, so as not to wear them out.

That the Van der Eckes mash their potatoes to a gravied cream with their forks and then suck the potato-cream off said forks in loud and satisfied unison.

That they call cheese thinly sliced "toenail cheese."

That their dogs get to eat from the table, just like people.

But their main failing, and the one from which many of the others seem to spring, is the Van der Eckes' religious life. It's not that they are unchurched, exactly; every Sunday Mr. Van der Ecke sits behind the wheel of the "new" car, ponderously drawing on his cigar and waiting for Mrs. in her cotton print dress, and the children, all eight of them, to pile in behind and beside him. Dorie never ceases to marvel at the fact that Zeke, the only boy, rides in front with his father, while Mrs. Van der Ecke is relegated to the back – "What must that woman's dress look like when she gets there?" – with all those girls.

Once all are ensconced, the family drives to Centerville, to the Dutch Reformed, a church tackily built in the shape of a triangle composed of streaky pink and purple panels; that lets its members drink liquor (a tired old story still goes around that, instead of a parish hall, the "Reformed" harbours a well-stocked basement bar); that worships Calvin and Martin Luther (the Devil, in other words); and that does not encourage birth control, obviously. Excess, deep, dark, and wine-coloured is suggested by everything that outsiders, Dorie in particular, suspect about that church.

Vanity and folly are duly and regularly noted. "No, I'll never understand what they think over there, those Van der Eckes. Making all those kids keep in their best clothes all day Sunday, and then spending the whole afternoon polishing up that car the way they do. As if that article was their god!"

And as if Dorie can talk about God, when all she does is stay away with her headaches and make Jenny take Sonny to the uppity old United Church, where nobody from their family is ever going to belong.

The real grievance about the Dutch Reformed isn't discussed, even by Dorie, only hinted at, which later will seem to Jenny such a Cumming thing. The Church of the Streaky Pink and Purple Panels is "from away." Apart from the Van der Eckes, nobody in Cumming goes out of town to church. Possibly, according to Cumming wisdom, Dutch people like to drive twenty miles to get to service on a Sunday morning, or perhaps – after all, there are six churches of respectable, recognized denomination right there — nothing in Cumming is good enough?

This idea does seem to be harder for people to digest than the fact that the Van der Eckes speak an eccentric brand of English; that they plant their garden differently from everybody else (who could possibly need all that red cabbage?); that Zeke, at the age of sixteen, is already allowed to smoke, and is rumoured to be "doing it" with the goats. According to Dorie, their choice of churches sets the Van der Eckes apart from everybody else, as if they consider themselves better, when anybody can see that this is not so.

2

Jenny and Anneli ignore all the grown-up stuff about churches and cars, which only comes up, anyway, when they're hungry. Getting hungry makes them mad at each other, and getting mad makes them thoughtful of the wider issues.

"Your family's going to hell."

"At least my family goes to a real church, and my dad doesn't smell like a barn."

"How do you know how your dad smells? He isn't even around, and when he is, he smells like a still."

"What even *is* a still?"

"My dad said it's where they pickle people."

Jenny doesn't mind the idea of having a dad who's a pickle; she loves the Heinz mustard ones, so sour and crunchy. "Better a pickle than a dad with no teeth."

Practical necessity finds them playing mostly at Anneli's. Jenny's house is too small, is perched on a scabby, treeless hill, and is rendered still less appealing by her peeing, pooping baby sister and by Sonny, with his thick tongue and his devious mumbling, his tricks, and his tantrums — not to mention his heart, which, according to Dorie, is frail, and which thus absolves him of all consequences. "How would *you* like to be a poor little Mongoloid boy?"

At Anneli's they do as they please, undisturbed. What pleases Jenny is imitating Anneli, whom she worships. Why? Anneli is not pretty. Her skin is sallow and freckled, her flip-flops, hand-me-downs from her sisters, are too small, she has a temper like a nor'easter, and Dorie's right — her teeth are terrible. But Anneli is in masterful possession of something very special: total autonomy over that ramshackle farmhouse surrounded by shade-giving chestnut trees, deep lawns, and calm gardens — and stuffed to the gills with all the paraphernalia, remarkably well preserved, that has accompanied the thrifty rearing of seven older siblings.

Jenny can never get enough of Anneli's house, or understand how, with so many people coming and going all day long year after year, it can always seem so cool and quiet, so deep and mysterious. Every detail she endows with significance: the real wooden shoes (brought to Cumming all the way from Holland on a ship) with ivy growing out of them, the grandfather clock that every hour makes its stately, melancholy noise, the pot of peacock feathers standing iridescent, goat-eyed, fringed, and fantastic on the pump organ in the living room. And all those cupboards filled floor-to-ceiling with folded sweaters and cat's eye marbles, with games and puzzles (every piece accounted for), with hand-painted blocks, china dolls, tin trucks and cranes, beads in bottles, and on the living room table, the round blue-green ashtray whose lid, if you push the little button down, spins and spins, until the ashes simply disappear.

All Jenny wants out of life is to be a skinny girl with stringy blonde hair, licence to swear, terrible teeth, and outgrown flip-flops on her feet. Most of these things she can't hope ever to attain: her hair is black, her teeth white. She is not skinny. Since at home she is the oldest, her shoes and sandals tend to be purchased just for her, and therefore to fit. But she can approximate the fretful pout, as well as the Van der Eckian dialect, though *ence* (meaning: otherwise) *I'll send you home* is said by Anneli to Jenny, never the other way around.

There are rules to be obeyed. Since Anneli reigns over the spinning tops and the matchbox cars and the hula hoops and the circus sets, words are Jenny's (that's all that's left), and Anneli can only say Jenny's favourites – combine (the grain harvester, not the verb), Madagascar, Byzantine, and perpetual, with Jenny's permission. In all other areas it is understood that Jenny waits humbly for Anneli to take the initiative. If it suits Anneli, they will pound on the chilly-sounding old piano in the verandah or make little houses with the boxes and blankets under the sewing table, or read aloud to each other from a battered copy of *Greek Myths for the Young*. Or they may get out the dolls (Anneli always gets to have the one with the real teeth and hair, a velvet tongue) and saturate them with powder and maudlin affection until the need for contrast sets them smearing tent caterpillars across the back steps, throwing cabbages at the cow, or stripping naked and sprawling in the grain field, "to get a tan *there*."

Should Anneli be feeling particularly magnanimous, they might sneak upstairs into Isa's room and snoop amongst the lipsticks and perfumes, posturing rouged and smooching before the mirror, or pull the latest *Secrets of Young Brides* from its hiding place under Isa's bed and parade to the altar as though they were its be-laced and buxom heroines.

Or . . . they might go somewhere.

3

A late-summer day so flat there is barely air enough to dry the Van der Eckian laundry, so dead even the dogs won't stir from their dirt beds, so dull Anneli is starting to smile in the way Jenny dreads. The smile can mean anything from: "You're so chubby you're starting to get titties, you should ask your mom to lend you a bra, ha ha." To: "You better smarten up, ence I'll send you home."

Jenny has to think fast, not to be sent home, but thinking fast is one thing she seems to be pretty good at, and suddenly her mind shows her a picture of puffballs, a sudden and celebratory fungus that mysteriously springs up along the shrinking banks of the river at this late hour of the summer. Last year at this time — just before the start of school, when they were bored with everything, like now — Isa took them down along the riverbanks, where the water had shrunk to a trickle, the full cows lolling on the cracked mud to get cool. Puffballs were everywhere, secret and swollen, purple as organs, hiding in the short-cropped grass, where they waited to be found and stomped on, torn open, forced to release their hordes of spores. The two girls became obsessed with puffballs, with purple, with spores. Possibly this was because they did not really know what the strange growths were, whether beneficial or sinister, whether they might bite or spread contagion, be magically capable of changing the skin of children into dead crepe like their own. It was the puffballs' mystery they wanted, their secret they longed to squeeze out of them.

Puffballs might be worth a try. "Remember last summer, when Isa took us to the river?"

"What if I do?" Though a gleam of interest shows below the dull bangs.

"Why don't we get her to take us today? We're allowed to go if –"

"Hello, Isa's got a job now, remember? At a certain Zellers store? And Ma'll kill us if we go down around the river without asking her." Anneli grabs up a sprig of pineapple weed, twists its yellow head to a fruity smear between her fingers. Then she thinks some more. "I know where Zeke is, and he owes me."

Normally, Jenny prefers to avoid Zeke. He doesn't bother with her and Anneli much, but when he's bored enough, he'll hang around, order the two girls about, involve them in endless negotiations over toys and territory – with him, nothing is free – and he is forever saying, *none of your beeswax*. What do bees and wax have to do with anything? The phrase in its inanity seems less a statement than an attribute of Zeke himself, part of his attitude, his mean, unclean handling of everything.

Also, he is ugly, with his loose, sullen mouth, the deep dimple in the middle of his chin, the fuzz that is beginning to grow in and around the dimple, and the smell of oil cans and cow that, even on Sundays, clings to him. Mostly Jenny avoids looking at him, but Anneli sees advantages to keeping in his favour, she humours him. And he is good for some things, it cannot be denied. For a package of SweeTarts, he will leap onto the cow's horns and ride her the entire length of the pasture while she bellows and tries to toss him. For two packages, he'll offer caps from his gun to explode on the back steps, while a promise to show Zeke one's underpants is good for anything from a ride on the tractor to a peek at *Playboy*.

In the kingdom of Anneli, Jenny knows her place. "Okay."

4

"Can we go to the river?"

Mrs. Van der Ecke lifts her freckled hands out of her bread dough. "No'm." (She closes her lips over the "o" when she's really annoyed. Has Dorie been talking to her?)

"Aw, Ma, it's just the right time to go looking for puffballs!"

"I tol' you already, many times: If you are twelf you can go by river. You are eleven only. You stay by home ence you are in beeeeeg trobble." She pauses then, as though considering. "Or ven someone go vid you. Only ven someone go vid you."

They find Zeke in the workshop, taking apart an engine. Jenny hopes, as her eyes grow accustomed to the murk, that he hasn't discovered the pictures of naked ladies she and Anneli drew in the bottoms of the tool drawers the other day.

"Hey, Zeke?"

"Buzz off," grunts a shape in the far corner. Cigarette smoke is in the air, "I Fall to Pieces" on the tinny transistor. "Bzzz bzzz bzzz."

"Ma said we can go looking for puffballs if you take us."

"So?"

"So, can you?"

"Mind your own beeswax and get the hell outta here."

"Shit, Zeke . . ."

"Yeah," Jenny echoes weakly, "shit . . ."

Zeke looks up then, slightly smiling, but only at his sister.

And now, a rare thing to see: an answering smile, slanting back from Anneli.

5

Evening. Supper and baths over and prayers said, the grown-ups doing whatever grown-ups do when the bats begin to fret the sky. Today, Dad happening to be around, Dad and Dorie are busy fighting or making up from fighting, so there's more leverage, more leeway for Jenny, than she usually enjoys.

She slips out of bed as soon as she hears their raised voices in the backyard, and puts her shorts and top back on, no socks, she can find only one.

Down the narrow stairs and across the kitchen toward the front door, such a long way with them sitting right out there, endless. Then to the driveway and out onto the road, where Timothy grass and Queen Anne's lace are beginning to cast long shadows. Strange to be out at this hour and on the sly, it's so quiet, no sound but the swallows twittering on the telephone wires, not a soul around. Still, a promise was made, and a meet-up with Zeke down by the swamp seems a slight price to pay for an entire afternoon – Zeke unusually agreeable for some reason – spent wandering over the moonscape of the river meadows, kicking the tops off cowpies and running from horseflies, scaring each other with what-ifs about the bull, and stomping the disturbing daylights out of a bonanza of puffballs.

She lets herself through the barbed-wire fence behind Van der Eckes' workshop and heads past their garden, down to the creek, the world so different now than in the daytime. Up on the hill behind her, the grass still waves white under the pale bowl of the summer sky. But down here, night is already underway, as if all there is of it at this hour has begun to collect like water in the hollow places, the roots of trees, the deep hoofprints made by cows. Crazy shadows reach out from cattails, from pussy willows. The water, warm and cloudy in the afternoon, has gone clear, dark, deserted looking, like the windows of a haunted house in a cartoon.

Anneli and Zeke are both there, she spots them now, waist-deep in bulrushes, waiting for her. For a second she catches an odd, absent look on Anneli's face, as though she is imagining she might be somewhere else. Then Anneli shoves her finger in her nose, business as usual. But something seems amiss, some small and sensitive weight to have shifted.

"Hi there, guys." Jenny smiles uneasily, waiting as always, for Anneli to give the go-ahead.

But this time, Anneli's waiting for it too.

As Zeke nods to Anneli then moves quietly toward Jenny, she begins to sense that the plans have changed since they parted for supper. It isn't any longer, it seems, a case of Anneli and Jenny allowing Zeke to see their underpants in exchange for the afternoon trip to the river. By Anneli's slow signal back to her brother, Jenny sees that their after-supper meeting has become an opportunity, provided by Anneli, for Zeke to exercise his sixteen-year-old powers on something other than goats.

Zeke flicks his cigarette into the bulrushes. "Come 'ere."

"I better go," Jenny stammers, "My mom doesn't know I'm down here, I'll get in —"

"Wait just a minute here, I thought we had a deal."

"A deal?"

Zeke grins sideways at Anneli, who could be about to polish her shoes or catch the school bus, the way she stands, almost boredly, chewing her hair. "You got an awful short memory; don't you, li'l girl? This is how you pay me back for your puff, puff, puffballs," a wider grin, "by doing something real nice for *Zekie's* balls."

He gives his crotch a grab and then he's pulling on Jenny's shorts with one hand and working at his pants with the other, as Anneli, come back to life suddenly, claps her sweaty paws over Jenny's mouth to hold her in place, and keep her from calling attention. Jenny can feel her shorts coming down, feel her feet sinking into the cold swamp mud, can taste the greasy sweat of Anneli's palms pressed over her mouth, see cars passing by on the road high above, unreachable as rescuers on the far shore of a nightmare. He's going at her from behind, so at least she doesn't have to see his scrawny nakedness, but she can hear his grunting, feel his gyrations as he pushes himself against her panties, which he seems not to have realized are still on her, until she feels something hot and wet, hears the helpless groan, so unlike his usual bullying swagger, of Zeke's release.

He can hardly get the words out, as he shakes the blind and wilted worm of himself back into its slimy hiding place: "There, *now* you can say you done it." Though soon, a darker look pulls taut his face. "But you tell anybody about this down here, and . . ." He makes a strangling gesture, puffing out his cheeks for emphasis, crossing his eyes.

"I won't tell, Zeke. Cross my heart and hope to die."

6

The wash is in progress when she descends the stairs next morning, the kitchen floor organized into the weekly gauntlet of whites and colours. Bright squares and rectangles of sunlight tremble on the linoleum, just the same as any old day.

"My word, aren't you a sight," mutters Dorie, barely looking up from her sorting. "Take that rig off and put it in with the rest. Colours in this pile, whites over there."

Jenny looks down. She's still wearing her clothes from yesterday, sneakers and all; somehow, she cannot remember how, she must have managed to get herself home and into bed unnoticed, though not undressed.

"And take a good look around your room while you're at it — under the bed, too — and bring me down anything else dirty."

These ordinary words, heard every week, spoken the same way every week, have a strange effect on her this morning.

"What in the world's the matter now?" demands Dorie wearily, as Jenny runs back up the stairs.

7

She keeps her word not to tell, partly because there *are* no words, and partly because she knows that if Dorie ever finds out, she'll keep her home looking after Sonny and Rose for what remains of the summer.

And — for, what else is there, in Cumming, to do? — she continues to turn up over at Anneli's, careful as usual to avoid Zeke, and duly deferential with Anneli's toys and privileges, though no less tenacious with her words, even adding a few extra humdingers to the list of already banned ones. Something has formed in her during this long hot summer, some new small cube of bright ice or clearness, and what she is clear about is that, from now on when it comes to her words, even if Anneli says *ence I'll send you home*, she will not give in.

Though it isn't long after this that she begins having dreams about Mr. Van der Ecke burning kittens, to see in her sleep the flames surrounding their tiny blind faces, to hear their infant claws squeaking against the incinerator's rusted sides.

To smell that smell.

It's after this, as well, that she finds herself more tolerant of Dorie's irritable, useless question, as reassuring as the seasons, and as predictable.

PARAFFIN

Here it is, washday again, and it's Jenny's job to keep Sonny from bothering Rose the Baby. Good luck. Trying to keep Sonny from bothering Rose is about as realistic as making a plan not to grow. Though for now, Rose the Baby is safe and sound behind the stove where Jenny put her, fingering electrical cables, tasting dust.

The things a person has to do around here, to get a minute's rest!

Soiled clothes loiter over the floor's black-and-white linoleum squares, and every few minutes, more of them whoosh damply down the narrow stairs. Behind the stove, Rose the Baby sucks and whimpers.

Jenny stands meanwhile at the counter, gazing toward Anneli's house through the fly-splattered kitchen windows. To help the time to pass, she licks lime Jell-O straight out of the package as slowly as she can, testing the endurance of her tongue, savouring the powder's wicked green. What's that, though, amidst the Jell-O's cruel sparkle? A delicate slanting, a veined shining – she suspends the spoon – a wing?

A creak on the stairs. Jenny looks. There stands Dorie with Sonny by the chubby hand, as so often, possibly worried, more likely mad.

"Jenny, where's the baby?"

Now she's in for it. She waits to get yelled at — the half-empty Jell-O box clutched in her hand, Rose the Baby not around, and her mouth a telltale green — but instead Dorie holds out her jewellery box. "I guess you may as well have this stuff for dress-up, I won't be needing it." She pauses. "Just remember, though, you can't play with it anywhere else; it has to be played with here."

A crystal tear in a web of silver shimmers below the box's beaded lid. Jenny lifts out the bauble and fastens it on as Dorie quits the room. Pretty soon as usual, "Shenandoah" floats out of the living room, Dorie's voice wobbling along with the record player. "Oh, Shenandoah, I'm bound to see you, fa-a-a-a-r away, you ro-o-o-o-lling river . . . O Shenandoah, I long to hear you. Away, I'm bound away, 'cross the wide Missouri . . ."

Jenny hates when Dorie sings about the Wide Misery. It's like the clothes on the line, a damp flapping. Against the music's sorry saccharine, she craves sour again, reaches for the Jell-O box and dips in, her tongue hungry for green. Maybe this afternoon she can show off her newfound bounty to Anneli, herself a sudden queen.

She lifts the bitter crystals to her lips, looks down. A fat, dead housefly glitters in her spoon.

Now that the wash is hung, Dorie's pickling. Blood from Swiss chard mists and trickles down the wall, filming Rose the Baby's forehead so wide and pale, and settling into the horrible pulsing thing Dorie calls the "fontanel."

Dorie snatches off her hair rag. "God all fishhooks, I'm out of wax just when I need to seal my bottles." Into Jenny's hand she stuffs a bill. "Take this two dollars, and I want you to run to the Five & Ten, get me a pack of paraffin." She pokes a Cheerio into Rose the Baby's teething mouth. "And don't go over there to Van der Eckes, and bring me back the change."

But Van der Eckes' is on the way to the Five & Ten; nobody's going to be the wiser if she stops in for a minute on her way to get the paraffin.

—

Over in Holland where the Van der Eckes come from, the people are *way* better than the ones here. Anneli says so all the time, and she should know, she's one of them, even if she didn't get born there. Furthermore, everyone in Holland—and next door—is allowed to swear. The Van der Eckes don't just pee, they "shake the potatoes dry." They don't simply fart, they "cough in the pants." Anneli calls gloves "hand shoes" and she curses like a witch. Shit, fuck, arsehole, she'll yell, plus *Godverdomme*, damning things in Dutch. She's supposed to wash her mouth out with soap, but she won't. She calls the milkman a moron, the dog a cunt. She drinks the dregs out of Mr. Van der Ecke's beer bottles, she tattles and flaunts.

Her withering glare can make a table leg wince.

She claims she has an appetite for ants.

And even though she's the youngest, she never gets in trouble for what Dorie calls her "nonsense." Instead, she can have chocolate sprinkles on her bread, and she never has to brush her teeth or go to bed.

Anneli's got it made in the shade.

—

There she is now, pale gold, perfect Anneli, crouching on the cracked cement step, her trim little bum propped against an overturned apple crate. A burning smell is all around her in the air as she works at exploding strips of caps, the pale down on her arms and legs shimmering in the soft June light.

Jenny positions herself such that her new brooch can catch some of that light. "Hi, Anneli."

"You look like a who-er," Anneli observes, not looking up.

Jenny's heart beats a little faster. "I've got a whole big box of jewels," she reports proudly. "I got it today."

Anneli leans forward, her sharp chin digging into her knees. "Such a lit-tle who-er." Tenderly, she sings the words.

"I've got earrings and brooches and necklaces and –"

"A retarded brother." Anneli lets her tongue loll wetly out of her mouth.

Jenny replies, *So do you*, though not out loud. Never out loud, *ence* . . .

"Ka*boom!*" crows Anneli as three caps go off together. "Godverdomme, that was a good one!" A flash of her decaying grin. "Where'd ya get it from, then?"

"From my mom." Jenny angles her plump shoulders so that the teardrop necklace can be touched by the sun.

Anneli's thin lips curl into brackets of scorn. "By the way, your mouth's all green; how come your mouth's all green?" As if at her command, a column of ants marches up and down.

What made her think she could ever be a queen? Jenny sticks out an ungolden foot, twisting a few of the ants into oblivion.

"That's not nice," Anneli croons with gentle menace, her clever toes pressing the smooth yellow ovals she has worn into her flip-flops, her red heels extending an exquisite inch past the thongs' hollowed-out ends. "You better be careful, ence I'll send you home." The grin again. "Who-er."

A slam of the back door, and here's big sister Isa, sashaying past with a basket of fresh washing balanced on a newly womanly hip, a jam-tin of clothes pegs clamped between her sturdy teeth. She's wearing a brand-new red circle-dress with a wondrous froth of crinoline underneath.

"Out of my woad, you two," she bosses around the clothespin. "I gotta get these damners hung out before my shift."

Since turning fifteen and getting her part-time job at the Five & Ten, Isa has begun to redden her lips to set off her new dresses, her bare legs strong and white against nylon and rayon and blushing satin. With one hand she gives the clothesbasket a practised hoist to her solid waist; with the other she advances the squeaking clothesline, deftly hooking in the heavy separators, just like the married woman she intends to be. Already she has started her trousseau; all she lacks is the fiancé.

"Hi, Isa." Jenny gives a small wave, hoping the necklace will catch the older girl's attention.

Isa lets out a soft whistle. "Godverdomme, what's *that* you got on?"

Jenny smiles, happy to be seen. "It's my jewels, Isa! My mom gave me a whole big box full!" She pushes out her chest, proud as a spring robin. Then she remembers where she's supposed to be. "I have to get Dorie some stuff for her pickling."

"I'll be on this afternoon," Isa drawls importantly, using the lingo of her new job. "You know where to find me."

Jenny loves the Five & Ten, with its Chinese Checkers and Happy-Apple cookie jars, its "real-tears" babies and bendable Barbies. She loves to wander the dim aisles, studying the Cellophaned Mattel dolls, dreaming of how well she would care for a Mitzi, a Tammy, a Bridal Girl.

The door gives its usual cheerful tinkle-and-woosh as she pushes it to go in.

"Hey, there."

Is Jenny in trouble? Jenny's always in trouble. But it's only Isa in her same red dress and matching halter lounging at the counter, her plump enamelled fingers dipping into a bag of Glosette Raisins as she studies a crisp new fashion magazine. "Well," she pouts, not looking up, "wouldja look what the dog drug in and the cat wouldn't drag out."

Jenny chews her hair, tugs at her pedal-pushers. "Hi Isa, did you remember that my mom needs me to buy some wax? For the –"

"Housewares, aisle two," Isa replies with a self-important, adult-sounding grumpiness, "and it's called *paraffin*, for your information." She returns to her magazine.

Housewares: Flour sifters. Eggbeaters. Canisters, mixers. Turn the corner for aprons, oven mitts, bubble bath, flip-flops.

Flip-flops! Green, pink, blue, yellow! She digs through the sandals until she finds a suitably too-small yellow pair, grabs a pack of Bird Brand paraffin, heads to the counter.

"All set?" Isa draws her gum out into a long pink strand, lets it drop almost to the counter, tongues it languidly back.

Jenny holds out her money. "Here's for the paraffin." She shows the flip-flops. "And I'm getting these."

Isa sucks in her cheeks, looks up and sideways, rolls her eyes. "You might want to find some the right size."

"These ones," Jenny nods fast, "it's these ones I want."

"Up to you," smirks Isa, "but don't say I never told you nothing."

Jenny sprints home in the too-small flip-flops. Their narrow straps cut into her feet like wires. They are too short to flip, let alone flop.

Except for being brand new, they are just like Anneli's. All she has to do is wear them out.

When Dorie sees the flip-flops, she blows up. "Do you think I can afford to buy you shoes that don't fit?" She slams the fridge door, making Rose the Baby squeak. "You're going to march those things straight back to the store and get the money back. If your father were here . . ."

Jenny stands in the dark doorway, the afternoon light loud behind her. Stewed chard and canning bottles drip and stew everywhere, as Sonny sits pulling a seam of loose wallpaper, and Rose the Baby sniffles and gums in her little chair.

Jenny thinks that "your father" is darn smart not to be here.

"What are you standing there for?" demands Dorie. "You march yourself back and return those foolish things."

"Back again, are ya?" Isa smirks as Jenny chimes open the door of the Five & Ten for the second time this afternoon. "What happened, sun melt yer li'l wax wings?"

"I don't have any wings."

"I mean like that Icarus guy, dummy, in the book we got up home, them old stories you and Anneli read at all the time." A tired fly buzzes on the window, its wings glittering in the afternoon sun.

"I'm not allowed to keep these." Jenny thrusts the flip-flops, now unceremoniously wound in an empty Ben's Bread bag, across the counter, her chin beginning to tremble as her necklace shimmers with a moment of caught light.

A look of gentle interest crosses Isa's round face, as though she's remembering something. "Aw, now, what's wrong . . ." She slides off her stool and rustles over to the door, where she turns the blue and white sign from *Open* to *Back In 5*.

"Tell you what," she murmurs, turning to push Jenny's sweaty hair behind her ears, just like the nicest mother ever . . .

Jenny wants Isa to keep smoothing her hair and talking to her in that nice mother voice she's never heard before. She makes her eyes squeeze out a tear.

Isa takes a look out to the street, extends a dimpled hand. "You just come with me." And she leads Jenny by the hand to a door that says *Employees Only*.

"Here, baby doll," Isa smiles, patting a shelving stool, "you come sit."

"Where's your chair?"

Isa settles herself on the stool. "Right here, silly. I'm gonna sit right here with you." Now comes the monkey out of the sleeve. All in one motion, Isa draws Jenny onto her wide, soft lap, deftly removing the crystal drop and sliding it beneath her motherly haunch. "We wouldn't want you to lose it," she smiles dreamily, "now, would we. We'll put it back on before you go home."

Something about Isa's unexpected kindness makes Jenny start for real – not pretend – to cry. "My mom said Sonny might die." She rubs a drop of snot from her upper lip, remembering how she pushed her brother down the toad hole. "From his bad heart. I heard her say it to Mrs. Button on the phone, and I –"

"That's real sad," croons Isa, starting to sway Jenny back and forth just as if she was her own little baby. "Do you like that? Do you like for Isa to do that?" She kisses Jenny's nose. "But even if he does die, she's still got you and Rosie. Plus, you know, they're not meant for keeping, *them* little ones."

Isa rocks and strokes, rocks and strokes, as gradually Jenny begins to grow drowsy, her eyelids dropping low, then lower. The room shimmers with watery afternoon light off the river. In its temporary sheen, spiderwebs sway and mannequins lean, white and thin and alien as bone.

DAMAGE DEPOSITS

When Dad's around, Jenny gets to hang out in his pickin' room, which is really just the storeroom at the back of the butcher shop, where he practises his banjo. She likes how he lets her say swears and gives her Wrigley's gum right from his mouth to hers, then says she's a bad little girl, but all he really means is she's Daddy's girl, D.G. for short.

Best of all about the pickin' room: no Dorie or Rose, and no Sonny.

Right now, D.G. is perched on a stool in the banjo pickin'-and-storage room (Dad and Bill the Butcher are buds, so Dad gets to use the room for free), where Dad, a.k.a. Daddy, practises his jigs and reels. Daddy is one mean banjo man!

While Daddy's working on his picking, the comics are open in D.G.'s lap. She never gets tired of when Popeye the sailor man squeezes his spinach can and the stuff splurps out, and he gets so strong he can do anything. She's saving up to buy Daddy a can of spinach to make *him* stronger, so Dorie-Worry won't have to keep saying he never does anything, which isn't even true. Dad works so hard on his banjo!

Though, right now, he's over in the corner drawing funny pictures of naked ladies, and having another beer.

Dad makes sure not to let Dorie see his naughty pictures, so no worries there. He keeps his girls (that's what he calls his naked ladies) right here in the pickin' room where Dorie never comes, so she doesn't get to know about them; only D.G. can know, because she's the real Daddy's girl.

—

D.G. — though these days she goes by Jen — slouches with Ricky Thompson on the couch in Dorie's living room. In the semi-dark flicker of the TV, the two of them are surreptitiously groping each other, while across the room in her recliner and slipper-socks, Dorie is nodding off in front of the Lawrence Welk show. It's getting to the end of the program, and the Champagne Music Makers in their yellow voile dresses (matching three-piece canary suits and white loafers for the guys) are giving it their all in the wrap-up song. "Good night, good night," they chirp and tweet, "until we me-e-et again, adios dum-da-dum, au revoir dum-da-dum, auf wiedersehen, my friend!"

"Thank yuhm so much'm for joining us tonight-uhm," the maestro beams, beating time on his open palm with a short white baton, "it wouldn't be the same without you'm." Pleased with his mild wit, he turns to smile flirtatiously to the gals and guys and the grinning band, as Ricky's doughy paw finds its way under Jen's waistband.

Ricky is quick to cash in on Dorie's TV-induced snooze.

"Wanna get outta here?"

"Where?" Jen wonders. It's a stormy fall night, and she's not eager to get cold and wet. "Where would we go?"

"Hole-in-the-Wall, where else?"

At some point in Cumming's dim history, someone got the bright idea of creating a drop-in centre for young people. To that end, a few cans of institutional-green paint were splashed on the basement walls of the drugstore, and the back door was left unlocked. Centipedes hang out down there, and the town's tough kids are fond of kicking holes in the walls (hence the name) and scribbling graffiti about which girls will do it for free, on the peed-on beams. The place has all the ambience of the final scenes of *Carrie.*

"I don't know . . ."

"Oh come on," urges Ricky, "where'd you rather be? Sittin' here with your mother watchin' Lawrence Welk, or down't the hole, neckin' in the corner?"

Jen acknowledges that he has a point, but. Ricky's smell, a mixture of toe jam and bus terminal, combined with a subtle layer of cigarettes, unwashed jockeys, and low-grade anxiety, wafts moistly out from between his short, stubby legs as he leans forward to gauge Jen's willingness or lack thereof. When was the last time those jeans got clean? Suddenly she thinks of Lolly, Ricky's anxious, pudgy mother, with her thinning, black-dyed hair and her seven children, her sad back-road trailer. Right then and there, she decides that a Lolly life is never going to happen to her.

"Well? You comin'?" Ricky wants to know.

Saved by Lawrence Welk (show's over) and Dorie. "Jenny, say good night to your guest, it's time to turn in."

Ricky gives Jen that look of, *I knew all along you were nothing but dirt*, as he jumps to his full height of a teapot.

And he's out the door into the rain, and just the way life works out, Jen will never share a couch with Ricky Thompson again: *adios, au revoir, auf wiedersehen!*

Though eventually — word gets around — she will learn that her initials and phone number have been carved for all eternity (and a good time) into Hole-in-the-Wall's venerable beams.

Jen and David Faun the minister's son are down by the brook in the afternoon sun. This is before David's fall from the roof of the chicken house, when he still can walk and smoke and take dares — and after he calls her up using the number carved on the beam down at the drop-in centre. When Dorie asks her, "Who was that on the phone?" Jen says it's the fish man, and Dorie answers, "I hope you told him we don't need any."

Admiring his reflection in the brook, David Faun resembles an actual faun, mischievous, lean, and white of skin. The soft swell of his muscles is dusted with fine gold down, his hair is a heap of auburn silk, his freckles like sesame seeds floating in milk. Jen can't help staring at him. The bright bow of his mouth curves down with amused scorn, as his shoulders grow rosy in the afternoon sun.

The two of them call the brook the Panting River, for the way it gushes and spurts from the culvert under the road in the spring. Down here, hidden amongst the cattails and snapdragons and Dr. Pepper cans, spring has sprung.

In celebration of the season's first warmth, David's starkers, his scrawny bod speckled with blackfly bites and small nicks from the kiss of Timothy grass, his apple-shaped buns, like his shoulders, beginning to glow pink in the pale sun. Every so often he reaches down with bemused irritation and bats at a knee, scratches a blackfly-bitten foot, his willie dangling between his legs, impudent as clam spout.

"Dare you to pee in this bottle." Jen grins.

David Faun will always take a dare. Though, not for nothing; he might be a minister's kid, but he's not stupid. "Dare *you*."

"You first."

"You're chicken."

"Look who's talking."

"I will if you will."

"I will if you pay. Pay me a dollar and I will."

"I haven't got a dollar, besides, it's not even."

"What do you mean, it's not even?"

"You've all got your clothes still on. It's not even-Stephen without you taking some off too." David Faun puts on a pretend English accent. "You must remove your bloomers."

Down go the bloomers, their descent suspended by a tuft of eel grass. "Happy now?"

"Lift the skirt."

"What if a car goes by?"

The minister's son makes a dismissive sound. "I knew it, you're the one who's chicken."

The skirt is black-and-white polka dots. Jen lifts the front, so only he can see. "Okay then," she says, "now you have to pee."

"Keep your skirt up and stand with your legs apart, or no deal."

As she opens her legs, what's between them starts to feel achy and strange in a not-unpleasant way.

"Here goes." David Faun hunkers closer, shoves his willie into the bottle, and waits. A minute or so goes by.

"Ha, you can't," Jen smirks, her polka dots still raised.

Pretty soon, though, a thin stream begins to roll palely along the green glass, to pick up speed, grow wider.

Jen's eyes grow wider, too.

David Faun finishes, removes himself from the bottle, taps off the last drip, looks up. "Open 'em some more."

Jen squints through the long grass. Nobody around. No sound but the wind, the purl of the stream, a tied dog crying. She moves her legs further apart. Their eyes meet. David slides a finger between her legs and then inside, gradually beginning to slide the finger back and forth. All on their own her legs open further, and all on its own, her hand grabs his hand, pushes it deeper. She feels like laughing. A sound like laughter is bubbling up from deep inside her, shuddering, rushing, unlocking bones, the ache increasing, the quickening rhythm becoming deliciously intolerable until Jen herself is the Panting River, awake and shaken, relieved and dazed.

David Faun grins. "Didn't know I was good with my hands, did you?"

This is her first time. She doesn't even know what she's done. Though Dorie, who has been talking with the mailman, has an idea. "If I find out you've been up there in the grass with that boy again, I'll be telling your father next time he's home."

That old song.

Later, it will be winter, and Jen will be older. It will be night, the temperature dropping, a hard wind breaking branches, driving sleet. Dorie will be out at a meeting of the Women's Institute, and Jen will be wrestling with the baffling angles of Grade 10 geometry. That same night, David Faun will be holed up in the henhouse with Clemmie Russell, smoking rollies. *Dare you to walk the ridge pole. Dare you. Double-dog dare.*

When Jen learns of David Faun's fall, she will carve his initials, a D and an F, bright and arterial. Eventually the letters will scab over and turn pink, then white, a small, barely visible damage deposit.

Jen and the math teacher are sitting in two pushed-together desks in his empty homeroom. It's June; their trysts will be over soon. Except for the distant plonk-plonk and referee-whistle of intramurals, it's eerily quiet in the deserted halls. Jen adores being here with just the teacher, far from the madding crowd of daytime and of home.

Being here after school, all alone, with him – what more eloquent proof could she need, of her secret belief that she is meant for fortune, if not fame?

The teacher's tweed elbow cozies up to her cotton one, his flannel slacks making common cause with her bare leg, while between them a page of figures stares up at her with its strict inanity. Reflex, right, obtuse, straight, what do these signs mean? It hardly matters: once again, the teacher is acutely considering Jen. His name is Ralph (deliciously pronounced *Rafe*) Brooks, a.k.a. *R.B.*, initials she has blissfully doodled, bored, and scored into various and sundry surfaces, including hers). Also, he is tall, dark, and sallow, with pitted skin from chronic acne, wide pale lips, and square front teeth showing a rakish space between. Apart from the fact that his eyes are so close together, he is handsome, to her, as James Bond in *Diamonds Are Forever*, which she swooned over last year. And he can do anything: for example, he runs the Grade 11 chem lab at the same time as he teaches Jen's class math. When he's mad at them for making him interrupt the lab to come discipline Grade 10, he goes, "If you guyths make me come acroth thith hall wunth more, I'll fail every thingle one of you!"

She adores it when he talks dirty.

September was barely over when R.B., a.k.a. Rafe, determined that Jen was going to have to be kept after school, and not just once. Since then, the two of them have evolved a bit of a pattern. When the bell rings and people start sighing with relief and packing up, Jen quietly heads for the Girls'. Keeping in mind that the coast won't be clear for about half an hour, she takes her good-looking time getting there.

Who knew there were so many things you could study after school! Calm as a curator, she examines the goofy artwork on the bulletin boards in the hall, then slips inside the gym and takes in a bit of basketball (the boys her age look so dumb, so hopelessly lame), pours interestedly over the forlorn and unseasonal artefacts on the lost-and-found table. In the washroom she dawdles in front of the mirror, applying Max Factor, filing her nails, fooling with her hair. Finally, she turns to inspect her profile, sucks in her tummy the way Dorie's taught her, makes smoochy faces at the mirror.

Today, R.B. has been catching her up on the subject of planes, especially about how much he loves the horizontal one. Nuptial scenes of petal-strewn divans float through her mind, her horizontal self virginally adorned, Rafe angled to tenderly or passionately or indifferently deflower her, their love, as in James Bond, an eternal flame.

Though for the moment, the clock above the blackboard reads dinnertime.

"Lookth like it'th time to take you home." Rafe assumes a mock-sad face, his big pale lips curving downward in a tragicomic mask of grief, as Jen stares at his large hand, which is whitened with chalk dust, strewn with fine black hairs. She wants to smell it, lick it, hold it in her own and keep it warm. She can't wait to carve his initials. They'll look so sexy in a notebook, a desk, the secret crook of an arm. She wants to engrave them on her very bones.

"Parting is such sweet marrow," she intones.

Not for Jen the three-thirty mayhem of basketball and band practice, the after-school spitball-ride home on the bus; fortune-favoured Jen gets to coast past lawns and storefronts and houses and Hole-in-the-Wall in a blue-and-silver Buick Electra, the teacher's big hand resting lightly on her bare knee, said knee sending her other parts unmistakable jolts of electricity.

All too soon they are rolling into her driveway.

"Here we are . . ." The teacher executes a smooth U-ey in front of Dorie's lilac trees and affects a pout, languidly stretching his arm along the seat back behind her. "Well," he sighs, "another night when I don't get to kith a pretty girl good night . . ."

Beyond the teacher's tweed shoulder, Dorie's permed head bobs like a Hallowe'en apple in the kitchen window. It has bobbed there before when Rafe has driven Jen home, but tonight it looks different, an angry pumpkin-grinner lit from within by a hot bulb.

When Jen returns to school on Monday, she discovers that she's not in the math teacher's class anymore. And when she sees him in the halls, he pretends she's not there. Luckily, it's almost the end of the year; his retaliatory attempts to get her shunted into the vocational stream — also foiled, Jen will learn much later, by a finally-wise and furious Dorie — go nowhere. When the school doors reopen in the fall, there's a new math/chem teacher stalking the halls.

"Good riddance to bad rubbish," sighs Dorie, "that's all."

It's a hot September night, and *Sgt. Pepper's Lonely Hearts Club Band* ("it's *the* classic album for stoning"), is wobbling away on Garnet the market gardener's record player. Under Jen's bare legs Garnet's vinyl couch is slick as sin, but right now that's the least of her concerns. This is her first time being stoned.

A minute or a lifetime ago when she walked across his living-room floor, the carpet woke up and started walloping like a swinging bridge with an elephant on it, dodging and fleeing, then playfully smacking up against the shocked soles of her feet, bucking her like a straw man in a rodeo gone south, her heart, lungs, liver, and guts firmly relocated to her mouth.

No one's getting her off this couch. Not now, not ever.

This is the third time she's tried getting high with Garnet. The second time she made the mistake of saying nothing was happening, bragging it wasn't possible, Jen and her big unstoneable brain. Tonight, good ole Gar has ramped things up with *Sgt. Pepper* and supplied a water pipe of hash, a sizeable dark ball of which lolls in the bottom of the bottle like the hard day's work of an industrious dung beetle. She takes a toke, masters a retching spasm, dutifully sucks back another one.

"One more for the road," Garnet demands, "and let's make it a good one. This time we're gonna make it happen."

Like dear old Dad before him, Garnet calls himself a Jack of all trades. Though unlike Dad, who adds to this designation "master of none," gardener Gar takes pride in his magpie versatility. The income he reports to Revenue Canada comes from teaching life skills to cognitively delayed people, a job that requires him to keep business hours, wear shoes, and assume a reasonably unsardonic face. For all this official hardship he makes up with his off-the-record green thumbing, which is carried on behind his house. Whenever he's not teaching his clients, he's living his legume life, grimy, black-nailed and happy, polishing a pumpkin, praising a melon, sharing a toke or a suck with whoever has happened to wander in.

While waiting for Jen to get stoned, he disappears into his garden, returning a hundred years later with an English cucumber that should have been harvested months ago.

"What d'ya think *this* is?" he asks friend Jen after her third hard suck on the hookah. Something in her head swells, recedes, bulges again. She doesn't dare look at the fly-away floor; not only that, she's terrified the police might drive by, hear *Sgt. Pepper*, and know that people are breaking the law in here. She is so scared her heart is racing and her knees ache, so scared there is some sort of insect-buzzing in her ears.

"We should close the window," she suggests, longing for the first time in years for Dorie, juddering with fear.

Not the response gardener Gar was looking for.

"Look again," he grins, giving the vegetable wand in his hand a gentle twirl, "what does it make you think of?"

In the background, the Lonely Hearts Club band crackles away about enjoying the show and letting go.

The last thing Jen is able to do right now is let anything go.

"Okay, *who* does it look like," sings Garnet, more or less in rhythm with the record.

Jen's hands are freezing cold and simultaneously sweating, her eyes on the window, canvassing for telltale signs of cruising police. "I actually don't know," she manages to grind out between clenched teeth. She needs to do some carving, just a little cut or two, to ground herself. Even the thought of it helps with her brain's cold panic, the jackhammering of her jaw.

"Come on," croons Gar, "doesn't it look like someone (or some*thing*) familiar?"

The former cucumber looks like no one, and no *thing* with which Jen feels, or wants to be acquainted. Who can care about a cucumber — much less what it stands for — when she's been released into outer space and detached to drift untethered through black galaxies, back from which she will never find her way? Never again to lie down calmly in her own clean bed, to walk to the corner store for milk, eat Corn Flakes, inhale the smell of fresh laundry. Those things can only be done by citizens, not by the likes of Jen, who, thanks to her own bad choices, has become a little piece of space dust, weightless and lost. Meanwhile the night has turned cold, watchful, malevolently planetary. Stars whiz by without mercy; a grinning alien is seated beside her, trustworthy as a virus.

"I give up," she says, hoping that, once she fails the guessing game, the alien will be kind, and go away.

"It's your hap-*penis*," Gar grins, one hand tenderly holding up the discouraged veg, the other massaging his groin, "now do you recognize him?"

At midnight Jen is still stoned as a loon, and the fear is becoming, if anything, worse. The ache of it has spread from her knees to her own groin, and her heart is going like a washing machine, she could practically come, right now, from desperation.

"How 'bout we take a little stroll," posits Gar, who is not completely without the faculty of fellow feeling, "the walk'll do you good."

She nearly weeps at the normal, nourishing words.

The two of them walk until two a.m. through the stilled city streets, Jen taking comfort in the absence of Sergeant Pepper and in the sight of ordinary things she understands: signs, metres, parked cars, garbage cans. If these things can so calmly consort with gravity, perhaps she may one day again be subject to it, too. Standing in front of those good, earth-bound cans and signs, she makes herself a promise: if she gets through this, she will swear off chemicals and the people who go with them, forever. Perhaps there is still a chance, if there's a God and he's listening, that she will wake up tomorrow and all of this, including gardener Gar, will be over.

The walk ends at Jen's place. Her own sane little house. There in the dark, waiting for her, stand her tiny garden, her sweet gate, her white door: all of it real and whole, and still there! She wants to kneel and kiss the welcome mat, but instead she says good night, sleep tight, call you in the morning, and all that. Breathing gratitude, she locks her door and goes upstairs, carrying what is left of her Sgt. Peppered nerves.

While she's pretty sure nothing like tonight will happen again in her life, she must never forget it, either. Once safe inside, she gets out the gauze, takes a deep breath, and carves.

For about a week after getting successfully stoned, all Jen needs to do is think about The Beatles, and she is out there again, spinning in space, knees locked, ears cocked, tongue furred with existential terror. By around day six the spinning finally stops, and she calls Gar, to tell him it's over.

"Been a slice," he says.

A month or so later the phone will ring and it'll be him, calling to let her know his new girlfriend has developed genital wens, and he's just wondering . . . did the new girlfriend get the virus from him, or will he be contracting it from the new girlfriend? "Like," he wonders with hardly any shyness at all, "did you ever get 'em?"

"So far wen-free," Jen's pleased to say.

There is a pause and a moment's static roar, like the surf delivering a fresh load of pebbles to the shore.

Just like Dad used to do, she blows a slow, voluptuous Wrigley's bubble into the receiver.

Then, though she knows Garnet won't see it, she takes a bow. "Bye, now."

Jenny is sitting beside Dorie on a couch in the neighbours' living room, watching Dad on their brand-new TV, since he's the star, tonight, of *Don Messer's Jubilee*. Even though the neighbours say she's only knee-high to a grasshopper (which means practically a baby, which she isn't), she knows her dad's not really in the TV. Still, when the camera focuses on him, and those brown eyes of a bad boy beam right into hers over his fretboard, she waves frantically, and dives into the pillows to hide from the amused laughter of the grown-ups, and from the terrible onslaught of love.

Tomorrow or the next day he will be home again, still feverish from the spotlight and the dancers and the long night of partying, after. As sure as he's hungover, he will imagine he is on the cusp of a real career, that he is going to be a star! And just to seal the deal, he'll bring his Jenny a memento: a pack of Wrigley's, or a roll of nickels, or if she's lucky, a long-legged, bendable doll.

After all, she's Daddy's girl.

ACCIDENT

Here's Jenny and Rose in the back seat, arguing about who can make her treat last the longest. Jenny knows she'll win this one, because A) she's older than Rose, and B) she's smarter than her. Way back when Sonny was still here on these Sunday afternoon rides with their parents, Jenny learned that an ice cream — Rose's babyish treat of choice — disappears tons faster than a bag of chips, which, while perhaps less glamorous, can be prolonged indefinitely, plus used to torment the empty-handed loser. Watching Rose dribble and devour, Jenny takes her good-looking time. She savours. One salty orange curl, then another. Predictably soon, the silly ice cream is gone, Rose is sticky and cross, and (ha ha) Jenny is still firmly in possession of a tidy half bag of Tom Thumb's. Even when the chips are finished, she'll be able to crumple up the foil bag and see a galaxy of tiny stars twinkling inside its foil universe, and guess what. Those stars will be all hers.

In the far country of the front seat, Dorie and Dad are busy with grown-up problems, Dorie warning Dad what will happen if he gets into Uncle Archie's homebrew again this afternoon. They are on their way to Grandma Elsie's house on the North Mountain, the same as every Sunday at this time, rattling past abandoned shacks and clumped dark evergreens and wild raspberry canes that reach all the way to the dusty car windows and squeak like bats against the glass.

"I'm telling you, Reg" – since Sonny died from his bad heart, Dorie's been quicker than she used to be to let her crabbiness out – "I catch you into his damn jug again, you'll wish I hadn't."

Jenny hopes it was Sonny's bad heart that made him die, and not herself. What if she hurt his heart that time she tried to stuff him in the toad hole? . . . Or when she filled his mouth with peanut butter just to see what would happen, and for a whole long minute he couldn't remember how to breathe. Or that other time – this was the worst – when he was lying on Dorie's bed, and Jenny pushed his legs up over his head, and he pooped himself?

Should've thought of that before you decided to be so mean to your poor little brother, she scolds herself in Dorie's voice.

"Dorie, Dorie puddenan' pie," drawls Dad, gallantly unperturbed, "nags her man and makes him cry . . ."

Thanks to her need to provoke and ignore and subdue her sister, Jenny's only half-listening – but she hears the strange adult words, reminiscent of the gangster movies she's occasionally glimpsed on TV (Dorie has one now) on her way up to bed. What does Dorie mean, "you'll wish I hadn't"? Into Jenny's mind comes a jailbird version of Dad, foul smelling, striped and roaring, a sorry monster. Not so different, really, from how he is when he gets home from playing his banjo at a house party, or an evening at the Legion.

Dad goes, "Don't you worry your pretty little head about it."

"Worried's the last thing I am." Dorie darts a hard look into the layers of spruce and fir and tamarack crowding up to her side of the car. "I'm *telling* you, is what I am, and you better listen."

Cars at this time don't feature seat belts. Free of constraint, Rose and Jenny roll about in the back seat, a pair of sweaty, farting bear cubs, pawing and hissing, nipping at each other, their bear mother warning them in that special growl she uses at such times, what they had better do if they know what's good for them. Rose, as usual, becomes tearful. Also as usual, Jenny simply moves to her own side of the seat and elaborately enjoys a saved-up chip, as the car rattles over the potholed mountain roads.

She despises and fears this pilgrimage with Dorie and Dad (when he's around) and Rose (who never stops being around), and with the empty space in the middle, where Sonny used to sit, giggling and rolling his eyes, tugging his ear. Apart from the fact that Sonny's not here, it's always the same: the close-crowding trees; the triangular yellow signs that warn of Falling Rock; the dread as the road begins its improbable ascent through steep clearcuts, cruel and grammarless; how Dorie starts to darken as Dad, carefree and cavalier, snaps his gum, just to get to her. What keeps the car from losing its laughably slender purchase on the terrible road and crashing down the bank into distant water with all of them in it, dead? Jenny does. Her own praying or bargaining, or dazzling will-power, is all that is keeping the car from realizing that what it is doing is impossible and falling away from the world without so much as a sigh of regret. If she relaxes, if for one second she lets up repeating the magic syllables and crossing all her fingers and toes just the right way, the whole jig could be up: *Family of Four Found Dead at Bottom of Ravine.* Every time they make the trip, she believes they all will surely expire, and each time they survive, Jenny knows it is because of another furious exertion on her part. Reliably each week, she reaches the top of the Mountain tense and bad-tempered, the others unwitting and ungrateful around her.

At last, they crest the top. The day is cloudless, the ocean air fresh. Dusty black-eyed Susans fringe the dirt road, strayed from the front yard of the dilapidated house at the top of the hill, in front of which can be seen two cars, jumbled together like discarded chocolate bar wrappers.

Dorie gasps as they approach the eerily peaceful scene. "Oh, dear God –"

Even Dad sucks in his breath. "Get down," he barks to Rose and Jenny, "get right down on the floor the both of you."

But it's too late; Jenny has already seen. Probably Rose has, too. The crumpled hoods, the buckled doors, the still-escaping steam rising off the exposed engines. And there's more. The windshield of the worse-off car is shattered, splintered like ice around a hole that a head must have burst through; guts are everywhere, gobbed, clumped, and quivering, a blood pudding.

Not to mention the smell. Harsh and foreign, like sucking on a penny, or the stuff Dad cleans his paint brushes with.

The smell of death.

No more worries about Uncle Archie's still, or Dad's possible mischief in said still. No more back seat squabbling. No more anything.

Just Dorie's harrowed whisper. "What . . . Reg, oh dear God, what can we do?"

And Dad's quiet answer. "It's all over and it looks like they've got 'em to the house; we'd just be in the way."

As though in a dream, they glide soundlessly past the two bloodied wrecks, past the merry daisies waving in the ditch, past the house, with its horrifying contents, to Gramma Elsie's cottage, down in the harbour.

When this happened, the harbour had a number of pleasing features. A rotting wharf bleached white by the sun. A great many lobster traps, some with bits of claws and shells still in them; colourful fishing boats with names like *Fundy Girl* or *Sea Witch* or *Wave Queen* leaning over on their sides, waiting for the tide to turn and lift them; a stony shore ripe with the smell of decomposing fish, and yielding to the beachcomber bits of amethyst or quartz, or green bottle-glass rubbed as smooth and cool as jade, mysterious to look through; old shoes, their rubber soles curled up in a drunken leer; charred remains of campfires; devils' wheelbarrows, a kind of sea-bladder stranded by the tide and sun, their blackened feelers good for scaring Rose with; periwinkles to collect in a cup and cook and dig the meat out of with the dull ends of sewing needles, for snacks; gooseberries, tart and luminous, striped with seams of pale pink and growing wild everywhere, excellent for pies, better right out of your fist. And always the falls, tumbling menacingly down the sheer, never dry rockface behind Grandma Elsie's tiny house, into the harbour below.

Of course, as well, there was often the not-so-pleasing feature of Uncle Archie, parked at Gramma Elsie's with his wife Aunt Phemie and their multitude of hungry, smudgy, pale children, so many Jenny only knew two of them by name — Lucy, the youngest and therefore still cute, and Cal, who was her own age, and whose thin face looked as though it had never once in its life seen this side of a washcloth. Though they went to the same school, she acknowledged Cal only at the harbour, where there was no choice, and where none of her friends was around to notice. While the adults did whatever they did, the kids would roll around on the tire swing; trap bumblebees in Elsie's roses and see who could dare to confine them the longest; squeeze snapdragon pods to make the seeds jump out; press their noses to the screen door, demanding bread-and-molasses.

That is, Jenny would demand; Cal and the others would marvel and admire.

This was a hot day. A slow, still, airless afternoon with locusts sawing, blue bottles buzzing. Dad and Uncle Archie were as usual where they shouldn't be, and Dorie was in the house, helping Elsie scrub down the kitchen with water hauled from a neighbour's well.

Rose and Jenny, outdoors in the heat, were hungry and thirsty and starting to get cranky; they'd had enough of clunky tire swings and trapped bumblebees and nameless cousins, and so they set about getting Cal and the others, who would likely never have thought of such a thing on their own, to join them in pestering the grown-ups. At first, they were nice about it, please-please-please. Gradually, when no one gave them the time of day, they became more insistent.

"Dorie!" Jenny demanded, using her mother's first name, a reliable showstopper.

Nothing.

So, she stood on her head in front of the door.

Ditto.

Finally, she gave Rose a good hard pinch, to make her cry.

"Git in the car then."

Jenny looked up.

There stood Archie, a recently cashed welfare check in his hand, grandly offering to take all the kids to the store (there was a general store-cum-bootlegger operating out of somebody's basement about a mile away) for ice cream.

Amidst the victory-whoops of the cousins, Jenny felt an edge of something cold. The fact was, she was a little afraid of Archie, who was as wiry and scrawny and fast-moving in his falling-off pants as Aunt Phemie was bloated and slow, who had a smile made Hallowe'eny by many dark gaps, and whose red-eyed stare had about it something furtive, sideways, not quite tame.

But she wanted that ice cream.

"Giddy up." They all piled in on top of each other, the door was slammed shut with a loose rattle, and before they'd even had a chance to untangle their legs and find enough spots for everybody to squeeze into – supposing there had been such a thing as seat belts back then, there would never have been enough for all of them – the car, with a gravelly lurch and a cloud of dust you could taste, had started up the hill in the direction of the store. Pretty soon it picked up speed, more dust churning up through the floor and around the door, many small loose stones smiting the underside of the car.

Suddenly, the door bounces ajar, and out rolls Cal.

Unthinkable.

Appalling.

True.

Over and over in the dust and spitting gravel and flying stones behind the car, which keeps right on going, her shy cousin is rolling and scrabbling, being tossed and jostled as if he were nothing more than a stray scrap of newspaper. There is blood, too, plenty of it. Streaking across his legs and arms, out of his nose, down his dust-smeared face, which, as if he were asleep or watching a movie or not there at all, does not even appear to register what is happening, but has an almost private, smug, and sealed-up look, the way a dead person's has. As she watches out the back window, Cal is getting farther and farther away, becoming a small off-white and brown and red and distant bundle, moving less and less, swallowed, finally, by the roil of road dust.

Could she have seen all this? Could Jen really have seen the ghastly rolling and the blood and the curiously closed-up face of Cal? Certainly, she'd been aware of things – the odd shift in air pressure, the change in road sounds from muffled to bright, the shocking weeds and raw ditches streaming brazenly past the car's open door – and anyone could see that her cousin was no longer where he had been sitting before.

And all the kids yelling and hollering for Archie to stop! Stop! *Stop!*

He did stop, eventually. In just the same way as if he'd had to go back and retrieve any old sack or piece of possibly useful garbage that had got away, Archie eventually hit the brakes and hopped out with demonic agility, grabbed the bloodied boy, opened the door, and tossed him into the back seat amongst the rest of them without a word of surprise or interest or recognition or condemnation. Then he slouched back behind the wheel and kept right on going.

Without a word.

No particular commentary or interest or inspection, either, from the other cousins, or even from Cal himself, who simply stayed where he had landed, gazing out the window as the trees once more began to stream past, dreaming of a chance at ice cream.

Was there ever ice cream? Did Archie manage to get them to the store? Were there choices, flavours? There certainly was Dorie, when they got back to the harbour. "Don't you ever," she hissed at red-eyed, gap-toothed Archie, "don't you *ever again* take a child of mine in any car of yours."

—

All the kids around had to be bussed to the Valley for Grade 4. When Jen got to the gaunt old Victorian school with its scribble of iron fire-escapes (long since torn down for a paved parking lot) behind the United Church, Cal was in her class; in fact, his desk was near the front of the same row she sat in, with just two or three other children separating them. She was used to seeing his pinched profile, his poor transparent mousey ears and sharp nose and dull hair, and the way he seemed always trying not to be noticed by the teacher, Mrs. Porter, who showed no mercy when he did not have his lessons done, did not know, even, what book they were supposed to be written in, and who made an example of him because he was not clean. "Doesn't your mother own any soap? Hey? You tell her *I'll* give her some soap if she doesn't have any, and she better use it, or you're not to come into this classroom again. You tell her. Coming to school smelling like that."

Another way Cal came to school: hungry. That must have been why he always seemed so drowsy. His head, on those dark winter mornings with wool mittens dripping on the radiators and the fluorescent lights sleepily buzzing, would wobble for a while as though too heavy for his skinny grey neck, then drop down suddenly, to be pulled smartly up with a small private snort, his long lashes fluttering, his half-open mouth twitching and watering. A habit of his was to stick his sharpened pencil up into one of his back teeth and retrieve a particle of a meal earlier enjoyed, study it tenderly for a while, then eat it back off the point of his pencil, savouring. A display that, along with his smells and his pallor and his dreaminess — which looked for all the world like stupidness — seemed forever to exempt him from the human race.

One morning Cal seemed farther away than usual. There was the customary wobbling and fluttering and avoiding, the careful half-conscious gaze at a point not far from his nose, the watery open mouth. No inspection of the pencil today though, no tender savouring. And this time, instead of the snort and the start, the abrupt and bashful return to consciousness, the head went right over the edge of the desk: flop. Soon a bubbly, yellow, viscous puddle appeared on the floor and grew larger, encompassed greyish bits of half-digested food, sent up a shocking smell. It could be seen that he was throwing up – except that "throwing up" seemed too energetic and confident a term for the sorrowful dribble that was listlessly stringing out of Cal's mouth – right there in the middle of long division, in the sleepy Grade 4 classroom.

Even to country schools, a time was going to come when someone like Cal might be calmed and comforted, a cool hand held to his forehead, an encircling arm offered to help him to the sickroom, a call made to his mother.

Not in that school. Not back then. Then, and there, the teacher, a jowly middle-aged woman with a crown of permed curls and arms like capons grabbed Cal by the scruff of the neck, hauled him, half-conscious from his seat, and made him clean up his mess himself, while Jen sat in silent paralysis, watching the whole thing, along with the rest of the kids.

It's true. She did that.

You would think that she might once in a while have granted her cousin some shelter – it could have been as small and secret as a smile, a furtively passed piece of her sandwich, a heads up, whispered in the cloakroom, on the homework for the day, in the world of school. You would think so. To have done that, though, she would have had to show affiliation, to demonstrate connection: to be tarred with the same brush. But her own position in that world was not so secure that she could afford to let her connection to Cal be suspected; she went all through that school without ever speaking a word to him, or to any of his brothers or sisters, her own cousins, the same ones she played with in the woods and went with for ice cream in Archie's car, and who sprouted like pale weeds here and there in school, over the years. If it was at any time suspected that they were related, none of them ever let on.

Eventually she passed into high school (to her relief, none of those children showed up there) more or less unscathed, and after that would come university and marriages and miscarriages, divorces, and so forth, all conducted in other, safer parts of the country.

Apart from the occasional funeral and one hapless good Samaritan experiment of Dorie's, she never saw any of those cousins, or Uncle Archie or Aunt Phemie, again.

There never was any accident in front of the house with the black-eyed Susans. No blood and guts, no brain detail, no death to smell, which in any case at that distance wouldn't have been possible.

Jen learned this from Dorie during one of those late-night phone calls where you realize everybody's getting old, and you should try to find out who died of what cancer, and which marriages are still intact, what Rose is going to do now that she's left the church ("an *eBay* business? Rose the great theologian? You're kidding!"), and if Uncle Archie was simple, or just cosmically disenfranchised.

He was both.

But Jen could not be satisfied. She described, again, what she had all her life not been able to unsee. The ramshackle house "on the left side of the road as you're going up the hill, remember?" The grassy ditch, the daisies.

The crumpled, steaming, reeking cars.

"Oh Jenny, dear, we've been over this so many times before." Dorie sighed with her usual confusion. "I think you must have dreamed that, and no wonder. It was always pandemonium over there."

Jen does think sometimes, now that everybody's getting older, about Cal. Apparently (she found this out at a high-school reunion she happened to attend) he managed to get a grip on life. Just as she herself did, he grew up and got married, held jobs, had kids, paid bills. Presumably he gets enough to eat now, and is treated decently when he doesn't feel well.

Suppose life in its haphazardness had landed the two of them in other families, gentler circumstances. What would it have been like to have played with, studied with, gone for coffee or a drink, compared notes with Cal?

To have known him.

Eventually Jen decided she must accept Dorie's stubborn account of the accident; after all, she'd only have been nine or ten at the time, and she'd certainly had an imagination. Though nobody can tell her she dreamed up that chilly old school, her cousin's pinched profile, her own passive cruelty.

Is that why, in the rear-view of memory, she still sometimes sees that far distant day? The dust and the blood, her cousin hurtling away.

ARMDALE

These days, Jen was hanging out with Wanda up the road, not with rot-toothed Anneli next door anymore.

One drowsy late-summer afternoon, out comes Wanda with, "You should see this girl I know. Well, woman actually, I should say *woman*. What a babe." It was three weeks from the start of high school, and the two of them were down in the orchard, sprawled in the back seat of an abandoned car whose doors had long since been carted away. Wild grape vines and burdock canes and deadly nightshade had found their way across the windows, under the floorboards, around what was left of the rear-view mirror. A smell of souring fruit and hot leather was everywhere.

"Oh?" Jen didn't for a minute believe Wanda knew any babe, though she did need a diversion, so she decided to test Wanda's powers. "So . . . what about this so-called babe?"

"Well, her name's Pat and she's from Halifax or somewheres up there, and Jenny, she's about *eighteen* or something, and she's got clothes like a friggin' movie star, and *makeup*" — Wanda's eyes rolled back worshipfully — "you should *see* the makeup, I'm tellin' ya."

Despite her habitual skepticism where Wanda was concerned, Jen could feel a stir somewhere inside her.

"Where does she live then? And I've told you, like, five million times, I don't go by Jenny anymore."

Wanda puffed out a scornful acknowledgement. "*Jen*, then, la-de-da. *Pat* lives closer than you might think."

Jen smote a blackfly. "You're such a bullshitter."

For once, Wanda was equal to Jen's scorn. "For your information," she enounced elaborately, "she lives with the Bennetts. They brought her down here from Halifax — well Armdale, actually — to look after the kids during the day."

It was true that the Bennetts both worked; more than once Dorie had spoken disapprovingly of Mrs. Bennett, who as a rule was not to be found at home with her children.

Jen gave the front seat a good swift kick. "Armdale, you say."

The Bennetts lived just down the lane from Wanda's place, in a house that used to be owned by a farming family that had moved out west. If such a thing as a babe at the Bennetts' had occurred, Wanda, if only by virtue of proximity, would quite possibly be the first to know.

"'Course she's not the first one they've had in there, there's been two or three in before her, but they never stick around for long, they always seem to end up gettin' in *her* bad books and takin' off after a few weeks. Must be hard on them kids, poor little buggers."

This was all news to Jen; it began to dawn on her that there might, after all, be more to Wanda's claim about the hired girl than met the eye. "So," she said with as much indifference as she could muster, "what's she like then, this Pat?"

What Jen thought, the first time she walked into the Bennetts' kitchen, was that if she had been a girl brought in to look after those children, she might have run off, too, out of sheer discouragement.

The second thing she thought was that discouragement did not seem to be a thing that Pat had much familiarity with. Anybody else might have deplored the filthy floors, the empty cupboards, the stacks of gritty, unwashed dishes, the almost complete absence of any furniture.

The smell.

Pat seemed not only undaunted by this state of affairs; she was, Jen gradually understood, somehow unaware of, even in some strange way above the general mayhem. It was not that she ignored the squalour; instead, she seemed focused on some other reality, some higher, worthier, *believed-in* thing.

What was that?

That was for her to know – with a thick-lashed wink, she soon said so – and for Wanda and Jen to find out.

What did she do, then, from the time Mr. and Mrs. Bennett left for work in the morning until they presumably returned, at supper time?

Oh, she said, she kept track of *them* (the two little boys) – rolling her Egyptian eyes to make it clear that that was no mean feat – and fed them, and did the housework, you wouldn't believe the housework! There was the laundry, the cooking (*what* cooking, Jen wondered?), the hosing down and mopping up and airing out of the house, and the animals to feed and the garden to weed, and God knew what-all. Any leftover moments must be devoted to the time-consuming task of her personal upkeep.

She must go around looking like that all the time, then.

This visit, the first one, took place a few days after the conversation in the old car — and the weather, which had been stifling then, had not improved. August had reached the point where everything in the world is covered in white road dust with not a leaf stirring, and though the sun burns on day after day, there seems to be no real light in the sky: it was the part of the summer when just standing up makes you whimper, when simply catching sight of someone you're used to can light your temper.

Pat seemed about as aware of the heat as she was of the state of her employer's house. Instead of wearing a tank and shorts like anybody else, she was modelling one of the full-length bellbottom jumpsuits popular at that time, and she wore a long-sleeved (cuffs to the elbow), many-buttoned rayon blouse, pantyhose, and snappy patent-leather slingbacks, just as if she was all set to go out on a big date.

Not only that. Her short dark hair was impeccably teased back from the bangs in a soft mound punctuated by a pink satin bow, her kiss curls were perfect — how did she manage that, in such humidity? — and she was made up like a mannequin and seemed to sweat about as much as one; plus, she had long glossy witchy red fingernails, just as promised.

All, in fact, as promised.

Seeing her that first time, Jen recalled a line of poetry she'd once read, about a demon woman, *a virgin purest lipp'd, yet in the lore of love deep learned to the red heart's core* . . . The virgin part was debatable, but the red lore and the heart's core sure were a fit. Glamour, sex, mystery — Pat was all that.

Compare this to Wanda and Jen, with their frayed pedal-pushers from the year before, their dirty bare feet and smelly adolescent pits, their tame aspirations concerning the boys in Grade 10.

Excited, competitive, wary, they followed Pat around as long as she let them, which was most of that still and stifling afternoon.

But when five o'clock ticked into view, she had them out the door in a hurry.

Which only added to the mystique of her. Jen couldn't stop thinking about those kiss curls. Those lips. Those insatiable eyes. "I don't know what anyone would ever see in *that* hot thing," she carped, as she and Wanda went their separate ways.

Naturally, they were back there the very next day. And the day after; in fact, every chance they got, they were padding down the dusty lane and around the corner to the Bennetts' tilting establishment. It became their habit to wander in there mid-morning — the "little buggers" went down then, for their first nap of the day — to sit on the back step with Pat, listening to her transistor, admiring her makeup and outfits, which despite the deadening heat continued to be fresh, on point, and immaculate, and devouring her stories of the boys, the dances, the dates to be enjoyed in Armdale.

"In Armdale," she reflected, her thick lashes brushing tantalizingly together at the thought, "there's this guy? His name's Cheetah — well, his real name's Donnie Something-or-other, but everybody just calls him Cheetah because he's so wiry? — and every girl, I mean *every* girl is crazy to dance with him, and last weekend — I was home for the weekend? — he asked *me* to dance, and afterward he kissed me *French*." Her eyes closed completely at this thought, then slowly reopened. "Do you know how an Armdale boy shows if he likes you?"

How? Wanda and Jen were eager, anxious, desperate to know.

"His thing gets hard, and he pushes it against you from behind" — the thick lashes closing again — "and he kind of rubs it back and forth, like this." Here she made a startling movement with her pelvis at the same time as her candy-pink lips curved up in a savouring smile. "That's how you know when an Armdale boy *really* likes you." Her glance fell momentarily on Jen. "In Armdale," she continued, "it's an honour to be carrying a hippie's baby. If an Armdale girl's pregnant by a hippie? She dances like this, with her hand on her belly."

Now she spread five perfectly manicured fingers across her own firm abdomen – "See? Oohm . . ." – and closed her eyes again, pouting like a ripe raspberry and swaying to music only she could hear.

Soon Jen was forgetting to keep track of how many days to go until school started; boredom was a thing of the past. Her first thought on waking each morning was, What will she have on, what colour will her lips, her fingernails, her eyeshadow be, how will she have her hair today, what will she *say?*

Somewhere along the line these afternoons began to take on a different character, to acquire a sense of purpose, a focus. This was launched by a formal introduction to cigarette-smoking, an activity new to Jen, though not to Wanda, and which, according to Pat, neither one of them did with any style. Or possibly it was their woeful ignorance in the matter of toners and sloughers, their outdated, hand-me-down, babyish summer clothes, their useless youngness. Whatever it was, their afternoons at the Bennetts' gradually morphed into lessons of a sort, Wanda and Jen becoming Pat's grateful and devoted protégées in the countless subtleties of grown-up femininity.

And not a moment too soon, apparently. What hopelessly rough material she assured them they were, what smokin' stuff they were going to be, by the time the school doors opened in September. The Grade 10 boys, she promised, would never know what hit them.

They were shown how to walk with a provocative undulation of the hips, which Pat, in her stylish outfits, could pull off, but that, when Wanda and Jen tried it, appeared demented.

"Look at the cow on ice!" Jen cackled, watching Wanda's lumpen attempts, only to be hooted at by Wanda when she herself doubled over and went cross-eyed, trying to inhale.

"Cut it out, you dumb-asses," warned Pat with an expert drag on her own cigarette, "there's nobody here but us, so smarten up and try," a slow wink, "try, again. You want to know how to do this by the time school starts, don't you?"

Soon they were initiated into the complexities of creams and foundations and the removers of same, instructed in the steady-handed application of eyeliner and mascara, shown the great many varieties of lipstick and rouge – "you don't want the powder kind, you want the stick, like this, it's easier to blend, see" – the artful application of false eyelashes and nail polish, the best way to hold the hairspray.

They learned how to backcomb, how to tease, how to round-brush their hair so that, whether they wanted it over or under, it would flip just the right way.

Then came dancing, which took place in the milk-and-rice-crispy-strewn kitchen with the top forty cranked up and the curtains closed, to make it seem more like a dancehall. Though there seemed to be no particular steps or routines to learn, there was a succession of mechanical movements and gestures that could not be deviated from, and which were all the rage in Armdale.

Waltzing, though, was another thing. They couldn't stop snorting and recoiling at the need to get pressed up against each other and shuffle in circles; Pat had to keep lecturing them as to the serious nature of what they were doing; the promise that it was for a future, better cause; and the fact that they were being immature, an accusation she knew they hated to hear.

"Grow up, you two; if you want to act like babies, go on home and hang around your mommies, I got plenty here already to keep me busy without wasting my time on the likes of you."

Recoil or not, Jen never seemed to get enough of this dancing, performed in the weird afternoon intimacy of that derelict kitchen, the hot, pale sun ball pressing on the tired curtains, the transistor radio crackling out "Blue Velvet." When she waltzed with Pat, she tried to memorize the smell of her mysterious unguents and grown-up body odour (she did sweat, it seemed, after all), to follow the intricacies of her ear's perfect coil, to accidentally brush her kiss curls with her cheek, as if, by an adoring osmosis, she could somehow absorb her, resemble, become her.

Though there was one thing, one niggling question, that managed, annoyingly, to penetrate the fog: why did Pat feel the need – surely all that housework and child minding couldn't be doing her beautiful outfits any good – why did a girl from Armdale have to dress so perfectly every single day, just to be a housekeeper in a hellhole like the Bennetts', in the middle of nowhere?

So, one afternoon when Jen was her waltzing partner, she whispered the question into Pat's dazzling ear.

A minute movement of one shadowed eyelid was all that indicated what might have been a momentary lack of assurance; the next instant she looked Jen straight in the eye. "Well," she said matter-of-factly, "I do have a boyfriend, a *sort of* boyfriend down here, and we go out when he's off work, after *they*" – the Bennetts – "get home. He comes to get me right at five o'clock though, and what with these little monsters to run after all day, there's no way I'd have time to get ready if I waited 'til I was done work." With one glossy fingertip she pressed a shimmer of moisture from below her eye. "I have to start first thing in the morning, and just make sure I don't get dirty."

Jen thought that was a fishy story. She agreed it was a prudent measure.

She noticed – it was the first time she had ever examined Pat at such close range – that her nose was ever-so-slightly irregular.

In that part of the country there will sometimes come a late-summer event that the locals call "a terrific storm." This can involve anything from hail to hurricanes, and never fails to bring high winds, thunder and lightning, bruised apples, beaten-down grain. People anticipate the terrific storm with stoicism and, depending on how long the weather has been unbearably muggy, not without a grim sort of anticipation, agreeing that it should at least soon be possible to breathe again, for a while anyway.

Though until the storm breaks, it's as if something has sucked every little bit of air out of the world, all you can do is wait, and sweat.

The worst of the hot weather, the flat dead eye of it, had been going on for about a week when Wanda and Jen made what turned out to be their last visit to the Bennetts'. That day, neither of them, padding through the soft white dust of the lane, felt much of the usual enthusiasm about the afternoon's instruction; the heat had gotten to them; they were silent and introverted, ready to be offended.

"You knocked into me."

"I did not."

"You did, you knocked my hip, you know you did. *Ow*."

"Hips that big, no wonder they get knocked."

"Least I've *got* hips!"

"You're pathetic!"

You're pathetic!

Pat herself, when they arrived, seemed a little less perky than usual; Jen was startled to note dark rings of perspiration under the arms of her pale-green paisley blouse, a shiny caste to her makeup. A fine film of moisture stood out on her upper lip, beading in the soft down of dark hair in the corners of her mouth.

Even her kiss curls looked discouraged.

"No dancing today," she sighed when her students came stumping up the back steps. "Let's just go sit in the backyard under the lilacs, that way we can hear if the boys wake up."

When they got to the lilac bushes though, it was clear that the temperature was no different there than anywhere else, so back they dragged themselves into the house, pulled the heavy living-room drapes against the sun, flopped on the couch, and got out the cigarettes.

By now Jen and Wanda could pass for seasoned smokers. They knew the ways of holding, gesturing, and blowing shapely smoke rings, and Jen was fairly good at concealing the fact that she still didn't inhale, so they had graduated to cigarettes of their own, snitched from their parents' packages, instead of just being offered training drags on Pat's. The combination of the darkened room and the cigarettes made them feel sophisticated, worldly, pleasurably jaded. Inevitably, the conversation turned to boys and what you were supposed to do with them, a subject that reliably made Pat move her hips, moisten her lips, close those deep-set eyes. Wanda and

Jen exchanged glances through the haze; Jen began to feel warm in a way that had nothing to do with the weather's pall; a comfortable buzzing in her head made her think she must have forgotten herself and started to inhale.

Pat said, "The rugrats won't be up for a while, why don't we practise kissing?"

Now they were instructed that kissing broke down into "necking," "petting," and "French," and that it could result, if you weren't careful, in dirty-looking mouth-shaped neck bruises, called "hickeys." Jen felt her eyes widen. Though Wanda, scornful of her friend's inexperience, seemed to have had a lot of this material before. "Dummy, why do you think Lorna Pineo always wears turtlenecks to school?" she snorted with quick little shakes of her head. "Where've *you* been?"

"Reading a book sometimes, unlike you."

"Just keep readin' your dumb books, see how that works for yuh."

"The important thing to remember with French," drawled Pat, who had automatically slipped into teacher-mode, "is to let just the littlest bit of your tongue show through your teeth, like this."

There, between her lips, peeked Pat's dainty tongue.

There, too, resembling a slab of ground beef, thrust Wanda's serviceable one. Mindful of Wanda's snarky comment about hickeys, Jen snorted with amused disgust. Then, remembering to keep her own tongue thin and flat like Pat's, she tried it.

"You're going to be a good necker," Pat crooned. "Oh yes, you *are*."

That was enough for Wanda, whose efforts had not been complimented, and who was half out of her head with the heat. Muttering something about not having to take this sort of B.S. from nobody, she flounced out of the room.

With a distant thwack, the back door slammed.

Jen, pleasantly foggy, looked over at Pat, with whom, she realized, she'd never before been alone. Leaning against the cushions on the other side of the couch, smiling in her strange way, her cigarette dangling from one slender hand, Pat blew a smoke ring in the direction of Wanda's exit. "That's an improvement, eh?" she murmured. "You are, you know," (smiling again), "going to be good."

"I am?" Jen said weakly, hoping the words didn't come out in too much of a squeak.

What had she imagined the woman meant? Further discussion? A brief treatise on the history of smooching? The next instant Pat was on top of her, her hands moving under her thin summer clothes, her tongue, far from peeking discreetly through her teeth as shown, invading Jen's own. Dorie by now had taught her all anyone would ever need to know about sex: stay away from it. Still, the cigarette's poison distanced and pleased her, enabling her to experience a mild subterranean stirring mixed with good-natured curiosity, almost as though she were a spectator, a mere bystander to the odd and sweaty business happening to her body.

She felt less like a spectator when sometime later – a minute? An hour? – a car door banged, and Pat was up the stairs like a shot, leaving Jen to get herself vertical, and to greet a startled-looking man in dirty green overalls.

"Must have fallen asleep," Jen mumbled pathetically as she lurched past, leaving Mr. Bennett, she assumed, to wonder who the hell she was, and how she came to be sprawled on the couch with his hired girl in the middle of the afternoon.

"Go on home," he muttered as she booted it for the door, but his eyes were on the stairs.

It occurred to Jen, as she scrambled through the first

fat drops of rain, that Mr. Bennett must have come home to cover up his old cars against the storm, which, while she and Pat had been lolling with the curtains pulled, had finally started darkening toward its moment.

"Where've *you* been all afternoon?" said Dorie, pulling down a window as Jen hurtled through the kitchen door.

"Oh," Jen said, gladder than she ever meant to be, to see her mother, "nowhere."

Hurricane Edna lasted a week, overflowing the swamp, backing up the sewers, and turning the lane from dead white powder to impassable muck. By the time it was safe to come out, school was only a few days away, and suddenly everyone was cheery, in a hurry, briskly busy. Jen spent the cool, brilliant days driving around with Dorie, who'd hired a sitter for Rosie, buying school supplies and new shoes and material for dresses ("shifts" were all the rage that fall, slab-sided sacks for which her flat chest made her grateful) to start Grade 10 in.

Though she pretended not to care, she was already calculating the marks she would need going forward, in order to someday sneak into a university.

Wanda's mother, Shirley, had an appointment with a specialist over in Wolfville, so Dorie and Jen took her along on one of those school supply trips. In the back seat, watching the turning trees stream by, Jen half-listened to the conversation in front. The storm was discussed, its destruction deplored and admired, the cost to the farmers considered.

Then Shirley mentioned the Bennetts. "So, they fired that hired girl."

"That so?" said Dorie, calculating a pass. "Another one?"

"Them people go through girls," mused Shirley, "like shit through a tin horn."

A week is a long time when you're fourteen. Already by the time the school doors opened, thanks to new shoes and crisp notebooks and fresh dresses to start school in, Jen had mostly stopped thinking about Pat and who, or whatever, she'd been.

But she hadn't forgotten boys.

What came to her, as she and Dorie stopped in Kentville to buy the one pair of Levi's that would have to last her all year, was the realization that there might actually be an Armdale somewhere.

And that, if there was an Armdale, what else might there be beyond Cumming's marshy borders?

"So, anyway," continued Shirley, "that's what Juanie Coffill was tellin' me. Guess she knew the girl."

"What do you suppose it was this time?" Dorie wondered with a glance, to see if Jen was listening, in the rear-view.

"We'll never know," said Shirley.

"No," sighed Dorie, "we never will."

HOW IT'LL GO

Dorie in those days was always looking for ways to make a little money. During the Tupperware era, their narrow, cramped living room had to be regularly made to look as not-narrow-and-cramped as possible, in order to accommodate the neighbourhood ladies who crowded in for squares and bars, and to see all the different kinds of containers that could hold the various squares and bars. The problem was that, while the ladies enjoyed the get-togethers and praised the baking — "Isn't this from the Best of Bridge?" "Oh, Dorie, you've *got* to let me have this recipe!" — they tended not to buy very many of the containers. At ten o'clock, there Dorie would be, resignedly putting the leftover Easy Apple Squares and Peggy's Pumpkin Bars into Frige-O-Seals and Stack-n-Stors, and muttering that "these parties are getting to be more darn trouble than they're worth."

After the Tupperware came a mail-order clothing business that involved carrying from house to house a folder of glossy pictures showing soft-eyed women in pastel gloves and pale spring suits, matching hats. Though mostly, thanks to all Dorie's household chores and childcare, it was Jen trudging up and down the roads with the folder. Stiff with mortification, she perched on the neighbour ladies' couches, nibbling one "would-you-like-a-cookie?" after another, while Dorie's potential customers examined her increasingly thumbed-through offerings. It wasn't long, to Jen's relief, before the mail-order business tanked; what had made Dorie think she could compete with the Eaton's catalogue? Or — by then, even some women were allowed to drive cars — with stores?

Chickens were next, along with a brace of African geese — "People will come to see the geese, and then they'll buy the eggs!" — followed by a go at selling used children's clothing (their own, mostly, that everyone had already seen walking around town on Jen, hung up and tagged for sale out in the sun porch).

An attempted art gallery brought on an antiques phase. For two years a Mastercard sign glared outrageously in the verandah window, and the chair Jen sat in at breakfast could not be counted upon to be there at dinner. Crocks and blanket chests, mustache cups and yarn winders, shoe forms and cradles, spindles and candles, where did Dorie find it all? For a while they harboured an actual piano, and Jen even took lessons on it temporarily, from an arthritic old lady down the road, her small fee paid in goose eggs.

It wasn't long before Jen began to catch on to music notation, to make tentative sense of the clefs and staves, to improvise a little. If pressed, she could play "Marche Militaire." That is: until the day she came home from school, and the piano wasn't there. (Lucky for Dorie, Jen was rehearsing adultness right then, she was fine. She took the tantrum that was brewing and turned it into a regimen of secret starvation, which, far from the desired appearance of a nineteenth-century heroine suffering from "galloping consumption," resulted after a week or so in the purchase of an entire box of Wagon Wheels and one very long afternoon in the bathroom).

Boarders soon followed the chickens and the art gallery. Somewhere Dorie found a dwarf lady who arrived with a budgie, a disconcerting cackle, and a wedge of iron-grey topiary for hair. Then came a widowed French teacher. After her, somebody's grandmother. Upstairs one after another, the old ladies would arrive and then after a year or so, expire, and depart to join their ancestors.

Until then, they had to be put somewhere. "Jenny, your room's the biggest; you'll just have to bunk in with your sister for the time being, there's nothing we can do about it." Jen could not see how that could be true; what was wrong with Sonny's old room? But Dorie wouldn't hear of that, plus once more, she had a scheme. How could any need of Jen's compete with the prospect of a ready income?

There was a brief lull between the old ladies and the new scheme, during which Jen felt somewhat safe. Then came the hot August afternoon when Dorie told her to wait with Rose, who was still just a baby, outside the church until she got out of her women's group, which met in the church vestry. "Just walk her up and down in the stroller 'til we're done; she's had a bottle, she'll be fine. And you never know, maybe there'll be a little surprise for you when I'm done."

It was about four o'clock in the afternoon, warm and dusty, the air flat and used up the way it gets late in the day at that time of year. Jen was hungry – she always was, back then – and eager to get home to their supper of Hamburger Helper and Kraft Dinner. Older girls in blue dresses and maple leaf ties had been around the week before; maybe there'd be Girl Guide cookies for dessert.

When she tired of walking up and down the parking lot, Jen pushed the carriage around the block to the front of the church, where she could at least sit on the steps and watch the people going in and out of the corner store. That was the first time she laid eyes on Laura Ward, who was also sitting there.

Laura might have been around nine or ten, probably just a few years younger than Jen, though she was so small it was hard to tell, and she was a stranger. In Cumming, everybody knew everybody, it couldn't be avoided, and Jen wondered why she'd never seen the girl before, why all of a sudden, she was waiting there, just as if she'd always been part of the town – didn't you have to live there to have a mother inside the church, to be waiting to get taken home for supper?

But who could her mother have been? All the mothers were taken.

Jen was on the pale and well-fed side back then; she envied the strange girl for being so thin and fine-skinned and tanned, though she couldn't help noticing a tremor about her, a kind of bodily hesitation, as if, not trusting her eyes, she might be uncertain where to put her foot down. There were dull purplish spots on her bare arms and legs and up the back of her neck, as though from long-ago sores that had healed and darkened, and the skin all around her mouth was red and cracked from being licked too often. As she stood on the step, she kept opening and closing a little plastic change purse, and quietly telling herself some story.

For a while she stood watching Jen pace back and forth jiggling the buggy importantly, and following her with those quiet, bottomless eyes. But gradually she began to edge closer, until she was walking beside Jen, one small brown hand helping her push the stroller. With the other, she held her purse close against her skinny chest, stroking the small gold knobs of the clasp with one thin finger. They went on like this for maybe half an hour — the mothers must have been having an extra good time that afternoon, maybe there was a new recipe or bit of gossip to savour — then Laura stopped and looked up at Jen.

"Are you my new mum?" she asked.

Pretty soon, Jen learned that Dorie herself was going to be Laura's new mum. Just like that, Jen had a second sister, though Dorie didn't call her a sister; Dorie called Laura a "foster child."

What kind of child was that? And why was this Laura being visited upon Jen in her own home? Jen already had her hands full enough with Rose the Baby and her shenanigans, she didn't need those of a second one. Also — and this was even stranger to think about — wasn't Jen enough of a daughter for Dorie? Why couldn't her mother have tried out something else to make money, candle-making, say, or pie-baking. What about magazine subscriptions, people always seemed to go for those.

But no, Dorie had to bring home a foster child.

How could she? Jen began to wonder about the other boarders, poor women who, for no fault of their own later in life, had had nowhere else to be.

A terrible thought: had they died of grief?

"A foster child is when the state, or the Children's Aid, actually, pays a family room and board to look after a little one who needs a home. Isn't that nice?" Jen didn't think it was nice, but Dorie didn't wait for a reply. "Laura's going to be part of our family."

Dorie didn't end up putting Laura in Jen's room, which almost made Jen like her, though not quite; there were the sores and the uncertainty, the chapped mouth to consider, and those eyes, those terribly still, dark pools with their grave and tranquil gaze. Instead, now that the gallery was out of it, Dorie gave Laura the sun porch, a room spacious and generous in appearance, almost a little suite in size, but not a bedroom, really. Windows on three sides eliminated any stab at privacy, and it wasn't insulated, which made it cold in winter, boiling in summer.

No one could seriously live there.

For a while Dorie took Laura places and showed her around and bought her things, as if she really was some long-lost child of the family. But that part of it gradually petered out, and at some point, it became Dorie and Rose and Jen in the main part of the house, and Laura in the far, cold country of the sun porch, set apart from the life of the family, fed and kept clean, not much visited. Jen might pass the door and see her standing there, always agreeable and hopeful, never insisting on anything, just standing at attention, shyly waiting, a polite ghost. She felt a little bit sick inside, seeing Laura's patient, hopeless standing-at-attention, but she was always in some hurry or calamity, some junior high commotion; who had time for an embarrassing oddity like Laura? After the first few weeks Jen began to ignore her — after all, she was Dorie's project, not hers — and to pretend there wasn't any Laura.

One hot September day not long after turning thirteen or fourteen, Jen came home from school, and just like the piano, Laura was gone. The sun porch was empty and tidy, Dorie cheerful and inscrutable, business as usual; you would hardly have guessed there'd ever been a foster child here at all.

Laura had long been history by the time Jen got a surprising scholarship and went away to university, met a boy named Eric, fell in love with his long legs, his big vocabulary, and his unexpected family connection to the local gentry, and brought him home to show off by getting engaged to him. "We're thinking maybe next summer. By then Eric'll be done his undergrad" — how she loved rolling out the lofty terms and phrases — "and I'll have finished third year."

Not even the African geese had pleased Dorie as much as Eric, with his beautiful manners and his Grade 10 in piano (they had a different one by then, for him to prove it on); she was thrilled and vindicated, and meant to stay that way, even after she found out that Jen wasn't so sure about getting married after all.

"What do you mean, you're not sure? I just finished sewing your dress! That dress is a Vera Wang. It's from a *Vogue* pattern, and it took me all winter. It has ninety-nine steps — and a *devil* of a lining!"

What could Jen say? The only thing that had happened was time, a fair bit of which had passed since the engagement announcement. As the semesters had gone by with steadily improving grades, she'd begun to realize she wasn't as dumb as she'd thought — maybe she could actually make a go at life all by herself — and that the prospect of marriage at twenty-one was getting her down. "That's all."

Dorie hit the brakes hard at a sudden red light. "If I were you right now, I wouldn't be 'not sure,'" — with an attempt at a snobby expression, she mimicked Jen's newly-acquired Upper Canadian tone — "*I'd* be swinging from the chandeliers!"

"Mum, I'm sorry." Jen made a regretful cringe to an alarmed jaywalker. "I'm just not ready. I thought I was, but it turns out I'm not."

No time to figure that out, canned cherries were on sale at the IGA, and they were on Dorie's hellbent way there, to buy a wedding reception's-worth of the gooey stuff for cherry cheesecake pie, which was all the rage at the time. As usual these days, Dorie was going over details – the hall, the catering ladies, the food, the flowers – as the fields, still dewy with morning, skimmed past the car windows in a dream. Dorie was deep in list mode: "We'll have roast beef and Yorkshire pudding for the main course, and of course the cherry cheesecake pie for dessert. The reception'll be at the fire hall, and the Ladies' Aid'll cater it . . ." She yanked down her sun visor. "Lilies by Ali will do the flowers, they charge an arm and a leg, but we're saving money by having the ladies cater . . ."

Jen gazed out the window. The grass and the trees looked blue, remote.

She didn't want ladies.

She didn't want flowers.

She didn't want pie.

The faster things went, the more she realized she didn't want Vera Wang or ninety-nine steps, or a lining, or any of it. She tried to tell Dorie. She tried. Dorie wasn't impressed; plus, she had her own reasons Jen's wedding should go ahead. "You're not going to make a fool of me."

All Jen's protests notwithstanding, getting engaged to the boy with the nice manners and the Grade 10 in piano was beginning to have an interesting effect on her social life. In about a week and a half she went from dormouse to debutante, from invisibility to front-page news. Girls who had all her life ignored her were suddenly inviting her to join their special cliques and telling her their secrets, townspeople she barely knew were nodding approvingly when they saw her on the street, she was being waved at and youhoo'd to by church people who had never before given her the time of day. In a small-town way, Jen was suddenly a celebrity. It wasn't long before she became the blushing object of showers, parties, afternoon teas, the recipient of the kind of attention she had always – expecting forever to be excluded from it – laughed at and made fun of. Carried now on its fulsome wave, she was cravenly starting to like her sudden renown, even to expect it, to feel it might somehow be her due. In fact, she was starting to think so well of herself, she was almost forgetting about not wanting to get married.

One of those teas was held at the home of Auntie Muriel, a friend from Dorie's Tupperware days. Welcoming crepe-paper bows and bells hung over the woman's front door. You had to put on a lacy apron and pick up a spatula when you crossed the threshold. Why, Jen wondered, was there batter in her future? The hostess had supplied a bulletin board where you could post practical advice for the happy pair, a couple's quiz, a game of bride bingo, cocktail napkins printed with snippets out of the *Good Wife's Guide*.

"Who wants coffee?" cried Auntie Muriel as Jen digested her napkin's advice about clearing away the clutter when *he* comes home, putting a ribbon in your hair for *his* arrival, quieting the children and being "a little more gay and interesting for *him*" – even, perhaps, depending on the season, adjusting the sprinkler, or lighting a fire. "Desserts through that door!"

And there, dressed in one of the silly aprons and handing out macaroni and cheese served as clever cupcakes, came Laura Ward. She was larger, of course, Jen hadn't seen her in years. Her arms and legs had filled out and her behind showed signs of an impending womanliness. Her scars, worn longer and stretched further, looked fainter. But those eyes Jen would have recognized anywhere. And they recognized hers. The eyes took her in, looked down. Jen's did the same; she wanted to look anywhere but into them.

"Laura!" she crowed in debutante mode. "How *nice* to see you!" She went hot and then cold with embarrassment then, but there was no going back, she had to keep on. "Is this your – do you work here?"

Laura smiled mildly. "I live here."

Dust came back to Jen then, a hot day, the pale dazzle of a late afternoon sky. *Are you my new mum?* Despite the too-warm room, an involuntary shiver went over her, a feeling of unsettledness, unseemliness.

Oh, who was she kidding? That wasn't true, those big fancy university words didn't describe her any better than "debutante" did, or "who-er" had. This sick and particular clamminess needed an old name, a Dad-never-home name. A Sonny-in-church name. An *ence I'll send you home* name.

Shame. That was what she felt, tricked out in her paper bows and her pretty scholarship, her assumed identity as innocent Eric's butter-wouldn't-melt fiancée. In her dark heart and gut Jen already more than suspected that she wasn't any more a scholar or a wife than Laura was an orphan.

Too bad. There Laura stood, balancing her tray of shrimp roll-ups and her mild smile. Shouldn't Jen step aside with her, invite her to speak privately, just the two of them? Shouldn't they at least acknowledge their brief, if peculiar sisterhood? But Jen was already being escorted into a different room, laughing ladies pulling and pushing her to a toilet paper throne shaped like the top of a wedding cake. Auntie Muriel was busy setting up the first game, in which blindfolded women and girls had to guess where the bride-to-be was, and pin toilet paper streamers all over her, to make a veil.

"Laura, *really* nice to see you!" she called over her shoulder, making a self-deprecating gesture in the vicinity of her foolish apron. "We really must talk!"

Laura smiled again, though not with full attention. She was busy showing people where to find things in the kitchen, and dispensing punch from a big, frosted bowl that stood on the dessert table.

When the marriage to Eric was teetering to its conclusion, Jen went home for a while, glad to have somewhere to be; by then, she wasn't doing so well in school, anyway. She told Dorie it had been a tough semester, that she just needed to put her feet up and smell the fresh sea air. Then she set about moping and bellyaching the way people do after the first one ends, staring at candles, walking in fields and so forth, both bitter and relieved that there had been no children.

This was some time after Dad, apparently on account of the superior music scene, had up and moved to someplace in Cape Breton. Dorie, by now well used to her husband's vanishings and peregrinations, was philosophical. "Well, that's your father. One day I turned around, and there he was, gone."

Dorie'd moved to the new, smaller place Jen found her in, at the base of the Mountain, a serviceable bungalow with cyclamen growing up a lattice. She complained of its lack of character. "I've always known I need something very unique when it comes to houses. And this place is anything but unique." She stared out the window, holding the morning to account.

They were having tea not long after Jen arrived, in Dorie's not-very-unique but bright breakfast nook, where she was catching Jen up on goings-on around Cumming, neighbours, people from Jen's Grade 12 class, town characters. Gary Rafuse from Grade 12 owned his own garage now, "over to New Minas. That's where they're all from, the Rafuses. He's done well for himself." Allen Johnson, who hadn't managed to graduate from Grade 12, had fried his brains with drugs. "You'll see him when you go down to get the mail, he's always hanging around the monument there. Hardly knows his own name anymore." She directed a shrewd look at the burgundy toenail poking out of her slipper. "He'll be happy to see you though, he can still shoot the breeze."

Jen had to ask. "What about Laura? Is she still in town?" ("In town." Another blush-worthy Upper Canadian expression).

Dorie got up to let the cat out. "She's been gone for years, Laura has."

"Oh? Where?"

"Apparently she's married to an art teacher and living somewhere out in B.C." Dorie swirled her cooling tea, a clear sign she didn't want to talk about the real reason for Jen's visit. But then she brightened. "Oh, but Muriel keeps in touch with her. After her time with us, Muriel took her, and pretty much raised her. Muriel's a nurse, remember, and she was better able to manage her care. She was in here just the other week with some pictures. You'd hardly recognize Laura anymore. That eczema she used to have's all better, and she's got a lovely home and two of the dearest little girls you ever saw. You never know, do you," Dorie sighed, choosing a ginger snap to dip, "how it'll go, with people."

"Are you my new mum?"

The afternoon sun is beginning to lean, bathing the gables of the church in a sugary blaze from behind, and opening a floorless blue vacuum in front, where Jen with her baby sister and the strange, motherless girl stand silently.

A vacuum opens inside Jen now, too. How could anybody have a new mum, any more than they could have three legs, or an ability to fly? Why would you calmly suppose a total stranger might suddenly be Her? The wicked gap widens further: Why not? In her mind she sees the church doors locked and Dorie gone, herself doomed to spend eternity walking back and forth with Rose the Baby's carriage and Laura Ward appended to her hand, orphans all of them. Lost silhouettes, they wander the world in that cruel blue dazzle, asking any kindly seeming soul Laura's hopeless question, grateful for a night's shelter, a cool drink, a gentle look, all the while getting farther from home, that distant haven Jen has not always approved of, and whose imperfect mercies, might not come again.

REMAINS

The turkey vulture takes its name from the Latin word 'vulturus,' meaning 'tearer,' a reference to its feeding habits. Carrion is a mainstay of its diet, and includes everything from garbage to hearts.

MILLS' GUIDE TO MARSH BIRDS

It's strange how closet time, marked in artefacts, can be capable of tricks.

Here's Jen cleaning out a cupboard that holds such a willy-nilly jumble of expired life stuffed willy-nilly away, you'd think she was done with it. Of course, that's one of the tricks.

The closet is more accurately a small and cramped catch-all behind the washer-and-dryer, that, on account of her knees, which are bothering her more these days, she hardly ever gets around to. In this cupboard or catch-all, she finds some things she hasn't seen in a good long while: an ancient Tinker toy that must have been Sonny's; her own defunct IBM Selectric; various items of outdated clothing from the Eric era (kept in case jumpsuits and peasant blouses ever came back in style), a litter box from some long-departed cat (Simon? No, it would have to be Javex, he would have needed one that size), and an envelope of pictures, photos that she had believed lost in some long-ago move.

Opening the envelope she has the same old feeling of prohibition, the familiar wariness and potential for dismay, but she cannot stop herself: out slides the ugly cabin they stayed in; then a touchingly young Eric, loading supplies into that rented canoe; next the odd little stone building – she had forgotten! – that they'd called the "charnel house"; now a night shot, a blur of feral eyes and fur: the bloody raccoons. But what is this one? She has to turn it sideways, then vertical, then back around again, to get a clue of how to read it. At last, she recognizes long grass and nondescript trees, with some sort of greyish bumps – animals? Birds? Hunkering on the lower branches: birds, she decides, what else can they be? And then she remembers the turkey vultures, and the embracing wave of stench from their kill, and Eric grabbing the camera in his rage.

And finally – even now she almost can't look – those shots of the body just before it happened: Eric's long limbs, sunburnt and unclothed, the unprotected toes, knees drawn up to the chest, eyes steadfastly closed. And look at his head, pressed down amongst the tree roots and pine needles and cushioning moss. Hoping thus to beguile her; patiently desiring, obediently waiting, there on the bare ground, for her to come down to him and offer herself to him, take him in. Looking for all the world instead as though he could be dead and waiting upon the judgement.

Well. With any luck his waiting has finally paid off; Jen genuinely hopes so, for his sake.

Back when she was finishing her psych degree, you could end the four-year program with a thesis, instead of with a final exam. A thesis was a pretty big deal, but still. No days-on-end study marathon. No last-minute jitters; no dire hours in a smelly, tension-filled examination hall.

So, instead of a final, she was spending all summer grinding at a thesis, for her laziness or cowardice. Maybe, in the end, a thesis was worse.

She was all set to head home from school one day when her supervisor said, "It's none of my business, but I honestly think you should tell Eric to take a break from all that research" (Eric was a promising anthropologist) "and the two of you just get the you-know-what out of town. Close the bloody books for a weekend, why don't you, and spend some time alone together just the two of you, you know? Just have a bit of fun. When was the last time you two had any fun?" The supervisor knew of a great little camp where furnished cottages could be rented for cheap, up on Canoe Lake. She could give Jen the number to call. "Would Eric go for that, do you think?"

Eric by then was close to finishing his PhD and had just arrived back from two months in Denmark, where he had been studying the leathern remains of people tortured and flung into a bog back in the mists of time. Jen didn't know what he'd go for at this point. She didn't know what *she'd* go for by now, either. At this time, Jen and Eric were renting an apartment from an absent prof in the anthropology department. It wasn't an especially nice apartment — recently Jen had seen (she was sure of it) something running under the kitchen sink, and the toilet leaked — but it was cheap, located in a nice neighbourhood of limestone houses and lilac trees, and it was biking distance from the university and the lake.

The man next door, who happened to be the very prof-cum-writer who'd taught her elective overview of English poetry way back in first year, was out on his deck when she got home from getting groceries one afternoon, all set to run Canoe Lake by Eric. Gordon (that was the neighbour's name when he wasn't selling sonnets to undergraduates) was barbecuing, as usual at that time of day. He was also, as befit the season, merrily caroling some ancient song about summer coming in. Jen waved slightly as she shoved the screen door open with one shoulder, wishing he wouldn't stare. She'd first become aware of her former professor and his more or less invisible wife when Eric was encamped for all those days in the Tollund Bog, analyzing the petrified ingredients in some two-thousand-year-old gruel, the ancient victims' last meal. Willow herb. Yarrow seeds. Hemp nettle.

Chives, spinach, and mint, meanwhile, were lustily bursting forth in the garden of the talented neighbour, who was also some kind of choral singer, and who liked to cook while working on his intervals. Jen could hear him over there late most afternoons, honing his minor thirds in his ferocious base voice, while grilling his homegrown zucchini in the mild spring air.

The prof's wife managed a yoga studio downtown and was hardly ever there.

Spring the year of the Tollund Bog had been sudden and warm. During Eric's months away, Jen was often to be seen propped between two lawn chairs, tanning and revising, while in the prof's pretty garden, the lilacs were coming out.

More often than not, so was the prof, at around three o'clock or so. That was when he would be wrapping up his own day's work (what lofty subjects was he writing about, Jen wondered, not without a sullen admiration), and wanting to sit out with a beer while he thought up just the right thing to cook for dinner. He took a mighty satisfaction in the virginal chives that were beginning to make an appearance along the fence, praising their delicate heat on the tongue, teasing, offering: *Here. Taste. It won't bite.* Laughing, too, in a not-unkind way. Holding her eyes in his gaze a little longer than was perhaps necessary: offering some oblique but palpable challenge.

He pointed out where he expected to find his fennel and his dill, his Italian parsley, when the ground warmed up.

"I didn't know there were different kinds," Jen ventured, "of parsley."

"You don't get out much, do you," he laughed. "There's common or curly, there's broad leaf (that's the Italian, that's the best, I think), then there's Hamburg and Japan, you can even grow lemon parsley if you want it, and there's . . . well, you get the idea."

Jen's curiosity got the better of her. "Why do you like Italian parsley, then?"

He laughed again, and Jen heard the familiar, ringing tones from his afternoon singing practice. "Why not? It looks better. It cooks better. I think it has a certain . . . *je ne sais quoi*" — stroking his greying light-brown beard with two long fingers — "kind of an urbane taste."

Urbane. A plant could be that way? Jen had never thought of food as anything much beyond casseroles and potluck suppers, fuel. And now with Eric away so much, dinner might be toast and peanut butter, a can of chili, a bowl of potato chips, half the time on the stale side.

"Care to join me in a beer?" the prof offered one day.

No. That was not what Jen and Eric did, would ever do, drink alcohol. She kept on saying no for quite a while.

But time was passing. The thesis was a chore; often enough, she was bored. Meanwhile, further botanical wonders were unfolding in the backyard next door. There came a day when it dawned on Jen that the afternoon was fine, and she was here, and Eric was somewhere in northern Europe, hanging out in a swamp full of dead people. Not only did she accept a beer from the writer, she went with him one day in his rattling station wagon out to Lake Ontario Park, where they spent the afternoon walking past empty playgrounds and talking about music and food. Was Jen aware that there were at least twenty-four different kinds of carrots, he wondered? That there were over sixty thousand species of snails in the world? That Bach's music was used to diffuse tension in airports?

The carrots and snails were news, but she knew about Bach. Did *he* know that Bach had fathered twenty children and might be planted somewhere other than his official grave?

He said she and that fine fellow she was married to thought too much about graves, and then he kissed her amidst the brand-new leaves.

All she wanted out of life, after that, was for him to kiss her again.

It became clear that the thesis supervisor's concept of a holiday was considerably more sociable than Eric's or Jen's could be, at this point in their lives. They found their cottage, a large under-furnished structure lumped in with four or five others of the same ilk, high above the water on a bare, sandy hill. Children and teenagers and dogs chasing and bruiting.

Frisbees zinging past, followed by hollering Frisbee whizzers. The steady thump of boomboxes. Hibachis. Heat.

Just down the sun blasted slope were stationed an impressively overweight – and, it seemed, hard-of-hearing – family, a mother and a father, a boy of about eleven, and two grandparents, whom Eric and Jen privately began calling "The Fats." They had scarcely opened their car doors on the afternoon of their arrival before the lisping boy from the family, clad only in a pair of dangerously low-slung Bermuda shorts, came wallowing up the sandhill to warn them not to leave any food around their cabin at night, on account of the "wat" (pronounced like pat)-"toonth."

"Wat-toonth?" said Jen to Eric after the boy had bum-cracked back down the hill.

Eric made an uncomprehending face. He was busy trying to get one of the swollen cottage windows to open, and wasn't interested in wat-toonth, whatever they were.

Late that night though, when, thanks to families of marauding raccoons, the campground broke into a bustling and percussive nightlife, they understood. In bed, the sheets in knots as mosquitoes whined invisibly around their heads, they gave up on sleep. Instead, they stood in their doorway and took unsteady pictures of the "wat-toonth."

They had paid their money. Eric's parents were collecting their mail, watering their few plants, feeding their cat, Pearl. They hadn't had a holiday since getting married and they were damned if they were going back to town.

The next day they loaded all their picnic supplies and sunscreen and books into a rented canoe and headed for the far side of a distant island. Soon the holiday noise slipped away, replaced by the lap of water, the creak of paddles in gunnels, a loon's haunting call far from land, the steady, light murmur of wind.

Jen, relaxing, pointed to a small limestone house or shed that could be seen through the trees along the shore. "Wonder what that is."

"Could be a boat house."

"But I don't see any windows or ramps, or anything."

"Looks a bit funebral, actually."

"What's that?"

"Well. Like stuff to do with burying people; funerals. The kind of building they used to put the bones in, back in the Middle Ages. To save space in the graveyards during plagues and wars. A 'charnel house,' it's called, or was."

"You and your bones," laughed Jen. "It does look like a charnel house, though. Creepy. I wonder if it is one." She got out the camera.

They went on, watching for a suitable place to tie up, and eventually found a deserted beach of white sand strewn with bark and driftwood, ribbed with fine, firm wave marks.

"What are those birds?" Jen pointed to a cluster of shaggy shapes circling a tree.

Eric pushed down his glasses, peered. "Turkey vultures, probably, up in that maple. They do that when they've got a kill."

"Charming," said Jen. "Let's go where they aren't."

Fallen trees lay here and there, half in, half out of the water. A wooded slope stretched up from the shore. They paddled until they could no longer hear the clacking and croaking of the gloomy birds.

Eric said, "How about here?"

Now that they had finally reached a place of quietness and privacy, the new stiffness, present since Eric's return from Denmark, reliably reared its head again. Jen found herself missing town, but forced herself to concentrate on exactly where they were, in order to avoid thinking about the neighbour, who had started sending her occasional typed letters, even though he lived right next door. The nerve. Though, without even trying to, she had memorized the heart-stopping openings of the letters. *You are the most dressed and the most naked of women.* Thanks to spying on her studying in her shorts and halter, likely. *All of me is molten.* All of him certainly was determined. *After, I suppose, my calling, I cherish nothing more than your condescension.* For a considerable while, she made plenty of condescension available.

You and the weather have started me running again.

To distract herself from thinking about the letters, she said, "Let's find someplace to eat." She had brought good bread and real butter; English cucumbers and smoked gruyere; kalamata olives and salmon steaks; new potatoes from the farmers' market and chocolate from Cooke's on Brock, plus beer and wine — Jen wasn't the only one, since Denmark, to have left teetotalling behind — and gin and tonic, and limes.

They hauled the supplies up the little hill, which agreeably steadied out into mossy woods, broken up by open areas: shadows and light interspersed with fallen logs, waxen buttercups, nodding trilliums. Jen laid out the extravagant feast, propped up bottles, found openers and condiments, dishes and napkins. She said, indicating the bounty, "All this could be one of your bog pals' sacrificial meals."

Eric agreed and held up his freshly cracked beer. "Here's to Tollund Man!"

They opened more beers. They ate, they drank, they drank more and then still more, until gradually, the combination of the alcohol and the food, and the exertion and the sun, were beginning to make them magnanimous, daring.

Eric said, "We should take our clothes off."

It was hard not to hear the hope in his voice. "You first."

Just like that, Eric began to strip, his untanned skin white as trilliums.

Giggling, appalled, Jen grabbed the camera.

"Hey, no!" cried Eric, but he was laughing, too, hopping out of one of his socks, his pale bum bobbing in the sun. "No photographs!"

"Aw, come on! I'll let you if you let me." She could tell that all Eric really was hoping for as an outcome of this foolish exercise was for them finally to have sex, to connect, again. And somewhere far underneath the rush of wine and sun and provocation, Jen knew that that was just what she did not, could not, want anymore.

Still, she played the teasing game, she played along with her own mean invention. And she photographed Eric: Eric lying outstretched, his skin growing pinker under the long afternoon sun. Eric on his back, hands crossed over his chest like a piece of graveyard statuary. Eric on his front, arms and legs splayed, a reverse Vitruvian Man, so trusting and so mortal. Eric on his side with his legs drawn up, obedient and fetal.

Until: squinting against the light (he had taken his glasses off, for the picture taking), he sat up in his naked state and demanded to know if Jen was — he could hardly make himself say the words — in love with someone else.

The one honest thing she did that day was to say yes.

Eric's family lived by the decent injunction that *unkind words are best unsaid.* In that gentle spirit, Jen could tell, he replaced his glasses, got himself dressed, and carefully smashed a wine bottle. Then he picked up all the pieces, searching for any shards he might have missed, after which he started packing up the food, the blankets, and – this became clear in the weeks that followed – his marriage to Jen.

(Though apparently in Eric's family, even if unkind words were best unsaid, they could be written down in a letter. The one that arrived soon after Eric had found his new apartment congratulated her on successfully tearing out his heart. Logical as usual, the Dorie in her assured her she deserved it.)

It was on the way back to the canoe, which they approached by a different path than the one they had taken away from it, that they came upon the death smell, the red muddle, the appalling bones. Then the great, ragged birds in their gruesome convention. "Here," cried Eric with bitter merriment, "why leave *them* out?" He grabbed the camera and shot them, too.

A favourite saying of English prof Gord's was: "You can't buy love, but you can sure pay for it."

When things between him and Jen had begun to take what had seemed a more serious turn, they took to driving out to the conservation area, which was not very busy yet, for greater seclusion. They would walk there, along the bosky paths under the great trees, or sit in the long grass above the water, and watch the gulls and tankers coming and going.

Jen wanted to know what he meant about "paying."

Oh, Gord said, he had a friend who always used to say that about situations like his and Jen's.

Like theirs? Was he saying that their relationship, which was about to upend her entire life, was not absolutely unique? That it fit into some kind of – category? That it was a – a "situation?"

Well, he sighed in a newly world-weary way, his friend had been talking about those things that are nothing to do with your life, with your real, permanent life. This person had apparently meant that when you get started on things like what Gord and Jen were up to their eyeballs in, you might never intend for them to interfere, but that they could sometimes have consequences – "That's the expensive part" – that you might not have been banking on. He cited untidy examples, from the experiences of people not careful, not smart enough, whom he had known.

Your real life. Interfere. Consequences.

Up until now, Jen had firmly believed that what she had been experiencing with Gord – even the bad parts, the hiding and the near-escapes and the pain and the unruly longings – had all been part of a new, justifiable, Real Life that would one day, once all the mess of the present was over, be theirs.

It had never until that moment dawned on her that while she was filled up with all sorts of fond plans and tender imaginings, Gord might be busily picturing something quite different. (She was twenty-six years old at that time and had not yet learned what fine and artful nonsense can be folded up in words.)

Not long ago, the Royal Ontario Museum brought the Bog People to Toronto. Jen thought she'd better go, *in memoriam*, as it were: getting to see them anywhere would be a once-in-a-lifetime chance, Eric used to say, way back before they'd lost each other. She had some banked time, so she took the train and spent the day wandering past the sad, leathery remains of the ancient victims in their traces of odd cloaks and caps, their boneless feet and frail nooses. According to the write-ups on the display cases, the murdered people had been staked through the heart, face down, in order to make sure they didn't turn up again. Good luck with that, thought Jen.

She was getting ready to call it quits and go find a latte somewhere when she came upon Tollund Man. The label on his glass case explained that it was believed he had been hanged and then deposited in the bog as part of a fertility ritual. *He has been dead for more than 2,000 years*, the inscription mildly continued, *but he is so well preserved that he looks for all intents and purposes as though he might merely be sleeping.*

Jen contemplated the touchingly tidy summary and for once resisted the temptation to crack wise. For a long time, she merely gazed upon the body, which lay folded up in the fetal position, the soggy football of a head tucked thoughtfully down, the brow knit in an expression of slight fretfulness or mystification, as though the long-dead man might be pondering a calculation that had temporarily stumped him, or be caught in some puzzling dream.

WORDS

Forever wilt thou love, and she be fair!

JOHN KEATS, "ODE ON A GRECIAN URN"

Jen couldn't put it off any longer, she had to get to the grocery store, and she was. Getting there. She didn't own a car anymore, so these days she was walking everywhere, telling herself it was good for her. Her boots were wet. The slush was climbing her pants. The snowbanks, what was left of them, resembled stomach contents.

But she needed cat food, milk, cereal. She needed a break. "You just had a break!" parsley-and-poetry Gord from next door had laughed when she'd told him she was taking one, whenever that was. October? November? By then they weren't neighbours anymore, so they'd been standing, as sometimes happened, on a blustery street corner, only this time, he'd broken up with her—his wife, his life, his "can't do it anymore."

She'd watched his duffel-green back and his stevedore rubbers marching resolutely toward his car. After.

"It isn't serious, but it could be fatal," was one of the truths he used fondly to aver. Too bad she hadn't thought a little more, back then, about what those worldly words might mean for her.

Today might be beautiful if a person were in the country, birds tossed by wind, black nets of trees dreaming of spring, the whole thing distant and misty as a Keats poem. Though the sun was invisible, a diffuse brightness on the stream of passing cars betrayed its presence. She was always surprised on certain late-winter days that the sun would choose to reveal itself through anything so prosaic as the hoods of cars, yet sometimes that was the only way you could tell it was there.

Maybe she should put that in a poem; lately life had driven her to poetry, both the reading and the writing of it – though what she put on paper was nothing she'd ever show anyone; even she could tell that her stuff was too raw, too callow, too – let's face it – hollow.

The cars went on and on, a luminous toothache. Funny, she thought as they hissed past, how much "luminous" sounded like "ominous." Badboy Gord would advise her to put that in a poem, too, he was always happy to tell her what she could put where.

A disturbance in the metal river caught her eye. One car, a wicked water bug, had detached itself from the others, and was swooping to a smooth and expert stop on the other side of the street. By now you'd think she'd be used to it. But the car's colour and shape and particular set of rattles and squeaks could still make her mouth go dry.

This was how he always arrived, plummeting suddenly and without warning, like some *deus ex machina* out of the weekday sky and then going on his merry way, leaving her shaken and changed. Always somewhere in plain sight, a store or a street, where he couldn't be seen to have planned the encounter, and where she couldn't run for cover if she wanted to. Not that she wanted to, stubbornly believing, as she did, that these visitations, however "fatal," were better than wondering if he was alive.

For this, for things like this, "you had the foolishness to walk out of a good marriage!" Dorie's voice, burrowing like a permanent worm in her ear. There'd been no point in telling her mother that the marriage's terrible goodness itself had been killing her, all that obedience and mild behaviour, the house rule against the raising of a voice or letting go of a swear. That the two of them had gradually been dying in that dry, polite air, growing one-dimensional as dolls cut out of paper, flat as placemats.

Dorie and her routine damnations. The least foolish thing they'd ever managed had been to end it.

"Hey there, you!" Gord strode against the red light toward her now, a small general advancing into battle, a homespun Napoleon on his denim shank's mare, charging forth to meet . . . no Josephine. Maybe if she were one, it would be clear to her why he always carried himself with such authority, what invisible armies surrounded him, awaiting his stubborn command. But she was never going to know more than what she was seeing at this moment: a slender, elusive, arresting man.

"You look like a woman on a mission," he called, raising his collar against the cold.

Standing very still, a caught rabbit, she tried to quiet the thumping in her chest. *Please, Mr. Fox, throw me in the briar patch.*

She managed thin smile. "If you call cat food and coffee whitener a mission."

"So, tell me," he launched in, as they began trudging in the A&P's direction, "about school. I want to hear about your program. And your poetizing. Sent anything out yet?"

Poetizing. Not: How's it going, or What's new, after all this time. "I want to know about . . ." As though they'd had breakfast together this very morning, and dinner last night, and his tossed questions were an extension of an ongoing conversation. She could never decide whether this was a matter of style with him, the need to streamline, to cut out the small talk and make it all count, the way he shaped his lectures and articles, or if it was part of some determination to keep at least a semblance of dialogue going with her, a simulacrum of what they'd been, or been reaching for. The thinnest thread of dialogue, perhaps, but linked and doggedly logical, as though they were real people, properly connected and knowing everyday things about each other. Or if it was just his way of protecting himself, establishing the boundaries of what could be discussed, by getting his word, his words, in first. From the corner of her eye, she could see the cloth of his coat, the one she remembered, the one she once was folded up and held in. The way he'd shelter her out of the wind and murmur, "Don't be askeert," using a made-up word that was personal to him.

His skinny neck sported the same narrow knitted scarf that looked like a child had made it. His child. His children. Did he say "don't be askeert" to them? Folded carefully across the vulnerable part of his throat, slick as a lock.

"I've been spending some time reading the Romantic poets," came her lame reply, referencing the elective she'd taken in his long-ago classroom. She didn't want to talk about her weary little poems or her tanked life, to be reminded of those first grinding months, when it had begun to dawn on her what she'd actually done in leaving her marriage — for him! For them! — when getting to class was all that had kept her connected to the known world. The schedule of essays and seminars that for a while had been her only companion. "Otherwise, I'm just working, sort of on a volunteer basis. For now."

"Let me guess . . . you're a glass blower."

She reared back from a car splash. "I blew the interview."

"A town crier."

"Way overqualified."

"I know! A professional mourner."

"More like: a professional learner. I'm part-time at the library. If they like me, I might get hired."

Another too-close car sent up a hurl of cold water, and both of them reared back, only to step into a deeper trough. Jen glanced behind her, puffed out a small laugh. "You're going to have a hike to get back to your car."

Hands jammed down his pockets, he ignored her attempted rigour. Maybe he was going to invite her to have a coffee with him, Mister Donut was close by, and he'd be careful not to get too much further away from the safety of his rattling chariot than there. Under his home-knit cap, his eyes surveyed the oncoming traffic, on watch for anyone who might recognize him. Napoleon sizing up the battlefield.

It was reading week. Maybe that was why he was out and about, dressed in jeans on a school day. More grey in his hair than the last time she saw him, more lines around those steady eyes. (What changes did he see in her, what folds and fissures? Probably it wasn't great for your look, being a professional mourner.) Everything else about him seemed the same, with the same molten effect on all parts of her. One of the great mysteries: looked at objectively, he was average enough. Her problem was the loss of the gift — what she'd considered a gift, the second sight or sixth sense, now lost — that would allow her to see him objectively.

"So," he demanded, "what are you doing for lazy week?"

She contrived a smile. "I guess you mean reading week. I'm not a student anymore, remember? And these days I can't exactly afford to travel."

"Whoops, right, for a moment I was imagining you heading down to Mexico with your school pals."

"Never been much of a one for pals. If you recall. And anyway, I need some time to concentrate." She could imagine what this sounded like to him; he was always so amused and mystified by her seeming lack of focus. What he hadn't known back then: she'd been too busy memorizing, hoarding, storing up details of his voice and face and scent against the time to come, to process the slightly less vital information, the words, tender or tantalizing, coming from his mouth. "Anyway, how's teaching going this semester? Got any promising students?"

She could barely hear her own words, thanks to the traffic, from which the sun had now withdrawn. So, she focused instead on the mysterious, kindly, challenging face in front of her, trying as always to learn, to read, to inwardly digest it. Knowing it didn't matter anymore, how hard she studied, how deeply she saw; no amount of memorizing was going to keep him there for many more minutes now. And she could guess what he was seeing: spotty old coat — "what have *you* been rubbing up against?" (one of his jokes) — and winter-white face and flat hair, nothing there but the real thing.

"There'll never be a student as promising as you."

"Oh, I was promising, all right." With one wet foot she gave a lump of slush a push. "I think you gave me an A-minus. In your course."

"I don't grade any higher. Anyway, I thought I told you."

A few visitations ago, no doubt, standing in some noisy intersection like this one, cars whizzing by. "Told me?"

"I'm on sabbatical. This semester. We're going abroad for a while, haven't decided exactly where, yet, but we're thinking Greece would be nice. You know what they say, publish or perish; gotta find a crag and a cottage, try to crank out some words."

He drew a long finger down his cheek, and she could feel, even now, the touch of those hands, the clean, startling nearness of his skin. But she needed to be witty. Wit saved lives. It should be part of the EMT curriculum. "You'll find some melodious plot, no doubt, complete with orange trees and nightingales. A good time for it, too." With a mittened hand, she indicated the monochrome view. "And don't forget to pick up some of 'the blushful Hippocrene' to enjoy on those fine Grecian evenings."

"Okay, Ms. Keats," he teased with another shoulder check. "Anyway, what's up for you tonight?"

His skillful advancing of time toward time-up was not lost on her. "Going to a 'flick,' to use your word." She zipped her coat higher, to keep the snow from finding her throat. "It's an oldie, down at the repertoire theatre."

"Oh yeah? Which one?"

"*The Commitments*."

"Mustang Sally! Great fun."

Jen drew her cuff across her nose, which had started to run.

They were both beginning to get edgy; this was about all either of them could usually take, what with the roar of the traffic and the pressure of the other words, unvoiced now, and from now on.

A cement truck was barreling their way, its tilted cone twirling idly behind with a kind of monstrous beauty. What would Keats have to say? *Ode on a Cement Truck?* "Thou unstill, grit-filled bride of chaos . . ." She felt a small chuckle stirring but kept the joke to herself.

"Well," he yelled, turning up his collar, "gotta run over to your library before it closes, pick up a book. Keep writing!"

"Right," she said back, the dead word swallowed in the howl of the passing truck.

On her way to the movie later in the day, she's waiting for the light to change when she glimpses his car again. This time it doesn't stop, or even slow down. Though it's dark and starting to rain, it's possible to tell that the car now contains a couple, going about its Friday-night errands. Momentarily revealed by the streetlight can be seen a husband and next to him his wife, her mouth open, forming words.

ARTEFACTS

FOR E.W.P.

The things you find when you're moving. Which, here she goes again . . .

- Antique cat-scratching post in hall closet. (Which cat?)
- Ancient sandwich (from the anorexic phase) in daughter's — make that, former daughter's — bookshelf.
- Bell bottoms and beads from long before the existence of said daughter.
- Bungee cords, rubber bands, a lightbulb.
-
- A Rubik's Cube.

And, as if on cue, here's the pics from that holiday weekend when Jen and Eric took the bus to visit his parents, in Niagara-on-the-Lake . . .

THE BUS STATION

There they are, Bob and Ilene, world's fittest retirees, Bob vigorous and tanned, a grower of grapes and maker of his own wine, never one to miss an early bird swim or a chance to read to the blind; Ilene ditto, plus she's a first-rate cook and domestician (a scary new word for Jen), as well as an enthusiastic altar guild lady at their church (Anglican), one of ten proud and cheerful second violins in the local symphony, a three-afternoons-a-week volunteer (library), and in her "spare" time a collector of art (still lifes, particularly). She likes to call her still lifes "memento mori" because they're supposed to make you think about life's ephemeral nature. She has enough paintings of breathing bouquets and leaning lutes and arrangements of fruit (who would ever need that many grapes?) to shame every memento mori maker from Holbein to Cezanne and back again.

Memento mori. Keep in mind that you will die. Back in Dorie-land, nobody'd be caught dead knowing a Latin phrase for life's brevity, or paying good money to go see a symphony, let alone calling themselves a domestician as they opened a can of Chef Boyardee. Most of which biases still (if secretly) hold true in the life of Jen.

The dust in the terminal parking lot hangs like theatre curtains, but Bob and Ilene are fresh and well-pressed in matching chinos and pastel polo shirts complete with those little Ralph Lauren horsemen on them, and looking, despite the blistering heat, like they have but slight acquaintance with sweat.

Hugs and kisses all around, the recorded voice blaring arrivals and departures. Ilene (she's driving) pointing the way to the BMW, her competent hands veined and tanned.

"You'll have to forgive the mess in back," she calls as Eric and Jen climb in over the fresh dry cleaning and bottles of expensive wine, and complicated looking breads, and cheeses Jen didn't know existed. "We figured since we were going to be out and about anyway, we might as well pick up some supplies for a special meal" – those terrifying hands skillfully manoeuvring the cherrywood steering wheel – "I always just think it's so nice to have a special meal when you kids are home!"

Jen remembers her manners. "Ilene, please let us help with the cooking and – things – while we're here . . ."

"Oh," Ilene chuckles, "you two didn't come all this way on your holiday weekend just to work, and I'm certainly not going to have you wasting your precious –" Expertly she shifts into second as they dash downhill. "Everything's under control."

The BMW slows, speeds up, hurtles out of town and shoots down a long narrow country road past crumbling walls, quaint bridges, mourning doves, musky grapevines. Pretty soon manicured bushes start appearing, and ornamental grasses, extravagant blooms, and then: Ilene's and Bob's trim rose-covered home is standing at attention right where they left it, across from the Botanical Gardens.

"Home at last!" Ilene pulls a smooth U-ey in front of the house, its well-watered lawns prim and stately and still deliciously green, despite the waning season, and barred with long, cool slants of evening sun. Eric looks over at Jen. Time to go in.

FRIDAY NIGHT

All but Ilene are seated in the softly carpeted living room, the bags stashed in the granny suite and Mozart stately on the stereo as the evening light pours like melted butter through the big bow windows.

Eric's busy making "paper knots" out of old newspapers for a fire they might have later, nowanights it cools down earlier, and Bob's in his favourite chair, concentrating on the new Rubik's Cube he got for his birthday, planning to figure it out "if it's the last thing I ever do." There's a trick to these things, he says, there's always a trick, you just have to work at it until you break the code. He makes a happy sleight of hand.

Ilene, meanwhile, bustles back and forth opening bottles, setting out snacks. "Just a few things I had around."

Asparagus and herbed cream cheese roll-ups. Warm brie baked in phyllo. Smoked oysters. Twelve-year-old port with Brazilian cashews and perfectly ripened Bartlett pears.

"Ilene," intones Jen in her best Upper Canadian, "this is so —"

"Oh, it's not much," Ilene laughs. "But" — wagging a finger at Eric — "you make sure you save some room. We'll be having just a light little meal, but there's trifle for dessert!"

"Oh, boy!" Eric tosses a paper knot for joy.

Following a dinner fit for the Romanovs, Jen sleeps like a baby.

BRIGHT AND EARLY

She comes to in the rosy dawn, all set to jump Eric's bones; after all, it's been a while, and there's something about being away, that wakes it up in her. Though, when she opens her eyes, Eric's dressed and ready to haul two old mattresses, an ancient preserve cupboard, and a bunch of paint cans to the dump with his father. Just a few little jobs Bob saves for when the "kids" are here.

"Oh, come on." She goes for his trousers. "How 'bout a quickie . . ."

"Jenny, oh, my, honey . . ."

Jenny. Instinctively, she bridles at her childhood nickname, which reminds her of dirt roads and compromised goats. "What?"

"It's just — with Mum and Dad around, you know —"

"Hiloo-hoo-hoo!" yodels Bob from the landing, as though in confirmation of Eric's intention to take things no further; that, or he's in need of a fellow patroller for the ramparts of Elsinore.

"Right." Jen zips Eric back up. "Have fun at the dump."

"Jenny, it's just that —"

But Jen's heading for the shower, despising herself while grabbing her trusty vibrator along the way. "Don't worry," she calls as she hoofs it down the hall. "Everything's under control."

Instead of heading up to the kitchen once her shower's done, she loiters in the downstairs rooms, not yet ready to take Ilene on. Through the sliding doors, she can see Eric out on the patio, hands in sad pockets, downcast of eye, and she knows she should apologize. But some combination of bad temper and stubbornness keeps her from going out there.

BREAKFAST

Or: Still Life with Pissed-Off Maritimer Sitting on Stairs.

Don't get in Ilene's way if you value your life. Tonight's the special meal. By the time Jen's cowering at the counter, Ilene's been at it since the crack with her choppers, gutters, and splitters, her gleaming weigh scales. The place looks like the Master Chef Test Kitchens at full throttle, Ilene hale as Hannibal.

"Morning," she barks mid-chop. "How'd everybody sleep?"

"Thank you, we slept gr —"

"Wonderful. I'm just doing up a quick batch of zucchini muffins for our breakfast." Briefly, she glances up. "This time of the season, they ripen so fast you just have to keep on them, the darn things can grow a couple inches a day. Oh, and tonight I'll be doing a brand-new lamb recipe I came across in this month's *Gourmet*."

Ilene doesn't talk about "cooking," she talks about "doing." In addition to the muffins, she's doing lemon-garlic tiger prawn shrimp appetizers (for tonight), followed by cold curried cucumber soup, her special chickpea and black bean salad, Beaujolais-braised summer lamb, herbed new potatoes in foil (also from her own garden), and for dessert – she's changed her mind – your choice of black-currant mousse or gooseberry fool. Jen feels a pang when Ilene names that one. It gets her thinking of how, back home, they all used to go picking down the bank when the tide was out, herself, Rose, and for a while Sonny, bringing home gooseberries by the bucketful for Dorie to put in her pies. Even now, her mind can hear the echo of Rosie's gooseberry discoveries, Sonny's subversive, delighted laughter, Dorie's cheerful threats and warnings.

"Coffee's in the urn," Ilene barks as Jen tentatively opens the fridge door.

"Can I do anything?" she enquires weakly, hoping to high heaven Ilene says no.

Ilene stands in the middle of the kitchen surveying the terrain, going over the annotated list in her notebook and pressing her pencil eraser into her bottom lip, pressing and rolling it, the big brown agate she wears on the fourth finger of her pencil hand snatching at the morning light like it owns it.

"Well," she says, not looking up, "you could stack the dishwasher." A fool's job, though in Ilene's kitchen, one not to be taken lightly. There's an exact place for every fork and plate and vegetable steamer, certain things that must go on the top rack, and others that can only be put on the bottom, and these are not to be confused. Plus, there's always more that can be got in than Jen can imagine, and ever such cunning ways of wedging them in there, you can't just toss them in any old way, some handles have to be up and some down, to prevent "nesting." And you're never to use the liquid detergent (God help her, she tried that once and nearly blew the place up), only the powdered Cascade with etching protection, and don't forget the Jet-Dry, with its special sheeting action. Plus, you're not to use the full wash-and-rinse cycle, that's wasteful, you always have to make sure to use the Water Miser.

"And then, let me see . . . you can polish the flatware."

Praise God, she knows what that is now.

Through the open kitchen window, Bob and Eric can be heard strolling companionably down the garden with their coffee, Bob pointing out all the hard work and husbandry that've been poured into the back half acre since they were last here. See the composter, see the Mighty Mack, look at the retaining wall; how about that deck! And all the while, the Saturday sun shining and the birds gaily twittering. She'd give her cat, if she had one, to be out there with them in the ordinary air, she'd give her firstborn.

She doesn't know much about life yet, but one thing she's sure of: there's no innocence for a woman in another woman's kitchen.

LUNCH

The four of them crowd cozily around the custom-made table in the kitchen "nook" in front of the bow window that Bob and Ilene built specially for bird watching. Dorie's not quite as snarky as she used to be, but Jen can't help imagining what she'd have to say about a window built just for staring at birds.

Plants, crosswords, and reference books are strewn in a pleasant jumble on the wide sill, plus two pairs of binoculars, together with notebooks detailing comprehensive lists of "sightings" complete with date, name of the bird, natural habitat, and markings.

So far today there's been two pileated woodpeckers, three purple finches, one grosbeak, and a load of common sparrows. Lunch, light leftovers from last night's spread (everybody on orders to hold back for the special meal), is finished and washed up, and Ilene's going over her list from this morning, while Bob scans the backyard, ever on the alert for something out of the ordinary, a hummingbird, say, or an oriole, or somebody's escaped parrot.

Ilene excuses herself from the table, and when she returns, she's wearing a crisp sleeveless linen shirt and belted khaki Bermudas, her handsome grey hair whipped into its customary crown. She takes one look at the rest of them, then holds out her compact with one hand, drawing on a masterful smile with the other. Rubbing her lips together, she observes to no one in particular, "I have to run up to the market to pick up a few more quarts of peaches to ripen, and some berries for tonight. Anybody need anything?"

Eric's good.

Bob's good.

Jen's fine: three hours, give or take, until further food preparation.

Now Ilene's rummaging in her purse, collecting sunglasses, car keys, the post office key. "I'll be back around three, to finish up for tonight. Jen, if you could take care of the dishwasher, that would be great. Don't worry about putting things away, just if you could empty it out, I'll do the rest" (she quite reasonably doesn't trust Jen to do it right) "when I get back.

Eric, while you're here I'd like you to clean out all that old stuff in your bedroom closet. I intend to set up my sewing room in there. Bob dear, the front flower beds'll need another good soaking this afternoon if you can get around to it, the impatiens, especially, I noticed, are looking a bit tired with the heat. Just to have everything looking nice for the special meal tonight."

And she's gone. You can feel the house let down.

STILL LIFE WITH DEAD PHEASANT

What Jen wouldn't give to be back on that bus right now. The special meal's cooling on the groaning board, Eric and Bob are God knows where, and Ilene's ready to blow. One thing you do *not* do is show up late to her table.

"Jen, please run and check the downstairs fridge," she goes, without looking up from her notes, "to see if the tortes have set."

Jen's never laid eyes on a torte in her life. This is long before Google and YouTube; how would she know if a torte's set, just chillin', or, like its maker, fit for lift-off?

"And you can pop out to the garden and get me some parsley, if you would. Not the curly, the Italian, it's the one with the broader leaf." She pauses, remembering. "Oh, and I could use a bit of fennel."

Jen doesn't know what fennel is yet, either.

As if reading Jen's dismayed mind Ilene adds, "That's the wispy stuff that looks like dill, but it's got a bit of a liquorice smell if you rub it in your fingers, like so." Her beginning-to-be-arthritic index finger strokes its neighbouring thumb, which is crosshatched with small dark lines from a lifetime of gardening, good deeds, and food preparation. "And bring it in out of the heat as soon as you pick it, so it doesn't wilt, it's very delicate." She draws her finger slowly along the lines of her recipe, and Jen can see harsh little hairline cracks in her work-roughened fingernails. "Be careful, though," she adds, "the wasps are something terrible out there this year." She tilts her elegant head, as though listening. "Have you seen any sign of the men?"

Jen's back in five, with one hand full of what she hopes is fennel, the other sporting a hot welt.

Ilene looks up from her Béchamel sauce. "Honestly, what is the matter with those two?" Then she spies Jen's hand, and away she bustles to get the baking soda, calling backward over her shoulder. "It'll draw out the sting."

Jen takes the next chance she gets to slip out to the lawn, where Bob's showing Eric the new sprinkler system. Like a possibly rabid coyote, she slinks up to them. "Um, you guys need to come."

Bob's head snaps up, he knows what's afoot. "Right you are. On our way!"

But it's too late. By the time the two of them show up, Ilene is grim. "Weren't we going to dress for dinner?" she enquires politely of the dining room ceiling.

Bob darts a conspiring look at Eric. "Whoops."

Ilene studies the Still Life with Dead Pheasant above the sideboard. "I'm afraid the lamb may be a bit overdone."

The food is perfection. The wine flows. Dessert follows. Bob opens the usual well-aged after-dinner bottle.

Ilene, in the kitchen between courses, sniffles only a little.

Though, thank the Lord for good food and wine. With a couple of glasses each or three, plus the saffron risotto warming their bellies, the men have relaxed, and Ilene has eased to the point where actual jokes can be told.

Bob: Where does the Commander keep his armies?

Jen thinks, You mean her armies.

Eric: Where?

Bob: In his sleevies.

Eric: Speaking of arms: How does a squid go into battle?

Bob: Search me.

Eric: Fully armed.

Jen (by now gladsomely wine-filled): What d'ya call an escaped parrot?

All: What??

Jen: A polygon!

Universal 'round-the-table groan.

Ilene: Never criticize someone until you've walked a mile in their shoes. That way, when you criticize them, you'll be a mile away, and you'll have their shoes.

Jen dreams of being a mile away, with or without shoes.

HANDS

Bob and Eric are relaxing in the living room with their sherry, the dishwasher is chugging, and the lights are turned down. Dinner, that harrowing mission, is accomplished, Ilene, for now, is at peace, the Alps satisfactorily crossed.

Exhaling praise to God for the survival of another special meal, Jen descends to the basement's cool obscurity, knowing in her heart of darkness that Eric's marriage, through no fault of his own, is not going to stand the tests of time.

Down here amongst the signs of Ilene's suspended industry, there's a twilit calm and further still lifes, though these are real, nothing like the framed scenes above stairs: Still Life with Ripening Pears and Ironing Board; Still Life with Preserving Jars and Pressure Canner (dear God, thinks Jen, let me be far from here when that job starts); Still Life with Gardening Gloves and Secateurs, the gloves still curled to the shape of Ilene's never-idle hands. Which by now will be double-wrapping the leftovers and emptying the dishwasher, scouring the kitchen to Kingdom Come.

Then – for it's after midnight – the silence of the tomb.

On the twin bed beside Jen's, Eric will soon be snoring, his belly contentedly digesting his mother's excellent cooking as he rests up for the long trip home in the morning. Now that all the stacking and talking and eating are done, Jen looks down at her own hands, still supple and unworn, compared with Ilene's well-used, ephemeral ones.

Tomorrow Jen will be grabbing luggage, clutching tickets, and waving through a dirty bus window at the bright, receding shapes of Eric's parents, full of being young, eager to get going, and unaware that someday, Bob and Ilene will be gone.

—

That was all so long ago. Trawling the internet late one night, she sees about Ilene's passing. All that upright elegance and gourmet efficiency, only to have it laid waste by something as ugly, unlikely, and unfair as a brain tumour.

By now Jen's been on her own three times as long as she ever was married to Eric, though she's never stayed in the same place for long. Who knew she'd end up in the home of beef, Banff, and bad driving? These days, she wouldn't have a clue if Eric makes paper knots, loves lamb, is satisfied, dead, or suffers quickies, but she knows when a torte's set, and, for what it's worth, she can stack a mean dishwasher.

The things you remember, a lifetime later. Bob in his plaid shirt and sock feet in the evening light, determined to find the sleight of hand that will crack Mr. Rubik's cool puzzle; the licorice smell of freshly-picked fennel; a young husband's reasonable modesty in his mother's house; a fond fire-starting ritual. The artefacts are innocuous, the ache they hold indelible.

Though she tries, as she shuts the computer down for the night, to grant herself the same half-fraudulent comfort she'd offer a child stung by a wasp; after all, when a person is as young as she was then, what can she really grasp?

HERE AND NOW

There once was a saint named Agath, who was placed in a torturous bath. Refusing to drown, she would only lie down, so they cut off her privates forthwith.

SMALL'S ANTHOLOGY OF WICKED LIMERICKS

On her day off, which is Thursday, Jen is updating her clients' files, those tales of brokenness, bad choices, depravity, and plain stupidity people accumulate and get attached to, and wondering if she should maybe take a break from it all and go teaching for a while; a mat-leave position has been offered, and she's interested. She's also half-listening, as usual, to the CBC. A woman writer from Newfoundland, according to the announcer, has come out with the story of a "dangerous friendship" between some famous genius or other and an unknown woman, back in the nineteenth century. Jen can't help herself; she cocks an ear and catches enticing bits about emotional cruelty and weird sexual hang-ups (the genius's), degrading practices (his too), elaborate humiliations and devious meanness (both of them, eventually), the whole thing verging on unspeakable.

She has to smile; she knows a thing or two about unspeakable. It's why she's ended up, after all, in this job; where else, she jokes, would she get paid so well to work on her own stuff? And she's lived life, read books, learned all about how we "create our own reality" and are thus responsible for every single thing that happens to us, which all boils down to the fact that no one else is to blame.

But there is someone she blames. Deeply, secretly, and in the candlelit privacy of her own bathtub, Jen blames God.

For one thing. She was a minor when God, who was after all so much her senior, first got hold of her, starting her down the path of admiring older men, with their mystery, their melancholy, and their seemingly magical powers. This was back toward the end of high school, when she was failing math, feeling desperate, and imagining that prayer and privation might help her get through Grade 11. At this time, she took to attending the Catholic Church, which caused some heads – her family was more or less United – to turn.

Catholicism had but slight, if any, effect on her math scores, but it did give her a taste for incense and plainchant, for solemn tomes about impaled saints and starving martyrs, and for all those pained-looking stained-glass Jesuses, with their softly waved hair, their womanish features, and their wavering oil lamps. Also, it must be confessed: for the priest, whom she got to call "Father," and who gave off a certain stern handsomeness in his miter and embroidered robes, his censer-swinging solitude. Solitude, after all, being at a premium where Jen grew up, across the road from Anneli's, with Rose the Baby, overworked Dorie, and – though only temporarily – dear, infuriating Sonny. Someday, she'd promised herself back then, she would be long gone from that impossible jumble.

Not only that. She was sure she was going to be remarkable.

She got to be remarkable, all right, though not in a way that impressed Dorie. "You don't mean to tell me" – this was down the road a few years, when Dorie found out that Jen and Eric weren't doing so well anymore.

"I tried to tell you."

"Tell me what, for Lord's sake?"

"Back when –"

"Oh. Back when I'd already spent the entire winter making that dress and the invitations were sent out and the whole town –"

"Yes, then. I tried to tell you I didn't want to get married. I tried. Don't you remember?"

"Oh, I remember. What was the point of all that education you got, if you can't even –" Dorie let out an exasperated puff of air. "I'm fed up with the pair of you."

No point trying to tell her mother that getting married after second year had been "just too soon."

"You made your bed."

Or that Jen hadn't – *couldn't* have – known enough back then, about what she really wanted to do with her life, to take a step that portentous –

"You were portentous enough about everything else you wanted."

Much less that, in the end (though she did tell Dorie this part), it was the Anglican church that had had a hand in her and Eric's final and for real demise.

"Well, at least you've said one thing today that makes some sense."

(This thorny conversation took place on Dorie's back porch one summer night, in that peaceful interregnum between the breakup with Eric, and the trying "one more time.")

They'd only been back together (in case a baby might be the thing that was missing) for a year or so when Eric, owing to his study of the bog people, had had go on another sojourn to faraway swamps in Denmark. Jen, though she'd gone back to school by now and finished her own program, had stayed on in town, living alone in their apartment (they'd sold their house, which Jen had never much liked anyway, and moved for a fresh start to one of those handsome old places down on King Street). The evenings were long, she didn't have a job or a baby yet, and loneliness soon reared its matted head.

A notice on the lawn of the Anglican church was mentioning a need for sopranos one day when she walked past. Wasn't Anglican pretty much the same thing as Catholic? To her considerable surprise, she passed the audition, and pretty soon was safely ensconced at St. Ursula's, delivering the Agnus Dei and the Dies Irae as lively as the rest of them. She liked getting to know the people in the choir and loved being lapped in the rigours of the ritual. It pleased her to sit in the chancel on Sunday mornings, dressed up as a virgin martyr in her scarlet choir gown and feeling the stained light from the Gothic windows falling upon her white, bent neck. Kneeling at the communion rail with the other choristers, she imagined she was one of the ecstatic girls in those gloomy old books she used to read, draped in crimson, ready to be stabbed.

Just around the same time, a job came up at the public library's circulation desk. What luck! Somebody she knew from the university was friends with the head librarian, who was interested to learn she'd volunteered at a library, and that got her an interview.

She got lucky that time, too.

A duty of the library job, and one she liked especially, was changing and maintaining the library's display cases.

One Saturday afternoon she was setting up an exhibit of prison artefacts in promotion of a popular new book by a local author. The book was all about long-ago convict life in the Kingston penitentiary, so she called around and found enough scary implements to make a forbidding arrangement of manacles and hacksaws, chains, clubs, prods, and other dire accessories. She was standing back to appraise her handiwork when her heel came down on the very polished toe of a handsome black shoe. She leaped away to steady herself, exasperated, apologizing, spilling torture instruments. "Jesus."

"Oh, my dear!" protested the man connected to the shoe. "It was entirely my fault for coming up so silently behind you."

Jen thought that was true and shot him a look that said so.

"Are you hurt? Is there anything I can do?" A vaguely British inflection, though without identifiable accent.

Jen said no thank you, that's all right, never mind. By now she had had time to tell that he looked like no man she had ever before laid eyes on. He was old, probably getting toward fifty, but striking in a severe and melancholy way, with fair reddish hair falling boyishly across his forehead, and startling blue eyes. He was wearing a suit of light black wool so expertly tailored it appeared to be a seamless extension of his body, which, Jen managed to notice, was both slim and sturdy. Another thing she noticed — was she getting the flu, did she suddenly need glasses? — he seemed to shine somehow or glow, as though he had swallowed a radioactive particle, or might contain a candle.

He held out a strong, well-tended hand. "I'm Gabe, and I *am* so sorry!"

She saw with alarm that he was beautiful.

"Oh well," she said, indicating her handiwork — "What do you think?" — and, regretting the anchovies in the Caesar salad she'd had for lunch, she joked, "I guess if pain's your thing, you've come to the right place."

"I think," he said with genuine admiration, "that it is perfectly *marvellous*."

Jen could not help wondering who on earth would use an expression like that, and for a torture presentation to boot.

Also: anyone could see that he was full of himself. "Well," she said, "nice meeting you. I have to get ready for the children's hour." She indicated the other librarian, over by the circulation desk. "Rozanne can help you if you have any questions."

That night, which was a Saturday, Jen had the strangest dream. She was back home with Anneli from long ago, and they were in the tool shed, making little people out of wooden clothespins. As usual back then, Anneli was the first to get bored and the quickest to turn mean.

Squat down, she instructs Jen.

What, here? says Jen.

Here, and now, commands the dream.

Jen does as she's told; after all, she doesn't want to be sent home. Next thing she knows, Anneli's got her tied up to the worktable, and is clamping the cruel clothespins onto her fingertips, her lips, her earlobes, even her eyelids.

As the pain approaches its peak, Jen begins to awaken, her legs kicking, the words *here and now* reverberating in her brain.

She woke to get ready for church the next day with an ominous feeling, left over from such shreds of the dream as she could recall. Clothespins. A worktable. Anneli's gently menacing smile.

While the choir was warming up on the versicles and responses, who comes walking—wafting, rather—into the practice room but the unusual man from the library. Though this time, he was dressed up as a priest, long gown, miter, stole, and all.

Jen did a double take. So did the man, whose name wasn't so much Gabe, as Gabriel.

The choir master, squinting up from his music and seeing him walk in, interrupted the singing and said to please welcome his old friend Gabriel Breene, who'd long ago studied with him at Hart House, who was now Bishop of Toronto, and who would be taking the service today, in the absence of the regular rector.

Bishop of Toronto. No wonder he looked like he had a candle in him. And *that* was who she'd covered with her fish breath, stomped on, and said "Jesus" at yesterday. Jesus! Behind her score of *O Vos Omnes* (it was Easter, crucifixion season), Jen felt herself go red to her scalp.

Too bad. Now it was time for the choir to line up for the procession into the church. As the great carved doors swung open to allow the clergy and choir's swaying progress into the sanctuary, Jen, who was carrying the polished crucifix and leading the way (the usual rood bearer was sick that day), happened to glance back to the end of the line. What she saw was Gabriel (Gabe!), looking steadily, unmistakably, and quite radiantly back at her.

At communion, which Gabriel served to the choir first, Jen was trembling. Kneeling before him, head lowered, she devoutly wished she'd washed her hair.

"The blood of Christ," murmured Gabriel, tilting the cold cup to her lips. She felt the burn of the wine, heard the creak of his polished black Oxfords and the rustle of embroidered brocade as he moved on down the line of communicants. She spied the glint of long red hairs on his divine hands. "Shed for you."

Gabriel was back the very next Sunday, brilliant as before, though this time not in his priest outfit. Instead, he wore the black suit from the library and a look of grave self-command, taking his place in the congregation along with everyone else.

The third time he turned up (why wasn't he back in Toronto, taking care of his own flock?) a rumour got going that he was suffering from fatigue connected with his priestly duties, and that he was therefore taking an extended holiday at his summer home, over on Wolfe Island. There were dark imaginings of illness, depression, and possible agnosticism, wonderings about his private life (did he have one?), speculations that he might be leaving the church. Satisfaction, that St. Ursula's was the alternative place of worship he had fled to.

Tongue-wagging, generally.

Pretty soon they were wagging about more than that.

After the first sublime look of criminal knowledge had passed between Jen and Gabriel on the way into the church on that fateful Sunday morning, things had moved along at quite a clip. For starters, Gabriel, who really was taking time off, contributed his serviceable tenor to the St. Ursula's choir, which meant that every Thursday night, there he reliably was, parked right behind Jen, front centre in the tenor section. The tension. The thrill up the back of her neck as she felt him take his seat behind her. The agony of waiting, if he happened to be a few minutes late.

And oh, the striving, ecstatic yodeling, once the polyphony got under way.

Soon bodily contact, in the form of accidental nudges or shoulder brushings during the choir's coffee break, were added. Further pointed glances were stolen. It wasn't long before phone calls were risked, confidences exchanged, entire life stories, bleakly meaningless until this moment, urgently shared.

Before long, it was revealed that Gabriel's public austerity was only a front for a shy but passionate heart, and that no one before Jen had ever been able to unlock said heart, mysteriously wounded long ago, hence the holy orders. Jen herself had so far, she felt, failed to experience much in the way of earthly passion, of agony or ecstasy, of Life. Both of them claimed to be in love with the chilly transports of English church music and Anglican ritual, mad for the punishing proscriptions in the Book of Common Prayer, determined that *there is no health in us.*

Meetings, both accidental and contrived, were taking place.

One time they ran into each other at the post office downtown, an event they took, with the inscrutable logic of lovers and drunk people, to be a sign from Above. On another occasion they stumbled upon each other in the reference room of the university library, that strict and silent haven for the hot to trot. One day, a letter arrived at her own library, asking her to visit him on his island. A creamy, heavy envelope, scrawled upon with thick fountain-pen strokes (who wrote with a fountain pen?), faintly, mysteriously fragrant, luminous with portent. Jen held the letter in her hands, for some moments blinded by the late afternoon light that was just then streaming prophetically in through the library windows, knowing (in that same way that drunk people and lovers, especially the forbidden kind, are apt to imagine they know things) that Gabriel was her fate.

That very night she went home and called Eric (he was due in a week to be home from Denmark) to say she thought she should live by herself for a while.

"I thought you were always telling me you're too much by yourself," Eric said reasonably.

"Just for a while, until I sort myself out."

Eric wanted to know what she had to sort out that they couldn't sort out together. After all, hadn't they only recently gotten back together? And he'd already been gone a good part of the year.

Well, she lied, she needed to be alone just a little while longer.

Eric wondered why she needed to be alone more than she already was. Though he understood he couldn't stop her; she could take time if she wanted to, he wouldn't be going anywhere in a hurry.

"It'll be just temporary," reasoned Jen, beginning to get the first inkling of what all this could mean. She would just try it for a couple of months.

They agreed to part for the summer, and Jen found a damp basement summer sublet.

Gabriel's place was one of the oldest on Wolfe Island. He pointed that out with a mighty pleasure the first time Jen visited, indicating the watery old glass in the narrow windows, the steep floors, the charmingly cumbersome latchkeys, for the doors.

"It's lovely," said Jen, who was entirely subdued by the handsome gloom of the place. It was early evening. Beyond the windows, swallows were skimming the lake, which had gone still and silver. There was nothing to be heard except the occasional call of a loon, the slightly asynchronous ticking of the antique clocks in the hundred-year-old rooms.

Gabriel took her by the arm in a way she found quaint but stirring, pointing out puritanical dressers and needleworked chairs, darkened paintings of grumpy-looking ancestors. "These" (an ancient-looking hand-tinted photo of three Brontë-era females) "are my aunts, my mother's sisters. They were missionaries, in India. A lot of this furniture, as well as the china" (faded flowers, maiden wreathes) "was theirs."

Jen studied the baleful faces, hoping to find a resemblance.

As though guessing her thoughts, Gabriel observed, "They were all born right here in this house." He corrected the angle of a frame. "As was I."

Jen managed a tiny sip of her drink, which was Cutty Sark, new to her, and marvellously harsh. She managed to murmur, "My goodness, how—"

"In that very bed, actually." With his own drink (a well filled G&T topped with hefty chunks of ice and lime), Gabriel pointed to an antique spool bed, just visible from an adjacent downstairs room.

"Do you still sleep in it?" Jen enquired politely.

"Absolutely. There's nothing so affirming, I find, as sleeping in the bed of one's forebears." He gave her elbow an encouraging squeeze.

Jen wondered how the forebears would feel when he was bouncing in that bed with her, supposing that happened. Though, the whereabouts of such an activity, should it take place, were yet to be determined.

Now he showed her the comfortable verandah, with its wicker lounge chairs, and the pot-bellied stove, the crucifix in the kitchen.

Jen had to ask. "You have a crucifix in your kitchen?"

Gabriel chuckled. "Doesn't everyone?"

Bottles of hauled-in lake water, lined up in orderly rows, on the counter. Other, more mysterious, adult-looking bottles, twinkling underneath. Garlic in a braid. A basket of lemons and limes. Cheeses. Chocolate. Good bread. Outside could be seen a biffy, more lawn chairs, a hammock, a cedar canoe. A tilting dock extended out from the ragged edge of the lawn into the lake. In the gathering dark, a weathered toolshed hunkered like one of the billy goats gruff. Did the property conceal a troll as well? Wondered Jen the children's librarian.

"But come," Gabriel said softly. So, she followed him single file up the narrow, twisting stairs, which creaked authentically as they climbed. "Come and see the one I like to call the Upper Room . . ."

This was another bedroom, considerably smaller and sparer than the downstairs one. Under the slanting roof stood a single bed, some books about the church fathers, and a sorrowful-looking icon of the Black Madonna, a Russian Virgin Mary who could pass in a pinch for the grim reaper. "I'm sure you know" — again pressing her elbow — "that it was in the Upper Room, according to Biblical tradition, that the flames of Pentecost descended upon the early apostles."

Jen whispered, "Um, I actually wasn't aware . . . of that." She'd give anything for a top-up of her scotch. "Who sleeps up here?"

"I do. When I'm in the mood."

She wondered what mood that was.

He was standing close to her, his fair and freckled arm just grazing her own. She imagined him coming up here alone year after year, performing his solitary, solemn, bishoply rituals, kneeling before the bed in his robes perhaps, or placing votive lights in front of the Madonna, his shining head bowed in the candlelight, tormented soul bared: *There is no health in us.*

"Take your clothes off."

Despite her own imaginings on the subject of sex with Gabriel – with a bishop! – Jen was startled when the invitation (was that what it was?) actually presented itself. She was also not entirely sure, now that it had presented itself so boldly, that she was up to the task; could God get you for taking your clothes off for a bishop?

"I'm so sorry; I didn't mean to be rude." He seemed genuinely alarmed by what he had told her to do. "It's only that I would so love to see you . . . as you were made, by God." Gabriel moved away, respectful, chastened, waiting, his face somehow drawn and elongated, a strange darkness – Jen remembered pictures she'd seen of an eclipse of the sun – gathering under the downcast eyes.

Here it was, that thing that so far had eluded her, and that she had long ago left home for: Life. It had never dawned on her fantasies that Life, once it got going, might have ideas of its own. But she'd come this far; she couldn't demur now, without looking lame. So she set down her drink and began slowly to open her white summer dress, one blue button at a time.

Though she needn't have worried. Gabe continued to stand chastely away, satisfied, for now, only to see.

Back on the mainland, life staggered forward. Eric kept his distance. Jen kept her job.

Centipedes, another large, hairy, unexpected and confrontational aspect of Life, kept things lively in the basement sublet. Though they seemed more or less to evaporate during the day, the centipedes did warm up at night, scurrying along – and frequently, audibly slipping off — the large canvas-covered pipes that carried warm water throughout the house below whose main floors Jen now found herself in residence.

Several of these pipes crossed the ceiling of the room that was her bedroom, and at night in bed, she had a horror of being fallen upon and bitten or stung, hairily invaded by these creatures. She listened for them, dreamed about them, thought about them too much. When she entered the apartment late at night, the first thing she did was grab the broom outside her door and take a run at the pipes, knocking down any of the unwitting critters she could dislodge, then working to kill them. They weren't easy to kill. One July day, she happened to come upon a specimen in just the place she feared to find one most: her bed. In a frenzy of outrage and fear she knocked the thing to the floor, grabbed the Raid, and sprayed until it was completely white, and yet — *O Vos Omnes* — it kept running and darting, and occasionally rearing up at her as though about to retaliate: an ugly, heartbreaking, unspeakable fight. Also, did it hiss? Jesus! Finally, she clapped an empty yogurt container over the weakening creature and, sobbing now, pressed a brick that had been holding up the window on top of its plastic prison.

The centipede did succumb, eventually. When, two days later, she timidly lifted the brick and then the container, she found it surprisingly shrunken and stiff and stopped, all the deviltry gone out of it. She sat down on the bed, then, and wailed.

Why did she do that? She had no idea.

And why did she hide her basement life from Gabriel? For she never did invite him there, or breathe a word of her arthropod adventures, or speak to him of the unease that was slowly growing within her.

The apartment was not far from her real house, the one she lived in, had lived in, with Eric and their tortoiseshell, Pearl. She had chosen the place, reasoning that because it was in a fairly handsome house, she might thereby be prevented from appearing too derelict to those who knew her — people from the choir, people from work, that uncertain woman who stared back at her, from the mirror. Eric, she couldn't let herself think about. But there was no confusion about how much she missed Pearl. The thought of the cat reliably could make her howl.

The main part of the house above her was occupied by an elderly British couple whose children had all grown up and moved away. Only the family dog, a geriatric black lab named Jacob Marley, now remained with the couple. For the most part, this dog was tied right in front of Jen's bedroom window, where he spent his days and nights intermittently hollering at passersby, shifting his heavy chain, and sleeping. When the air pressure was low, which it often seemed to be in that lakeside town, a dog pee smell made its strong and reliable way into the basement apartment.

Centipedes and Marley apart, a surreal sort of life unfolded in the underground twilight of the British couple's house. This involved Jen going to work at the library, pretending to the other library staff that she was arriving, as usual, from home; Jen on days not at work or on the island, staying in bed all morning, sometimes all day, listening to Marley on the stones above, then falling into dreams again, forcing herself to stay asleep; Jen prettying herself up (and hoping her clothes did not have too much of a dog pee smell or, God forbid: a centipede hiding in a fold), getting ready to meet Gabe at the ferry, and crossing to the other side.

Sometimes she would awaken in the middle of the night

when there was not a sound inside or outside the big old house. Then she would imagine rising up out of the rented bed in her nightgown and floating ghostly up the basement steps and past Marley, who for once would not look up, then down the driveway, and along the few quiet streets between here and where Eric would be lying alone in their bed; opening the front door – she still had a key – and slipping into bed beside her husband. Going home.

But she did not go home. With dazzling foolhardiness, Jen kept not going home.

Meanwhile, Gabriel was gradually getting over his good manners. As the summer wore on, pretty much every square inch of the island house and its grounds hosted the hellbent shenanigans of the Bishop of Toronto and Basement Dweller Jen. They got into a pattern, of sorts. Jen would arrive on the ferry at about seven in the evening, and Gabriel, who was a pretty good cook if garlic and butter counted for anything, would be assembling the things he had purchased earlier in the day at the farmers' market and the Liquor Barn and the fish store (he had stopped attending St. Ursula's, he had time to think about meals) in town. The red snapper and new asparagus and lemons and garlic and fresh pasta would wait patiently on the counter while the evening light failed and the clothes flew, and those two went at it as though for the first and last time, howling and biting, promising everything.

At last, they would resurface, wedged under a table or splayed in the wet grass on the lawn somewhere, cold and sticky, amazed and ravenous. They would eat then, usually a hastier and more workmanlike version of whatever Gabriel had originally planned, and (so much for Jen living alone) snore boozily tangled together in the big, mothball-smelling ancestral bed with the ferry churning back and forth somewhere out on the dark lake.

The next chance they got, they'd be at it again, never mind the faint stirrings, in Jen, of a sense of repetition.

And moments of lucidity in the fever — for the relationship with Gabriel or Gabe or whoever he was, was beginning for Jen to resemble the parched delirium of mono or measles, interesting for a while but wondrous to be done with — certain lucid moments had started surfacing, and with them some sobering questions, such as, Where was this whole business going? Could she really continue living under the ground with centipedes and a dog pee smell? What was going to happen in the fall?

One morning she jumped awake when the six o'clock boat started its engines down by the dock, which was not far from the island house. Turning over in the grainy light, she was shocked to realize that frost was sparkling on the lake-facing windows, summer was almost over, she had not made a plan for any sort of a future, and a whole different person than the one formerly presented was snoring beside her — not the sleek and golden wearer of robes and tailored Harley Street suits you might see during the day. A person, instead, with matted, greying hair standing up every which way, and folds of loose skin piling up at the sides of his face, and ears sprouting startling tufts of hair: a stranger.

She thought of Eric then, in their empty bed in town, the very same early light falling upon his face (was he asleep? Awake and wailing? Fatalistically smoking cigarettes? Eric would never do that. But what did she know, anymore, about Eric?), and felt a clamour stir in her. She thought of their bedroom, which they had been going to paint this summer (the paint was bought, it was stacked with the rollers and the turpentine and the trays, in the back room), and of their backyard garden, in which they'd meant to plant scarlet runner beans this year, since they'd had such success with them last. Had Eric put them in anyway? It was the kind of thing he would do, plant beans in a holocaust. Was there still a place for a garden? Was even their house still standing, after the thing, now getting to be public knowledge, that Jen had so unbelievably done?

But she couldn't seem to stop. Something was making her keep sleeping with centipedes and sneaking across the water to worship that dark angel, Gabriel.

A dream, this one from high-school days, still lodged in her somewhere and recalled from time to time at moments both crucial and banal: Jen stands alone on a dark horizon. Above in the iron-grey sky is suspended a beautiful, tragic, entirely motionless man. This man, who is frozen, is dressed in a military-looking greatcoat like something from the Nazi era, compete with a gold-braided captain's cap, leather gloves, a riding crop. On his feet shine the most cruelly beautiful shoes.

Noticing that a long thread is tantalizingly suspended from the greatcoat, Jen reaches up and gently draws the frozen man down to her level, whereupon she sets about breathing on him. Slowly but surely, he begins soften, to open and inhale, eventually awakening to a life only Jen's reviving powers can make possible.

On the earthly comportment and Necessary Discipline of the Weaker Sex, that they may Hereafter attain the Great Prize: Our Redeemer is so richly and abundantly generous that He wins mighty victories through the female sex and, despite their frailty, He confers glory and greatness upon women through strength of mind. By faith, Christ makes them strong who were born weak so that, when those who appeared to be imbeciles are crowned with merit by Him who made them, they may garner praise for their Creator who hid heavenly treasure in earthen vessels. For Christ the king with his riches dwells within their bowels. Mortifying themselves in the world, despising earthly consort, purified of worldly contamination, trusting not in the transitory, dwelling not in error but seeking to live with God, they are united with the Redeemer's glory in Paradise. Caesarius of Arles: The Liturgy of the Hours in East and West.

Gabe gave a satisfied sigh as he closed the antique book, fondling its gilt-edged leaves and tooled leather cover. "You would do well, my dear," he murmured, turning to Jen with a liturgical smile, "to consider these words . . . to read, mark, and inwardly digest them, as we say of the Mother of our Lord." They had just finished a typically uproarious episode of bedding; Jen was wearily (where did Gabe get so much energy?) sipping her topped-up drink and staring at the slanting ceiling of the Upper Room, whose Pentecostal flames were puny compared with the regular conflagration of herself and the Bishop of Toronto on the four-poster below. She didn't mind the old words about treasure and vessels and bowels and glory, in fact she rather enjoyed them, or had enjoyed them when a merrier Gabe had read them out for fun, exaggerating the somber invocations and punishing phrases and stern recommendations. Now, though, some of the fun was fading from the readings and being replaced, instead, with a new sonority, a daunting zeal; now it began to dawn on Jen when Gabe said she should mark and digest or whatever, that he might mean it for real. Should she be sitting like a milkmaid on a three-legged stool, taking appreciative notes with a dutiful pencil?

It was beginning to look that way.

(Also: it had occurred to her that she would welcome a change in their post-coital reading material once in a while. What about some of the dear old *Reader's Digests* she'd gratefully found in the outhouse? What about "Life's Like That?" or even "Quotable Quotes," or some of those stories of extreme danger, last-minute rescues, and happy reunions? How about perusing a *Burpee's Seed Catalogue*? She'd seen some of those, too, downstairs, in the pantry. What about Jen doing the reading sometime, for that matter?)

A small, repetitive puffing and bubbling sound had started up beside her, and she knew without looking over that Gabriel, his post-coital pontificating accomplished, had fallen profoundly asleep. Through the open window could be heard the lake nudging up against the dock.

Downstairs, in their various rooms, the old clocks ticked.

There were some places Gabriel had begun to like for love-making – he refused to call it "sex" or "fucking" or any other word smacking of impropriety or light-heartedness – better than others: in the toolshed, for example, amongst the mosquito-coils and lawn tools, up against the wall; down on the end of the dock late at night, with the fish jumping and not far away (could the ferry passengers hear that far, Jen worried?), the *Wolf Islander* churning back and forth; upstairs in the austere room with the Black Madonna and the church fathers and Christ on the cross (recently Gabe had added a new and gaunter Man of Sorrows) dangling like gloomy bridesmaids over the bed. That got to be his favourite spot after a while, and it was certainly more convenient once the nights started getting colder. Up there, under the sorrowful eye of The Crucified, they would flail and sweat and finally come with great calamity, marvelling at their own endurance and appetite and capacity to be transported.

Jen said, after one of these times, "Why do you like doing it up here best?"

Gabe was busy pouring them each another generous finger of scotch, the light from the setting sun kindling the red hairs on his long, strong arms and thighs.

"Because," he smiled, sliding in beside her again, "the union between a man and a woman is a sacramental act, and this is a sacred room, as befits it." He raised his Bohemian crystal glass. "Cheers."

Scotch was another of Gabe's favourite things, and, all things considered, it was becoming one of Jen's. The burn of it going down reminded her of their first communion, such a long time ago, it seemed to her now, and of her delicious alarm, as the chalice, and Gabriel, had moved along the gleaming rail toward her. She tilted her head back on the pillow, looking up. "Well, He makes me nervous."

"*Whom* do you mean?"

Jen jerked a thumb up the wall behind them. "Him."

Gabriel's blue eyes narrowed between the pale lashes. "Are you referring to *Our Lord?*"

Jen said, soldiering on, "I mean it's a bit weird having sex looking up at somebody dying horribly, that's all."

"It may be 'having sex' to you," said Gabriel in a relatively new, precise tone of voice, "but it is 'making love' to me, a profound gesture, one of the acts of Holy Communion, and it is therefore entirely appropriate that it" — the word was delivered with pickaxe precision — "that it, like all other acts of human surrender, should be conducted at the foot of the cross."

Jen thought, So when are we getting married, then, if it's so sacred. Lately she had been starting to wonder what she was going do, once her summer sublet was up. So far, she had been imagining that matters with Gabriel would settle themselves in some splendid and inevitable way, but it was starting to bother her just a teensy bit that this more practical eventuality, the end of the summer, had never yet come up their conversations, either before or after the sacramental act. What about Gabe's house in Toronto – the *deanery* or whatever it was – and his being a bishop? What about all that? Was he going to take her there someday? Would she go with him to the Cathedral? Of Toronto? Would he introduce her to his fellow miter-wearers?

And what, come to think of it, was he doing here on the island when she was away all day? Praying to the Black Madonna? Writing brilliant theological treatises? Hanging upside down getting his beauty sleep? Though, urgent as they were, such questions seemed a crass intrusion into the routine of cataclysmic and redemptive sex, post-coital scotch, and blanked-out nights of drunken sleep that the two of them had gotten accustomed to.

She said, "I think I'll go down and drain the calamari." (A word, like some others, that she had not known long.)

Recently Gabriel had begun complaining that Jen arrived too late in the evening, keeping him waiting. He wondered if there might be other interests. Medical interests, perhaps? He'd noticed her eyeing "some preening doctor" at that party they'd attended on the mainland last weekend; perhaps her schedule was getting too busy for time with a poor member of the clergy; he suggested that if she liked scotch so much, perhaps she could contribute a bottle now and then. Meanwhile, he continued reading aloud to her, usually out of the *Book of Common Prayer* or Thomas à Kempis, or some other mournful and reproving work, as though in the vain hope of bringing about a scrap of improvement in her character.

Sex was changing, too. Nowadays Gabriel preferred to fast-forward things past all the genteel preliminaries. He gave instructions, he exacted obedience: *Go upstairs. Wait in the shed. On your knees.* He wanted Jen blindfolded, in her underwear, outdoors on the cold grass, under the cross. He took to wearing his church robes, to tying Jen up, to twisting and wasting her, so that he could turn around later, and bestow forgiveness upon her. When all that was over, he had to gather up what was left of her and worship and cherish and murmur over her, as though Jen herself were the Black Madonna, or possibly roadkill.

Though sometimes Gabe was the one who got to be roadkill. *You're in trouble now, Buster. That's right, I want it all off except the shoes, and you can wear those* — untied — *over to the corner, where you'll stand until I've decided what I'm going to do with you.* — And so on, though her heart was not in it, and the only thing resembling a threat that she could come up with was Anneli's ancient *ence I'll send you home*, maybe because that was where she wanted to go.

August 19
Dear Eric,
It has been a very long summer, and I have learned much. I do not expect you to forgive me, at least not for a long time. But please understand that I still love you, and I think of you every day. I have often wondered if you got the bedroom painted (I loved that corn colour, with the red), or if you planted the

scarlet runner beans where we thought about, along the south side of the shed. What I am trying to say is, I am ready to come home for real, if there is still a chance that you would take me back. I want us to start over. I know, again. I want to sit on the deck with you and look at our garden again. Please write soon. P.S. you can send it to me c/o the library; I am still working there.

Late in August came an answer, though not in the form of an invitation to return. The letter was from a lawyer, bore an ominous-looking red seal, and was hand delivered, over Marley's enthusiastic protests, to Jen's temporary lodgings. Once unsealed, it informed her that Eric had changed his mind about not going anywhere in a hurry and was starting divorce proceedings. He was also moving to Vancouver, having completed his bog studies, to start a job there.

Could she blame him?

The next news was that Gabriel had been released (apparently, he had asked to be, long before he ever arrived at St. Ursula's) from his responsibilities in Toronto and would soon be moving to New York, in order to begin his new duties at St. John the Divine. He wanted to know, since she was familiar with liturgical music, whether Jen had ever heard of Paul Halley, St. John's celebrated organist and composer.

She had not. (She wondered if Paul Halley slept on a board under an icon of the Black Madonna; if he was fond of sacrificial sex with people half his age, in toolsheds; if, after the whole spectacle was over, he liked to beg forgiveness and conduct improving readings out of the Church Fathers.)

But Jen was done. The "measles" were over. Lucidity, for what it was worth, was here to stay. Very nicely and politely one day, she wrote and mailed on a sheet of specially purchased paper, "Fare well and fuck you."

There was one stroke of possibly divine inspiration in all this mayhem. It occurred to her to apply for grad school the following year (a year would give her time to sort herself out and earn some money), so Jen hurried up and did that — and luck being with her once again, she got in, nice and far away at the University of Calgary, for her sins. There she learned a lot more about human behaviour and what to call it, and best of all, how to make it pay the rent. Since life had brought them back within damaging distance again, she and Eric made a stab at bringing things to a final and proper conclusion, and Dorie — after all, what choice did she have? — managed to almost forgive Jen.

Is it the pandemic? The environmental crisis? The price of lettuce? These days she seems to be spending even more time than usual counselling the tormented affluent, who never tire of describing their folly, and who pay her well for her professional ear. At the end of the day, she likes to slip into her comfortable old bathtub with a finger of Cutty Sark, a throwback to one of her more "out there" summers. Sipping the pleasurably punishing liquid, she may think about the people she has seen and listened to in her office that day, going over their foibles and predicaments, their rash decisions, their wearying disasters. She has noticed that of all of them, it's usually the religious ones that are the weirdest and the worst-off of the lot.

(And she may from time to time think about God, that dirty old bugger up there in His nasty Heaven, the first of the old men and the last, and least forgiven.

There are a few things she's saving up to say to Him.)

INSURANCE

Jen is the worst driver. Rush hour, weather, a male passenger, any of the above can tighten her grip on the wheel, bring out a sweat, make her brain swell. She puts this down to the memorable lesson (the only one) she had with Dad, as a teenager. For starters, he didn't want to teach her to drive; how was that supposed to work when he was only there for the weekend and he had a million things to do, plus a gig to play? But Jen insisted, assuring him it would be a help to Dorie especially when he was gone, and finally one day — "All right then, Jenny, Jen, Jen" — he took her out for a spinny, spin, spin. She did okay, didn't have a crash-up, didn't do anything wrong, really, except terrorize her passenger. She still fondly remembers how he climbed the car door as she took the corner, the way he hung onto the vent window as though it was a rope paid out to some poor soul down a well, how sure he'd been that "You'll get the both of us killed!"

A lifetime or two later, she finds herself, not in Dorie's flier-strewn machine, but in a famous surgeon's sleek vehicle. Life can take strange turns when you're between relationships, tend to attend the parties of the pretentious (Gabriel Breene wasn't entirely without his uses), are soon going to be a very studious grad student in a province far from here, and might possibly harbour a death wish.

In other words, what's she got to lose?

The famous surgeon, whom already she secretly calls "Surge," is easily old enough to be her father; you can tell by the eyebrows, with their beetling disapproval, the rogue hairs, the ready scowl.

The car is a Peugeot, jellybean-black with a caramel leather interior and a real emergency-type telephone installed between its deep and sexy bucket seats. Surge uses this phone to get his minions started on his brain operations, a reliable turn-on, while shortcutting his way with Byronesque irritability through Toronto's crowded lanes and quirky streets, to his patiently waiting scrub room. In the bucket seat beside him sits stateless, rootless — and in Dorie's opinion witless — Jen, who never tires of seeing the hairs on the doc's powerful arms glisten while he switches between shifting gears and issuing commands into that sexy phone.

Earlier this same autumn evening, the Peugeot delivered Jen (newly arrived via train from her Kingston basement) and her surgical boyfriend out to dinner at one of those trendy little Cabbagetown restaurants with the skinny front windows on either side of a central dormer: the kind that, when the name "Cabbagetown" still referred to vegetables, used to be workers' cottages, but that now sport reddening vines and clever little signs whose utterly elegant, vaguely Armenian names are the only clue to the marinated lentils and smoked trout and duck confit on offer in their three small rooms. She'd sat across the intimate, candlelit table from Surge, savouring the lentils, admiring the lute, and imagining she was having dinner — after graduation from university, say, or before some debutante-type going-away party—with a father. Not with the one who occasionally turned up at Dorie's door. This would be with the one in her head, the well-dressed, urbane, concerned Dad not so different in appearance and bearing from the man across from her; the father who, after a long absence, or a coma survived, might embrace her ecstatically and brokenly cry, "Jenny, it's Daddy!"

She can dream, can't she?

"Araz" is the expensively understated name of the trendy Armenian restaurant, where, for the previous three hours Surge and Jen have been more or less anonymously ensconced, snarfing smoked trout, guzzling bottles of good wine (too many of them), and talking about his unfortunate offspring, who suffer from OCD, ADHD, and a DSM's-worth, it seems, of other acronyms, not to mention rockstar father syndrome. (Apparently, it's hard to shine when your dad holds the key to all grey matter, including your own.) Surge had meant to have smarter, brighter, more ambitious children; he expresses disappointment in them. He is also tired, so tired. After all, he's been on his feet all day, saving people. He yawns, nods to the maître d', and suggests they hit the road and the hay.

The prawns praised and the check handsomely paid, he drops the Peugeot keys into Jen's scandalized hand and drawls, "How about a big city driving lesson; you'll be the best driver in the west when you get back to your basement."

"What," she gasps, "like, here? Like . . . now?"

"No time like the present," he quips, then discreetly burps. "Besides, you've had less to drink than I have."

And about a hundred less pounds to absorb it with, she will think later, and far from here, and oh, so sober.

Right now, though, there's no time for the luxury of thinking. Instead behold Jen, blearily white-knuckling it "home" at the wheel of a standard (at this point she herself doesn't own a car, much less a standard) and in a city not her own, through the crazed Friday-night Church-and-Wellesley traffic, her clutch foot cramping in terror, as Surge chortles, "*Well* done, old thing, you're managing *mawvelously!*"

From the relative safety of the passenger side, he casts a shrewd eye on the crawling and bad-tempered cars to port and starboard, while giving Jen's knee a paternal pat with one of the famous hands. "Really *quite* mawvelously!" (He isn't even British). "But do remember," he chuckles parentally, "to put the clutch all the way in when shifting; we don't want to call attention, remember." A quick glance over his shoulder. "Almost there."

Almost there. The same words Dorie whispered one night in a far earlier car, after warning Dad, who was still more or less there, "If you don't get this car home safe, your name will be 'Mud.'" Jen thought that was a funny name and asked why Dorie gave it to Dad. "Your father's been into somebody's vinegar jug." One of those mysterious grown-up answers. How could vinegar turn one's dad into mud? If Jen had used vinegar, would she have had more luck turning her hapless long-ago frog into a toad?

They'd been visiting some of Dad's rum-lovin' banjo buds, and were now heading home, her father singing "Whiskey in the Jar" at the top of his lungs, and supplying the chorus too, *with a whack for my daddy-o.* Rose the Baby was asleep, lucky her, but Jen was never much of a sleeper, she had to keep an eye out. An eye kept out, she sat straight in the back seat beside furious Dorie, who held a weak and sleepy Sonny on her lap. The windows on the right side of the car were black — it would have been about nine o'clock on an October night much like this one, the moon ghosting over the dark wash of the Atlantic.

Surge at last directs Jen where to turn. She puffs out a terrorized gasp of acknowledgement — it's too soon for relief — as though acknowledging orders to bail from a bombed B-52, barks, "Here? Where?"

"Next set of lights," Surge murmurs, "*nice* and easy, there's a good girl. We'll be in beddy-byes before you know it, and tomorrow this'll all be nothing but a little headache . . ." As if to demonstrate his supreme confidence in their safe arrival home, he gets out his tobacco pouch and presses a dollop of Balkan Sobranie into his fancy French pipe, adding, "and you, my dear, unlike some of us here, will be able to catch up on your beauty sleep in the morning." He sighs importantly. "Never assume you know what an embolism's going to get up to."

Evidently, the same could be said of the Boys in Blue. They are close — tantalizingly close — to Surge's 'hood, when Jen happens to glance to her left and see the veiled form of a cruiser, tucked sly as a shark in a dark spot between a Burger King and a TD Bank. Before she knows it, she's been told to get out of the car (Surge huddling smug as a jug on the passenger side), stood against the door, searched to her bones, made to blow into their nasty breathalyzer, and — because God is a joker, she blows a hair under — given a fine and a warning, and sent "on home." Right now, she has no idea where that is, or why she doesn't know.

"I'll tell you why." Dorie, as usual, will eventually be quick to solve the puzzle. "Because you haven't got the sense God gave a goose, that's why!" Under her breath, she'll add, "You and your father: peas in a pod."

One night when Jen was five or six, dear old Dad, as often happened, didn't come home. Not until long after she was in dreamland, that is. He'd been drinking and playing hill-billy tunes down at the Legion, as was his wont when around on Friday nights, and by the time he decided to find his bed, he was blotto. This was before all the encouragements and punishments we have now, and it was tiny little Cumming with hardly a streetlight to its name, so there were no Boys in Blue, and somehow, he managed to find his way home unscathed. But not before he nearly struck, or possibly did strike, a person walking by the side of the road. He slammed on the breaks, swerved, heard a thud, and kept going, drunk as a skunk and all a-tremble. "Next morning, first thing I did when I got out of bed was run out and check to see if there was a dent on the car, or blood on the grill."

No dent after all, and no blood. No reports, either, of anyone dead. Dad was lucky; all there was, was mud.

Who knew mud can follow you all the way to Toronto?

Now, it's Jen sitting all a-tremble, but in Surge's living room while he clatters around in the kitchen, loopily singing madrigals about a dead dormouse (in addition to all his other achievements, he's a tenor in a respectable chamber choir), and fixes them double-rum toddies to make them feel better for what happened on the way home. "Look on the bright side," he trills from the kitchen, "at least you don't have a car to impound!" Then he goes back to madrigalling. "No sins had Dor to answer for," he warbles, handing Jen her hefty drink. "Repent of yours in time!"

"My what?" Jen enquires.

"Your sins," sings Surge, "of course. But don't worry about that silly fine," he says magnanimously. "Tomorrow's another day, as they say, and anyway, it's my car, I'll pay."

"And what about *your* sins?"

"Are you speaking of the sin of loving, not wisely but too well?" Surge smiles ruefully, beginning to stroke her thigh, and starting up the oh, so reliable commotion under the skin, the loosening and softening and liquefying of interior parts that tell her he's once again going to win.

"No, that would be me," she says, and he knows what that means. Jen's the one, after all, who has spun like a water bug between cities every weekend (because after all, people's lives depend on Surge), and lived in her rented subterrestrial digs while waiting for the green light to move in (at least, until she moves on) with her man, whose decisiveness in the operating arena has not followed him, it would seem, into the theatre of love. After all, there are so many things for a person of his stature to consider. His reputation, for one. How would it look if he suddenly set up house with another man's much younger wife? He's barely left his own! (A consideration at which, in the first astonished flush of their stolen romance, he hadn't batted an eye). Think how he would be viewed by his colleagues, his patients. Why, he'd lose his authority! "And what about you?" he wonders prudently. "What on earth would you do, uprooted from your own city, friends, contacts? You'd be miserable, and it would end up being my fault." He shakes his sad head. "Isn't everything?"

"First of all, I'm nobody's wife, that was a while ago. Second of all, I'm about to be uprooted anyway. I'm moving out to Calgary to study, remember?" She spurted an exasperated sigh. "Rootlessness is my . . . what do you call it? My métier."

None of these objections, however, holds a candle to the great, sorrowful, much more important stumbling block of his children (his poor abandoned children) with their disorders, their dismay, their famous name, their broken home.

"This is the year," he intones not for the first time, "that they really need a dad."

Jen mutters, "Don't we all."

Sin or no sin, they are soon on rum number two or three, and — this is always their way — before long the clothes are starting to fly. No time to make it to the bedroom: they strip each other and rut right on the living-room floor, gasping, lunging, knocking over rum, somewhere between Surge's briefcase and the leaded-glass door. As he approaches his final destination, he glares like an oncoming train into her eyes and cries out with admirable calamity, "Jenny, it's Daddy!"

Be careful what you wish for.

In the meantime, tonight Jen can't seem to make it to her own destination. All during the evening and the living-room shenanigans, something has been bugging her beleaguered brain, some little stone or unsolvable stain. Something to do with daddies, as a matter of fact, though under the circumstances, the source of the irritation, like most everything else, eludes her. For a while after Surge rolls off, she drifts in that dreamily rum-numbed state that can pass for rest, but as Dorie used to say: there's no rest for the wicked; ignore it though she may, Jen's head is starting to throb, and her throat is dry, so dry. Eventually she can't stand it anymore; she sits wobblingly up, hauls on her dispersed, reversed, dismissed clothes, shoves her hair back in its scrunchy. "You know what?"

Surge is starting to snore.

Jen prods him in the side, noting that he's getting a tad flabby, and he grunts unhappily. "We need to talk," she insists.

His arms fling out in a persecuted little flail. "What's going to happen to me now?" he cries, referring obliquely to the hell-hard way in which he spends his day, financing the kids, the boat, the ex, the expensive lentils. And now on top of it all: a half-his-age harridan is cruelly keeping him conscious! What's going to happen to me now? Jen knows what that means. It means that something could very well be going to happen to *her* if she keeps on, as Dorie used also to say. *If you keep on . . .* But for some reason tonight she can't leave it alone, can't stop keeping on. Soon Surge is sawing logs again, his furry belly winking at the moon, and the sawing makes Jen crazy. "Are you awake?" she says, and when the answer is a louder snore, "Can you wake up please? Hello?"

Surge is awake, and he is not impressed. He raises himself up on an elbow, stares down at her like an Old Testament prophet. Jeremiah with his lamentations. Moses with the tablets of stone. A pickled Pieta of the Living Room. "All right. You have my full attention. What is it that you want?"

She doesn't mean to, but Jen begins to cry. She loves this man, doesn't she? Unlovely and temporary he may be, but she's as mad about him as she is at him, and he is talking to her as though she were a stranger, as though she were some sad-assed delivery person or door-to-door salesman, sidling to sell him a magazine subscription. The more he stares, the more some ancient cave or cold cavern yawns inside her.

"All I want," she blubbers, "is for you to love me!"

The unpleased prophet gathers his dishevelled robes around him. "It is inappropriate for you to be producing tears at this time," he intones as evenly as though he were dictating the day's chart notes to his secretary.

So, she hits him. As with the tears, she doesn't mean to. She just hauls off and clocks him one in the chest.

And then they are doing that thing that happens at such times, with them. It's like a dance, a reel, a dark shamanic whirl that begins late at night when all the lights are off and the car is parked, and the trees are standing still as Clydesdales.

In its way, it's beautiful. The darkness, the deep privacy, the wicked commitment of it. Apart from the breathing, the force, the resistance they offer each other, they barely make a sound. It's not so different, really, from the devotion of lovemaking. Up the stairs they fall, and along the hall past the challenged children's empty bedrooms to the back of the house, and then they do the whole thing in reverse, pushing, pulling, twisting as hard as they dare, toppling into doors and tipping pictures off the walls, egging each other on until at two or three in the morning they end up in the master bedroom, clothed or half-clothed, parched and unconscious, piled in a reeking heap on the bed or the floor, to waken, in the grey of dawn, tender and sorrowful, with bruises they mourn, don't recognize, and console each other for.

Jenny! It's Daddy!

Though, that gum-chewing dude disappeared when she was born. And when she was two, and twelve, and fifteen, and twenty-one.

The night she was born, a Friday apparently, he was down at the Legion. When she turned two, he was recovering from a hangover.

Prior to birthday number three, Dad and his band went on the road for a year, or ten.

At fifteen there were sure signs Jen was female, and equally trustable signals that the man who could have helped with that project was AWOL.

At twenty-one, having misplaced the original one, she was unconsciously (she learned in Psych 101) on the lookout for an older man. A teacher, a surgeon, a stonemason – anything wearing a professional grin.

She wanted to be owned.

She wanted to be drowned.

For when a father is not there, owned and drowned can feel much the same; both take your breath away and nothing and no one can restore it, not even time.

History repeats itself, as they say. The first thing Jen does upon crawling, stiff and dry as a communion wafer out of Surge's splendid bed in the morning, is to sneak out and inspect the car. She goes over everything once, twice, three-and-a-half times before she's satisfied the world is still there, and bearable. It's a bright morning, the sun kissing last night's frost and softening the reddening leaves, Surge surging forth amazingly fresh, considering, and ready to begin another day of brain-saving. The falling leaves, the autumn air, a stranger she used to sleep with disappearing round the corner in his intact car. It all makes her think of a definition she once stumbled upon, of the cosmos: "beauty and good order."

Plus, bonus: as far as she knows, she's not a murderer.

Some months later, decently single in her new, brash city, she will buy a car, and she will have to purchase insurance for said car.

And when that happens, so much about that "big city driving lesson" (and its jocular instructor) will be revealed.

In the meantime, Jen waves the famous surgeon off to his operating room, walks over to that cute little neighbourhood store on the corner, and buys herself a lovely, exorbitant "fair trade" coffee and today's *Globe*.

Once the caffeine has begun its merciful work and she's sure Surge is deep into his first procedure, she will check the Via Rail schedule and simply — don't even try to stop her — disappear.

DIAGONALS

Follies often look like real, useable buildings, but never are.

ARCHITECTURAL FOLLIES IN AMERICA

Jen decided to take up dancing. Why not? She'd recently broken up with Frank Lloyd Wright. Not with *the* Frank Lloyd Wright, of course; with H., the Edmonton-based architect-cum-folly maker, aka God's gift to the gardens of the rich and the daughters of the poor.

By now, she was used to life on the bald prairee. After all, she'd lived there long enough to have a local's wry understanding that in Calgary it costs as much to park your car as to fill it, that rain there was as big an event as the invention of penicillin, and that all in the same day in good old cow town, it was quite possible to make good use of a toque and a bottle of sunscreen.

Not only that. On account of her subject of study, plus a little Naked Grape thing that had developed and then been more or less successfully dealt with somewhere along the way, she'd found herself a part-time counselling job in a treatment centre, and thanks to an extended house-and-dogsitting arrangement for a prof teaching indefinitely in another country, her rent was pretty close to free. For now, anyway. What could be better?

She liked to joke that she was shacked up with a needy bull terrier and a leaky water heater. "What is it with me and water heaters?"

Though, life in the man department could still be bumpy; to get over – or back at – the folly builder (who was also a ballroom dance enthusiast) she drank the absent prof's booze (within reason) and signed up for an evening jazz class at the university.

That's where she met Dawn.

WEEK ONE: DAWN

Jen walks in, looks around. What the devil is she doing in a dance studio?

It appears she's doing jazz runs, "spank-the-baby," "step-ball-change," and "Charleston." Jen can't do these things. Help.

She stands at the barre in her bare feet and Budweiser T-shirt, untoned belly pushing like an early pregnancy through the shapeless cotton, until she sees a flower, a flame, an ash-risen phoenix languidly reclining beside the boombox over in the corner. Jen can't take her eyes off her, and at the same time – so much has the woman arrested her – it's almost as though she doesn't see her, as though she's a weather system, or a fugue state: you're surrounded before you realize you're caught up in it.

Like Jen, the "weather system" is wearing tights, but hers, in contrast to Jen's, don't end in those goofy little elastic stirrup-things that go under the arch to hold down the leggings inside shoes, or boots, or what have you. Nosiree. *Her* tights disappear into thick pastel-pink legwarmers, inside which nestles a set of coltish ankles, followed, not by a pair of bare, bunioned plates of meat like Jen's, but by true jazz Oxfords, seriously scuffed and patinaed from eons, no doubt, of real, committed, and excellent dancing.

Jen has never wanted anything so much as to end in a pair of feet like that.

The phoenix has caught her staring and so she smiles, and then the phoenix does, too, and it's a slow blue dazzle, deliberate as the sun ascending over a calm ocean. That languid way she has of sweeping the eyes downward, as though she has just swept them down over Jen, too. She can almost feel the swish and stipple of them, so delicious and yet so grave, it makes her feel in some ticklish new way: alive.

To disguise the staring, she tells the phoenix her name.

In a voice as hushed and sweet as a secret on Christmas Eve, the phoenix breathes, "I'm Dawn," and Jen knows it's true.

After Dawn, it's diagonals, a form of torture where the instructor sends you – in pairs, if you're lucky – from one corner of the studio to the other, you and your equally knock-kneed partner flopping and skidding and colliding through an agonizing series of ball-changes or barrel jumps or jazz runs, your burnt bare feet (all four of them) squeaking pathetically on the studio's hardwood floor while the rest of the class, clumped in a damp herd against the back wall, waits its forlorn bovine turn.

Not so with Dawn. She sails out alone, her body long and smooth as Coltrane's saxophone, fingers shaped like wingtips, toes extended, ankles perfectly turned. It's as though the music, something jagged and sexy Jen has never heard before (why not? Where has this music been all her life?) is located not in the speakers, but in Dawn's hips and shoulders and arms and the insides of her Lycra thighs, like fury or like love, like Jen has never before in her life seen a human being move.

Two weeks ago, she didn't know there was such a thing as jazz, let alone a jazz run. By the time Dawn has reached the other side of the room, she knows she'll die if doesn't learn how to do one.

What a coincidence, Dawn just broke up with her boyfriend, too! Only she doesn't say "boyfriend," she says *my partner. My partner and I,* which Jen finds incomparably sexier. She learns this as they walk home together – amazingly, Dawn lives not far from Jen – through the yellow leaves and light rain and watery reflections of streetlights, after class that first night. But whereas Jen, broken up, is filled with anxiety and self-justification and plans for strenuously brilliant comebacks (hence the kamikaze jazz-dancing attempt), Dawn is relaxed and radiant, interested in the *process,* avid for her partner's growth, both *personal* and *artistic.* She pronounces it "ahtistic," and there, suddenly, is Marilyn Monroe standing over the air vent, dainty knees pressed together, white dress a-billow.

"He's actually over in Nepal right now," she beams, those amazing eyes dewy as the first daisies, "he's an *ahtist*" – the sweep of those lashes, that radiant regard – "and he's over there for the winter, living with some other ahtists he knows in a *craftsmen's co-operative* on the side of a mountain, I don't remember which one, they have so many over there, don't they! Anyway, he's over there just to chill, you know, and to get some fresh ideas? He always comes back with *so* many fabulous ideas! And we just thought – since he's going to be gone for so long this time – we thought, why not give each other our freedom!" The lashes descend, then rise again on all that dizzying blueness. "No sense doing the whole *possessive* thing and making a bunch of silly promises you can't keep, right? I love that saying that goes, 'if you love something, set it free. If it comes back, it's yours. If it doesn't – '"

"'– it never was,'" Jen chimes in, forgetting as completely as though she never knew it, how much that particular saying has always made her gag, and marvelling, instead, that somebody as beautiful and talented and free-thinking as Dawn would even talk to the likes of her, with her lumpy belly and Budweiser (Budweiser!) T-shirt and untalented feet; then she lets it drop, that *her* boyfriend (though technically not hers anymore, and not in Nepal) is an architect, actually: a folly designer. That's right, a designer of follies.

"Of what?" breathes Dawn beatifically. "A designer of what?"

Jen explains what follies are – she didn't shelve art books back in Kingston for nothing – sketching in a few choice details of H.'s unusual occupation as an inventor of fake ruins for the amusement of the rich and tedious, a calling that, fey attributes notwithstanding, has resulted in a timeshare in Bordeaux, a Peugeot, an intolerance of anything resembling snow, and an antique yacht no bigger than a basket. Which is lucky, since docking anywhere around Calgary is dear. Not that Jen cares anymore. "There's a branch of the public library right across from where I work; I can pop over on my lunch break and dig up some pictures of follies, if you're interested."

"That would be *wondahful!*" Dawn sighs again, her eyes gently shining. "I *am!*" And then she kisses – just grazes Jen – on the shoulder, whispers, "Bye," and melts away through the shimmering mist under the streetlights, leaving Budweiser to waft the rest of the way home in a dreamy jazz run, the dream of a jazz run, her feet barely skimming the street.

The only thing Jen can think about all week as she keeps an eye on the water heater and meets her new profs and offers wisdom to the addicted, is Dawn. How, before the instructor arrives, she stands at the barre, serenely cycling through the positions, first, second, third, plié, pas de bourrée, the exquisite hand floating out like a bolt of flung silk, over the professionally flexed knee; the way she doesn't just let her T-shirt balloon out over her leggings as though attempting to set up camp in the rain under it (like Jen does), but instead ties the loose folds into a stylish knot over one hip, so that her perfect waist and taut belly and lean flanks are prettily accentuated, limbered up, and ready for work. For jazz!; that hushed and secret way she confides things — *My Pahtner. An Ahtist. Our freedom* — as though for her listener's ears only. And how her eyes seem to get bluer and bluer, and impossibly bluer when she's concentrating — O ineluctable moment! — on Jen.

Though nothing's perfect. H. still calls two or three times a week, leaving messages containing urgent reasons to call him back. He has Jen's lapis earrings, for example, the ones they picked out at Birks, and needs to know what she wants done with them. Call him back, *beep*. He'll be in town this weekend, after taking Janey to recorder camp, to put his boat in drydocks for the winter. "We can have dinner at that place you like down on the waterfront. Nellie's? Willie's? Whatever. Call me."

Beep.

Drip. She knows the prof's water heater hasn't quit leaking (though, her belief that bad things go away if you just leave them be had allowed her to hope it might); the other day when she went downstairs to do the laundry she saw not just a stain on the floor, but a rusty puddle. At such times, she misses the architect, folly and all.

Oh, well.

"The tickets've arrived for the Architectural Society's fund-raising ball – remember that?"

How could she forget? Since the two of them had so much fun dancing. What was it he'd hissed into her ear that last time? "Don't follow the music, follow me!"

She listens to the messages one after the other, deleting them beep by beep. Bleat by bleat. All she can think about is: How many days until the next jazz class?

WEEK TWO: SHOES

She prepares much more carefully for the second class, running out after work to a dance store that, like so many things these days, she had no idea existed two weeks ago, to buy leggings resembling the ones Dawn was wearing, and jazz Oxfords, and an expensive arty T-shirt just long enough to tie a perky knot in. She spends hours tying and re-tying her new T-shirt, first at one hip and then the other, trying to determine which hip looks better, knotted. She thinks about knotty hips, about knots, their sizes and configurations, their history and etymology, their nautical names: reef knot. Square knot. Granny knot. Shroud knot. She's obsessed, she admits it. On a slow day at work, she goes next door to the public library, digs up a textiles tome, and learns that in ancient China, knots were used as a way of recording events. *The more important the event, the larger and more complex the knot.* She thinks of the event of Dawn's hip, secured by its frisky T-shirt knot. If that isn't something to record, she doesn't know what is.

Knots are not all. Like one possessed, she practises diagonals across the prof's hardwood living room, going over and over the moves, careful to scuff her new jazz shoes whenever possible, in order to make them look, if not worn, at least respectably broken in. For a mortified moment, there's a dim memory of Anneli and her hand-me-down flip-flops, way back when; a leopard doesn't change its spots, or something. Oh well, again.

And welladay, but things could be worse!

Before leaving her apartment on the night of the second class, she makes a note to call the plumber for the water heater – apparently it's not going to fix itself – and go over all the steps she can remember from the week before, apply a witchy little extra lick of Maybelline, arrange her hair in what she hopes is a balletic bun.

"Hi," breathes the phoenix when Jens slinks into the studio and takes her place. Her face is so radiant it's like taking a shower in the Aurora Borealis.

Though, honestly: what made her think she could keep up with the likes of Dawn? This time she's wearing a short-sleeved body skin with a deep, round neckline that shows off her perfectly toned chest and perkily upturned breasts, her peerless collarbones. To complete the look, a colourful silk Che Guevara-looking headband and sweats are rolled daringly low, exposing the lean waist and the Lycra belly, the perilous bones of the hips.

Until now, Jen hadn't realized that hips were supposed to show their bones. She takes a quick look down at her own: clearly, neither had they.

To cover her confusion, she says lamely: "I can't remember a *thing* from last week!" – and immediately cringes at her grandiose lie – can Dawn tell? – her pathetically admiring high-school enthusiasm.

Never mind. Dawn, as usual, is divinely unfazed. She closes those eyes, reopens them slowly (an easy epiphany Jen is beginning to recognize as her specialty): "Be my *pahtner!*"

Jen blinks uncomprehendingly, says: "Huh?"

Dawn laughs, a sylvan sound. "In diagonals, silly!"

Jen will so show that pretentious architect of follies.

After class number two Dawn invites Jen to a skinny little hole-in-the-wall frequented by the artsy types, and squeezed between a Chinese tea house and a second-hand clothing store; thanks to its frequently not-quite-fresh cinnamon buns, Dawn tells Jen, the regulars have slightly altered its name from its original Gristmill to a more fitting Mildew. But Jen and Dawn eat the buns.

Everybody eats the buns.

Though each in her own way. Jen, wary of sticky fingers, a gooey mouth, dissects hers with a knife and fork, cutting it into manageable pieces. Dawn, on the other hand, unwinds her bun and savours, dreamy as a disrobing geisha.

Jen follows Dawn's fingers, takes in their fluttering description of how she met her partner.

"It was actually on a walking tour of unusual homes in my neighbourhood, just after I moved in. He has this crazy place made entirely of cement – imagine! – with concrete sculptures of elves and mushrooms and grazing deer that he's made, instead of a garden, in front. That's because cement is so much more environmentally friendly than a lawn. Isn't that *amazing*?"

Yes! cry Jen's widened eyes, amazing!

"It's just like some darling little troll's house!" She chews, sips, licks her pretty lips. "And speaking of trolls, there he was, sitting on one of the mushrooms, happily stoned, with that little frizz of a ponytail sticking out behind," shaking her head, remembering, smiling her private smile. "Honestly, you could hardly tell him from one of his cement elves."

Cement elves, cement selves, Jen's mind doodles, as Dawn peels off a cinnamony spiral. "Well, he just gave me one of his famous grins — you'll see what I mean when you meet him, *nobody* can resist that guy's grin — and that was it! You know?"

About not being able to resist a professional smile? Yes, Jen, that serial siren of expert older men, knows about that kind of smile.

"And after that I found reasons to walk past his place every time I got the chance, until one day," the lashes descend, the pretty pink mouth bows upward, "he invites me in for a toke. And one thing led to another, you know? And there is nothing," she smiles, her eyes going dreamy as a Dairy Queen sundae, "like sex while enjoying a toke. You know?"

This time, Jen doesn't have a sweet clue, but she enthuses anyway.

Though now Dawn's luminous brow clouds a tad. "It's just that —"

Tell me.

"Well, *you* know." A mosquito-shooing gesture. "An elf-making dope smoker who lives in a cement hut?"

Jen furrows her brow into a look of: OMG, you're so right.

"Well after a while, I got to notice a certain — you know — pattern? I guess you could say. It was sex, sex, sex, basically. As if that's all he was programmed for, I mean, the man barely eats! It was sex in the bedroom, sex in the shop, sex in the rain on top of a cement toadstool! Don't get me wrong; I love sex, and I honestly have *nothing* against toadstools. Especially after a toke. It's just that . . . he's not quite father material. You know?"

Not really, Jen grins, not exactly having had one.

Dawn inhales her freshened coffee, takes a testing sip, closes those eyes, enjoying. "But enough of me," she beams gently, "tell me about your nameless *ah*chitect. Tell me about *H.*, tell me about *you!*"

Jen sighs. "That old saying is true, that it takes two to tango."

"Ain't it the truth," she eyerolled; "how'd you two meet?"

"I was at a conference in Edmonton, and he turned up at the same bar. Where a bunch of us went dancing. After."

"Oh, that's so . . ."

"So what?"

MORE WEEKS, FURTHER MOVES

Hitch-kick, hinge-push, hip-roll, hop. The weeks pass in a blur of H-named moves, as the trees grow more denuded, the phone rings less, and Jen's feet, though far from fleet, have begun to know a thing or two. She can now execute a somewhat credible pivot-turn, get through a jazz run without injury to herself or others, pull off a barrel-jump which now only slightly resembles a downed search-and-rescue mission; sometimes she can even follow all eight counts of a routine.

"Hello? Hello? Pick up, if you're there, I found one of your hair things." *Beep.*

Over in Nepal, the cold season socks in. Jen imagines Dawn's ex-partner, the artist, "chillin'" mid-mountain, his yurt dripping with winter rain and inspiration as the excellent ideas flood in. Come to think of it, H. could use a little chilling, maybe he should go keep the toadstool man company for a while.

"Does your artist have a name?" teases Jen. They're at the Mildew again, Jen as usual interviewing Dawn, the buns wondrous, even if they are a little burnt.

The "paused" partner's handle, Jen now learns, is Arendt.

"It's German." Dawn sighs as she delivers this news, the amazing eyes an invitation to share in the wonder. (Jen shares it, she does, though a nasty part of her can't help secretly thinking the name sounds like a knock-knock joke).

Knock-knock.

Who's there?

Arendt.

Arendt who?

Arendt you gonna ask me what's new? (These days, what isn't?)

"Arendt," she muses to Dawn, "any relation to Hannah?"

"Hannah who?"

"German philosopher."

"He should be related to her; he says the most philosophical things when he's stoned." A shimmering sigh. "But, nope."

"You're making a mistake. Call me." *Beep.*

Maybe she's making a mistake. Or maybe she made one the night she accepted H.'s first dinner invitation, only to find herself perched on the burnished deck of a round little wooden boat, drinking the last rays of the sun and a lime-splashed glass of Beefeater's Gin, while the water rocked them like a womb, and the evening light glistened in his thinning hair. So many mistakes, so little time; could it be that she made one when she hungrily, and for all time, memorized the scent of limes? Then again, perhaps she made it when she kept on with him, even after learning there was a not-so-ex-wife and three not-quite-teenagers, two nannies and a bad-tempered budgie, all of which had to be shipped back and forth between the not-so-ex-wife's place and H.'s, every Sunday night.

Or maybe it was when, his strong arms around her, he'd murmured, "I've built so many houses, yet I've never had a home." Gravely shaking his well-educated head. "My real home will be the one" – polishing his description of its dormers and decks like a poem – "the one I'll build for you."

And she'd believed it to be true.

"Why do you keep doing things like that?" (Dorie had been quick to demand); "Aren't you studying psychology?"

There was no point in telling Dorie that an education, even one in psychology, is no protection from the inherited mess with which we're let loose upon this life; that psychologists stumble and fall as hard, and with as much puzzlement, as anybody else.

CHEERY CZECH, WEEK SIX

The worst part of tonight's class is over, praise God — even with Dawn for a partner, diagonals still kill Jen; actually, maybe now they kill her even more, her and Dawn's combined progress across the studio floor resembling nothing so much as a swan towing a tractor tire — and the instructor, a cheery Czech, has finally lowered the lights for the cooldown. Her voice, a military bark during the active part of the class, has magically switched, with this transition, to a mother's caress: "Now I vohnt you to chust fooly extent your botty, chust feel each bone and muscle as it rests against za *vood* of za floor, chust feeeelink zet vood, feeling its smoozness, its coolness, and chust lettink everysing go, chust completely relaaaaxing . . ."

Jen sneaks a quick stare over at Dawn, who is poured out beside her like dark water, the points of her hips just breaking its surface: how can anybody be that peaceful? She is reminded of summer camp when she was a kid. While everyone else was snoring and whimpering and muttering about frogs and Tater Tots in their sleep, Jen was always wide awake, alert to every shift and cricket and creak of bunk, eyes glued to the impossibly high, grainy window, waiting for the first sign of dawn.

It would seem not much has changed.

". . . and I vohnt you to chust breeze in true da nose, out true da mout, *zo* . . ."

Back then — Jen was nothing if not perceptive — she believed that her solitary wakefulness in the face of all that communal oblivion had something to do with being neither especially pretty nor one bit rich. The skinny ones, the ones with the on-trend clothes and excellent connections, whose mothers played tennis and whose fathers ran businesses, somehow didn't need to be vigilant. Off they swanned into dreamland with the same insouciance as, in a few short years, they would enter colleges and universities, comfortable marriages. Whereas Jenny, with her round little belly, chunky untanned thighs and dim prospects, had to be on the lookout. She had to keep her eyes open, in case she missed something, or needed to give something a miss.

". . . and now I vohnt you to chust veeeggle zose toes, chust feel zet blode circoolating, zet skin glowink, feelink zet life poolsink in each individual toe. I vohnt you to *feel* za *life* in your toes . . ."

Dawn rolls toward Jen. "*Poolsink?* What's —"

"Pulsing." Jen strained to feel the life in hers. "As in blood. As in — you know — Life."

Was that what she'd been afraid of missing, back then? Life? The life in her toes and elsewhere? Was that what kept — what keeps her — watchful, that sorry belly of hers still awake and hungry, while the satisfied thin girl dreams on?

Dawn's eyes open now, bestowing the usual miracle. "Hey," she murmurs, her voice like melting butter, "how 'bout we go have a drink somewhere."

Instead of a house, H. gave her his boat. That is: he loaned her its keys. "You like the boat and you're a runner," he'd reasoned, "this way you'll have somewhere to run to, and at the same time you can keep an eye on her for me; never know what types might be hanging around a marina late at night."

Homeless females crouching on borrowed boat decks, perhaps? Thought Jen, beginning to awaken.

Though she had not yet fully realized that his visits were becoming less regular and more fraught, and that they were beginning to have a bit of a "conservation" plot: the children, the pets, his good name, his tight time.

At the same time, it had distantly begun to dawn on her by then that, while H. came to town to see his boat and of course her, Jen was never invited into his world. When did she begin to suspect that he had a secret? Because he did have one. And the secret was Jen.

"Do you mean to tell me nobody in your life even knows I exist?" she asked him late one wine-soaked night on the diminutive yacht.

"I never said that."

Though when pressed, he had confessed that until his divorce came through, he couldn't, shouldn't, mustn't, daren't; therefore, just for the time being, their relationship had to be kept, so to speak, under the radar.

In other words, Yes. He did have a secret. What H. didn't know: by this time, Jen had one, too. Or rather — it had her.

Dawn knows all the Bohemian watering holes. She leads Jen to a charming old place that could be straight out of Flaubert, and whose claim to fame is gourmet cuisine served in a nineteenth-century carriage house.

"A carriage house?" says Jen, who'd believed she was heading straight home, and dressed the part. "A for-real one?" Avoiding puddles, she keeps her eyes down, and sees: dear God, she's got on that Budweiser T-shirt she forgot to throw out.

"Welcome to Chez Vache," sings Dawn with a Frenchly ironic little lift of her perfectly shaped eyebrow, "or as the regulars call it, Chez Vachois."

Let's go have drinks at Chez Vachois. Jen has heard of this *Chez Vache*, or *Vachois*, or simply: *La Vache*, but until tonight, she's never been there. H., when he is available, prefers to grab a quick bite, as he calls the snails and truffles and filets mignon to which he is partial, at the marina's anonymous, reliably deserted and overpriced drinking hole, so that he can keep on polishing his brass and sorting out ropes — it turns out there's more work to sailing than he originally let on — and examining fittings, while Jen rubs (make that: rubbed) his hull with lemon oil.

How, she wonders, her eyes meeting Dawn's over the drinks list, did she ever do that? Where was her life?

Dawn smiles back, breathes, "What are *you* going to have?"

Grinning maniacally, Jen dives into the menu to hide her dismay: What, dear God, is a person supposed to order at a Bohemian watering hole called Chez Vachois? Over Dawn's svelte shoulder can be seen "the Vache" of Chez Vachois, a larger-than-life sculpture of a — surely pregnant — cow (cast in solid bronze! Made by a local craftsperson!), hunkering like a four-hundred-pound bouncer in the smoky echt-carriage house entryway, its unfoolable gaze drilling her right through the Budweiser logo: it can tell an imposter when it sees one, don't think it can't.

Privately, Jen vows to make very small dust rags out of the cursed T-shirt before the next dance class. Maybe she can use it to plug the hole in the water heater. She bets Dawn doesn't even have a water heater. Probably she channels the sun.

Now comes the server, a filmy creature with a basket of warm pumpernickel and curls like cold butter, serenely preparing to take their order.

Dawn, her slender arm unfurled along the table like a banner of surrender – even anarchists sometimes need refreshment – murmurs, "I'd love a White Russian."

The server beams upon Jen.

"I'll take one too. I mean, also." She cringes as Cold Curls darts away and disappears behind a wall of glittering bottles, while, in the corner, for her eyes only, the Vache, that baleful bronze mother-to-be, malingers and spies.

They will speak of many things as, in surprising numbers, the White Russians and Bohemians come and go, babbling self-consciously (the Bohemians) of things other than Michelangelo. Jen will learn, for example, that Dawn used to be married – just like Jen! But that unlike Jen, Dawn has a child, a little boy. His name, adorably, is Max.

"He's six," Dawn sighs, dance-dazzled, rum-warmed, reclining on the tranquil shores of successful maternity, "and he's *amazing*." She sighs softly, her beautiful skin glowing from all that exercise and booze, "And I can't believe how lucky I am; I have this wonderful job . . . you know? And an *amazing* salary plus commission" – Dawn doesn't just pirouette in leggings all day, she's actually a real estate agent for RE/MAX, home of the hot air balloon – "which meant that when I split, I was able to buy this *great* little house . . ."

Jen takes a big drink, the ice cubes banging like tankers against her teeth, and asks, interviewing again, what it's like to raise a child as a single woman. What she really wants to know but is too embarrassed to ask: how is it possible to have been stretched beyond recognition, bulged and rummaged like Chez Vachois' sneering mascot over there, and still have such tiny tits, such stunning abs. And the thing she doesn't yet even realize she wants to know: what is that country like? The country of Maternity. The mother country. That far, wild place whose gates, one rainy night, closed against her.

She hadn't been sure at first. A period can be late, can be skipped, can disappear altogether and then, like an underground river, simply resurface; it had happened in stressful times, before. This time, though, the river was over, and in its place: a vague queasiness, sore, itchy breasts, an ever-so-slightly thickened waist.

What she knew: a part-time counselling job would never pay the rent. Another thing: H. wouldn't be cheered, at this point in his life, to have discovered he was about to be a dear old dad again.

Was that why she hadn't told him?

"Hey," breathes Dawn, "you know what?"

Jen does not, but finds an eager expression.

"You should come over to my place for dinner sometime . . ."

Another big gulp sloshes down as Jen watches the room do interesting things, remembering. How some days she'd wake up calm and thrilled, studying her changing self in the mirror, aware of a new mantra, an irregular prayer, brave as a heartbeat: *baby, be there. Be there. Be there.* Another day, another metre: Baby don't. Baby don't. Baby—

". . . don't believe I married an accountant," Dawn is saying now, "can you believe I married an *accountant*? I mean, they're so limited. You know? So full of . . . limits."

The server appears, a pastel fish, all fins and filmy shimmer, swimming up to ask if everything's all right here, then flickering away again to whatever submarine grotto she hovers in, between tides. Meanwhile out of nowhere, a blues band has appeared, and is beginning to tune up in the corner. Sumptuous notes bloom like orchids in Jen's head. She imagines locking eyes with the lead, a guy with a straight nose and curly hair and tight jeans painted onto a pair of pencil-straight hips. She can feel the entire geography of her lips.

"I mean," breathes Dawn with a conspiratorial sip of her freshened Russian, "I don't believe in limits. Do you? I'm actually teaching him he has special powers."

Him, Jen blearily puzzles, who the hell is him?

Dawn sees her confusion, giggles, "Max, remember? My son? I'm teaching him there's nothing he can't do, if he sets his mind to it, because *he* has *special powers*."

Jen pictures a skinny kid balancing on the roof outside his bedroom, pre-flight in his Batman costume, thinks, surprising herself, Good luck with that.

"Dance Me to the End of Love" rolls out with its desolate irony and ecstatic despair from the band's dark corner, the singer stroking the smoky notes into his mic like a prayer.

"Do you miss him?" smiles a dreamy Dawn, giving her drink a little stir.

Again, Jen's in catch-up mode, her sodden brain galumphing after the scent of meaning, a feeble old hunting dog scrambling for a long-downed duck.

"Your *pahtner:* The mysterious 'H.,'" she hollers over the music in loud quotation marks. "The *ahh*-chitect. You hardly ever talk about him."

Jen tilts her head, she hopes affably, and shrugs a shoulder as the band sings about love being a shelter when all the threads are torn.

What is there to say? That she dreaded the Architectural Society's fundraising ball? That she sucked at the polka? That she slipped on the lemon oil? It all sounds so trivial.

When, for what happened, there are no words.

No worries. Dawn is off in her own world now, rummily undulating to the music and smiling her elliptical smile, her beautiful eyes at halfmast, glossed lips pouted in a potential kiss.

"One thing about Arendt," she croons with a slow wink and an intimate press of Jen's wrist: "No limits."

SIX WEEKS: A LOSS

It had been a rainy fall night like this one, a year before she first met Dawn. A last-minute decision to go for a run down to the marina and her borrowed boat, her aquatic folly, her womb away from home. Rough wind and swirling leaves, torquing cramps, towering waves. A smell then, harsh as a sentence, rising in shocking instalments between her legs.

But it wasn't the right time of month for her period.

Running scared and blind, dodging rain and oncoming cars, snatching a furtive look down, whenever she got the chance, to see how far, how fast the dark stain had advanced along the insides of her thighs. Jogging, dodging, counting in her head: backwards, forwards, back again through the weeks since she'd last bled, the brief life hardening like iron in her clothes, her head light as a red balloon.

Baby, be there. Be there. Be there. Baby don't. Baby don't. Baby—

Standing in the stall at the empty marina, yanking down her sweats. The bright cold of fluorescent lights, blank mirrors, ranks of gaping toilets. The way the sweats stuck and chafed like her peed-in snow pants when she was little, and that shame, so much the same. But not the smell. Smell of flesh and death, of life begun and then undone. The harsh, foreign, familiar whiff of a cycle gone wrong, followed by the discreet plop of something small and translucent, tight as a Chinese button knot, into the toilet. Until it dropped, she hadn't quite believed it was there; until she'd seen it, held for a moment in the stiffening shroud of her underwear: the closed bud of a hand, veined bulb of the forehead, inky anemone of an eye. The knotted cord of past and future, future past, teetering briefly on the water, light as a butterfly, a momentary folly.

Whether she saw all of this or not, she saw it. It was seen by her heart, recorded indelibly by her inner eye.

Then she'd flushed the toilet. Worse — and she can never unknow, unknot this — she'd felt relieved.

A RETURN — WELL, TWO

"I have some wonderful news," whispers Dawn over her shoulder as she and Jen move through the positions at the barre. It's a tender evening in April, long shafts of sunlight spreading like butter across the gold wood of the studio floor while the music, something funky and twisted with a beat that grabs Jen from heart to feet, bounces off the walls.

"Yeah? So do I," Jen hisses back, she's been at this all winter and still her spine sways in second position, a fact the relentlessly jolly teacher never ceases to point out: "Stend up *straight*, tuck ze bom *onder*," she giggles, "*zo*. You don't vohnt to look like auld leedy!"

Though by now she's gotten used to the instructor's teasing and provoking and scolding and giggling; she's actually begun to look forward to this class, even to diagonals, which, humiliation by mortification, she's developed a knack for surviving. And there are times now, when she's standing at the barre at the beginning of class, feeling the music pound through her bones and catching the sexy command of its beat in her gut, when it's like she's nowhere on earth but where she's supposed to be. Right here on this shining floor with nothing to navigate but space and music and hard-earned moves. At these times it seems as though all is resolved and she's alive, rescued and reformed, her grief both unleashed and pulled taut as catgut by a simple, saving count of eight: a thing she wouldn't admit, even — perhaps especially — to Dawn.

"Stretchink, pleece!" cries the instructor, and Dawn drops to the floor beside her, hands clasped around a toned leg, her long back effortlessly lengthened toward the stylishly flexed foot.

In this impossible position she turns her head toward Jen, so that her eyebrow and ankle meet: "He's back!"

"Who," Jen grunts through her stiff and nasty approximation of the same stretch, bones and brains knock-knocking the floor.

"Arendt, silly! Arendt's back from Nepal! What's yours?"

"My what?"

"Your news!"

"Oh, that." Jen farts; under the circumstances, it's hard not to. "H. is going to be in town next weekend. He says he wants to get together. To talk and so forth. And apparently, he's got some earrings of mine, I don't even remember whichever ones they were. I haven't seen him all winter. What do I *do?*"

Dawn turns her head away, the opposite eyebrow and ankle meeting, presumably, over some other unreachable body part. "*I* know," she breathes on the exhale, her belly a floral washboard. "We'll have that dinner you and I talked about last fall, and we'll invite H. and Arendt! We've all been apart all winter; it'll be a four-way reunion dinner, how cool is that?"

Jen smiles, nods like a bauble-head, thinks, good question.

TWO WEEKS LATER: DINNER

It turns out that Arendt – he and his bong are ensconced beside Jen, across from Dawn and H. – that Arendt isn't just an artist, he's a boat builder, too. In fact, he knows of H.'s boat, an antique Rhodes Wherry – a fine little specimen of a yawl, he's pleased to say.

"Oh yeah," he adds, helping himself to more of the main course, something featuring organic mung beans and arcane herbs, "I know a men," he says Germanly, "who makes these bohts, I think even I have seen this very boht here last year, at the Glenmore boht show? Was she not originally built as a birthday gift for a competitive sailor?"

"Indeed she was," murmurs H., not, Jen can tell, unimpressed.

"I seem to recall that she is built two inches to the foot and modelled on a sixteen-foot Maritime fishing skiff."

"*Well* done," H. affirms, with a gratified nod and a second helping of Dawn's health-filled yellow stew, "right you are, sir."

Since when is H. a mung connoisseur?

"I think it was Tom Goodwin, that fine Harbourmaster of Digby, Nova Scotia, correct me if I am wrong, who owned the original boht, a skiff about twelve, twelve-and-a-half-foot long?"

H. is fairly chuckling by now, and topping up his wine, a good sign.

"Oh, she is a pretty thing," grins Arendt, revealing a droll gap where a left bottom incisor should be, his head bobbing up and down with enthusiasm, eyes a-twinkle, candlelight sparking off the brassy frizz of his minimal ponytail, "I would not say no to a chance to look at her again."

"Why only look," smiles H., who, thanks to the hour and the plentiful food and drink, is beginning to lapse into boating lingo himself, "we'll take her out and test her mettle once she's roped and ready!" An image that causes Jen, though apparently not Dawn, who is abuzz with hospitality, an involuntary shudder.

H., in his fake British accent, adds, "I caun't *possibly* drop 'round before Friday night."

Arendt takes a good long suck on the bong, followed by a convulsive coughing fit. "One of" — cough, cough — "one of" — more clutching and gagging — "one thing I love" — he pronounces it luff — "about these bohts," he at last manages to somewhat clear his throat, "is that they are *unbelievably* buoyant. No person can *sink* a well-made yawl!"

Jen stares at Dawn across the table.

Buoys will be buoys, Dawn grins back.

And it's all keels and planking and spars after that, and it's lanyards this and it's halyards that, and it's more wine flowing and liqueurs a-glowing, and it's mung beans giving way eventually to something with raspberries and chocolate and a drizzle of Chambord, as the stereo plays more Leonard Cohen, and the candles burn down, and the spring night fills the gaunt old windows with its sudden mystery, and Arendt's well-honed hand settles companionably along Jen's thigh, rendering it so detached from her body it might as well be a plant holder or a fifth leg.

Drunkenly, she consoles herself that in time of need, she could reach down and unscrew the leg, lean it up against the wall, fight the Philistines, clock Arendt with it. Can the others tell? Surely, they can tell!

Though . . . possibly not.

Dawn is busy gazing at H., who for his part, is describing the way women at parties, mistaking him for a doctor – "it's the rugged profile," he jokes, "the intelligent sweater" – always want to tell him there is something concerning them, medically. All roll eyes and chortle, nobody at this table would ever do such a thing to a doctor, much less to a Rhodes Wherry sailor or a well-known architect, at a party. "Sure," he purrs, this time with an Irish inflection, "there was a lady at a party just the other day, wanted to tell me about her heart" – gazing heavenward and placing a pious hand upon his knitted one – "and I had to tell her what I always tell the ladies . . ."

"What's that?" cry Arendt and Dawn (Arendt's calloused paw still clamped to Jen's wooden leg, which at this point, she is too far gone to liberate) in unison.

H. gives his best diagnostic stare, lilts, "Nothing trivial, I hope!"

Eyes glued to a spot just between Dawn's and H.'s heads, Jen laughs like a chimp along with the others, thinking, Arendt-cha going to getcher paw off my pants?

THEN

When she picks up the phone a few weeks later, the elfin voice of Arendt is on the other end of the line, asking what she's up to – a knock-knock joke come true! – and if she might like to go and see a little thing some of his friends are in, at the Pumphouse Theatre. Like La Vache, this playhouse is something Jen has heard about, but never experienced – and the memory of gratuitous paws notwithstanding, she realizes that she's tempted; after all, it's been one long old yawl of a winter.

(Though, what about Dawn, she wonders, then recalls her friend's enlightened views on possessiveness and letting things go.)

Still, just to be on the safe side, she calls Dawn up to ask if she would be unhappy about a "play" date between herself and Arendt.

There is the very slightest pause. Then, "I'm so *happy* for you!" Dawn cries, as though Jen had just announced her full scholarship, plus living expenses, to Princeton. "For *both* of you! Go. Go!"

Jen can practically feel the spring sun beaming down the phone.

It shows in small ways at first, just in those insignificant little things that could so easily be something else. Like the fact that Dawn is absent from the next dance class. Possibly she is tired from all those hours on her feet, traipsing demanding clients through staged houses. Or: maybe this was the night she could not put off getting groceries one minute longer. Though, who knows – could Max's special powers have encountered an obstacle? A report card? A barn door? When Jen calls her to touch base, Dawn, in her same breathless voice, sings that she is just running out the door. "Tonight's parent-teacher interviews; gotta fly!" Click.

Slowly, Jen lowers the phone.

When, a few weeks later, Dawn does return to Jazz 101, she suggests that, now that Jen is getting so good at them, perhaps she can manage diagonals on her own.

Time passes, as do further dance classes. Dawn attends fewer of these, then quits showing up altogether. Also, she stops returning Jen's messages. Should Jen be craven, and call once more, this time to tell Dawn that she never even made it to that play with Arendt, on account of the revenge, that very night, of the professor's long-neglected water heater? Probably not.

Towards the end of summer on her way out of the A&P, she sees a poster advertising Spiritual Movement classes. The poster urges the reader to "express your soul's deepest longings through the language of mindful dance," and features a stylishly blurred photograph of that unmistakable body, those winged hands, the glorious shoulders, which look even more airborne than Jen remembers.

THE LIFE IN YOUR TOES

For old time's sake — and, it must be confessed, to listen to the guy with the curly hair and the straight nose — Jen takes to winding down after her Dawnless dance classes with her own late-night visits to La Vache. That's where, one night in September, whom should she spot but Dawn and H. in the eponymous bovine's dark corner, holding hands and guzzling White Russians to beat the band, both of them happy as clams?

Before she can hide, Dawn, that radiant mermaid, is flowing toward her, swimming up to Jen's table, and tugging like a little fish upon the morsel of her hand. "Hugo and I were just having a drink," she shouts over the music. "Come *join* us!"

Swallowing her confusion, Jen hollers back that she's meeting someone — as lies go, not the worst one she's ever told — then finds a seat with a good view of the band. (Though — subtlety was never her specialty — she can't resist one quick look over at the lovebirds' corner. There they sit, guzzling and billing. And doesn't it seem that, in place of the usual malevolent glint, there's a twinkle in the old cow's eye?)

It comes to pass that it's the last class of the season. As Jen helps the instructor, with whom she's begun to be friends, to pack up the boombox and the CDs and the extension cords, the woman giggles, puts an arm around her shoulders, which these days are getting almost muscular, and congratulates her on her "trrrremendous prrrogress," her newfound strength and suppleness, "like beauteeful Birrrrd of Paradise!" But then she suggests that Jen consider making dance a bigger part of her life, reminding her that she teaches the advanced level beginning in two weeks, and warning that "I vohnt to see you at ze barre!"

Jen has to smile at the riddle of life, with its slants and surprises — who knew she'd become a dancer? — its knotted cord of things that you can find, and lose.

Even as she tells the teacher she'll consider the advanced level, she begins to sense a secret stirring — she can't deny it — of the life in her toes.

STRAYS

Okay, I'm back. But not for long, I'll soon be gone;
just gimme a bite, and I'm on my way . . .

GARRISON KEILLOR, THE IN AND OUT CAT SONG

A cat decided to move in with Jen. This was, figuratively speaking, after the folly maker moved out. She'd graduated from the professor's apartment and bought a house by this time, a skinny place in Bowness, whose one selling point was that it was on the bus route into town.

The cat had turned up one late-winter day cold and hungry, and she couldn't help herself; she'd let the fleabag in. On account of its ginger coat and demonically tawny eyes, she gave it the name of Yellow, took it to the vet, and had it dewormed, defleaed, and put on steroids for its skin lesions. Even though it soon began to reveal certain rambling ways, she continued to feed and shelter the thing, to mourn its sudden vanishings, welcome its peripatetic returns. She attributed this to loneliness, and possibly to some unrequited ghost from her past, to Sonny or Eric or Laura Ward, or maybe even some needy younger version of herself. (Thanks to her studies, she'd read all about family systems and intergenerational this, and early childhood that, she could diagnose herself six ways from Sunday *and* get paid for it, plus, now she had a cat: she was all set.)

Much as she liked Yellow, however, it wasn't a cat she really wanted, and time was running out.

Some friends from work were having a party one Saturday night when she was meaning to catch up on housework, but the friends called and bugged her, so she changed her mind – the laundry wasn't going anywhere – and went. A well-made fellow named Kev happened to be there, just in from B.C. and staying for a few weeks "until I can get a place of my own." Kev was a mechanic, the serious type that read books and could fix anything – and there was nothing in Jen's house that didn't need fixing. Plus, he was not without a certain appeal. He wasn't thin but he wasn't fat, either; he had a nice warm-fuzzy beard, the most intense only-you-can-help-me-find-my-way-in-this-world eyes, and the kind of comfy little hairy belly that's not going to be an established gut for a while yet.

All that, and he wasn't a hundred. Was she finally growing up?

And even if he hadn't had all those nice qualities: if there was one thing in this world Jen could *not* resist, it was a handy guy who read books. If only she'd read more of them herself, instead of having such a good time before heading west. But back then, she'd been more into research, specifically on the liquor cabinets of alpha males, than reading. Though she'd always seemed, somehow, to have luck on her side. She still occasionally enjoyed the irony that it had been her "research," in the end, that had led to the work she'd ended up with.

Blame the wine. That very night the two of them made a bargain that Kev (all the partygoers said he was "*the* best") would move in with Jen until he found his own place, and pay rent in the form of house improvements.

It wasn't long before Kev and his backpack and his grin were standing, as promised, on the front step of Jen. "That gate of yours has settled," he said with an unimpressed glance street-ward, "that's why it's not latchin' properly." He took a slurp of his double-double, then pointed at the gate with his cigarette. "It's the frost, eh? Gets in there and puts 'em out of true something terrible."

Nor was he enraptured with her electrical panel. "When was this baby installed? She's not up to code, I'll tell you that right now."

Already she loved it when he talked dirty.

The humidifier on the furnace – Jen was an addictions counsellor, how was she supposed to know about furnace humidifiers? – hadn't been seen to for so long the filter looked like something of ritual significance recently excavated from an Egyptian tomb, and the little drawer-thingy you had to pull out to get at it was crusted shut with equally ancient mineral deposits.

Kev had it apart in half a second. "You ever get colds and coughs and stuff?"

Jen did have a pesky throat tickle, but so did everybody in her family, it was hereditary. "Because those little buggers, pardon my French, if they're not switched out regular, they're a *breeding* ground for shit you don't even want to know about."

Jen looked appropriately mortified, itched to touch the back of his neck.

And he had no lack of scorn for the state of her deck, when he got out back to see that. "You see them nails sticking out all everywhere here?" He pointed.

Jen saw them, all right, the nails drove her nuts in the winter, when she managed to find the time to get out there and ram a path through the snow.

"Every one of 'em needs to be countersank." Not minding Kev's grammar, Jen enthusiastically agreed; over time the protruding nail heads had turned the blade of her not-so-ergonomic shovel into a liability, and had many times infuriatingly driven her elbows into her gut when, pushing it on heavily snowing mornings, she'd run into them. She hated the nails unreasonably; she did not hate the gaze of Kev's critical eye.

Especially when, as it had begun to do, it considered her haunches approvingly.

It wasn't long before the fix-all mechanic ended up, not just out back with the tools in her shed, but inside, with his tool in her bed. Pretty soon, Jen found herself glazed over with sex (one thing about Kev, he was good in the sack), and hellbent to set about nesting and nurturing, and the whole foolish rigamarole. On the way to see her clients (these days: too often late and in hurry-up mode) she'd find herself thinking about how she'd make the oddly proportioned little upstairs room she currently used for hanging her clothes in into a nursery. She'd buy all those books about what to expect, and what to avoid. She'd take folic acid. All this would be happening while Kev was fixing the deck and making the tea-towel-sized backyard into a tiny, perfect herb garden, and coming home from being a mechanic, ready for the shower and a good romp between Jen's nice clean sheets.

Occasionally the fecund fog parted long enough for her to see that there were some things not domestic that needed looking after. Kev's teeth, for one. A constant fug of bad breath trailed him, and one day Jen got up the nerve to say something about it.

"What breath," he said, as though he had a different means of supplying himself with oxygen, than the rest of mankind.

"What do you mean, what breath, *your* breath, you dork,

your morning breath," (as usual, they were in bed), "your afternoon breath, your last breath, it's like living with a wet dog!"

"The only time I get bad breath is when I've ate garlic," he countered, "and I haven't ate garlic since I moved in here, because you never—"

"Eaten, Kev," corrected Jen, not quite as charmed as formerly with his grammar freedom. "You haven't *eaten* garlic."

"And you never talk too much."

He'd found a three-day-a-week job by this time and was making regular contributions to the laundry and the pantry; also, the hydro bill was up, and there were more sugary and salty snacks around, for Jen to try to avoid. "Or how about *you* cook a meal once in a while? As far as I know, vegetables haven't gone out of style."

Though he quickly came to adore Yellow, and wouldn't you know it? Yellow was into him, too. Which caused Jen to feel both jealous and needy—a new low—plus a potent combo. It made her unreasonably aggrieved to see how Yellow, who was practically feral, would let Kev wear him over his shoulders like a feather boa. A fur boa, she corrected herself, while secretly reminding Yellow who bought the kibble. A fleabag boa.

It appeared that Yellow, who'd switched allegiances with enviable ease, couldn't care less who supplied him with eats. Between the two males encamped in her anything-but-large living room, Jen was starting to feel abandoned and colonized, both.

And yet. And yet. Kev did the dishes without being asked, when the mood hit him. And he'd fixed the gate as promised, and he brought up clean towels from the laundry room, when Jen went for her bedtime shower. And he read—he actually read those New Age books of his – out loud, to Yellow, who had taken to shamelessly purring and grooming himself while hearing all about how to attract the desired energy into your life. (A subject, as far as Jen could tell, that Yellow and his reading partner were already well-familiar with.)

And he did, Kev did countersink those nails.

All of which, in Jen's soon-to-be-middle-aged eyes, added up to: Kev was a nurturer.

And nurturers made good fathers. The thought of Kev cradling a damp-headed newborn in the crook of his muscled arm could almost make her swoon. It certainly made her horny. And Kev in that department was unfailingly "at your service." Though he enjoyed replacing the last word in the phrase with "cervix," that tired old gag.

The tired old gag didn't stop Jen from getting him undressed when he came out with it. And fast.

Sack-happiness notwithstanding, pesky practical matters still had to be dealt with. For example: that Kev had gum disease, that his wet-dog smell was from perio-breath. So then, since he had none, she put him on her dental plan, and he had to have surgery and one of those Waterpik things, salt rinses, monthly check-ups, the whole nine yards. She was still hoping for that new shed he'd promised her when he developed carpal tunnel syndrome. How he could have got that she didn't know, since didn't you get it from repetitive strain, or something? And she never saw the man repeat anything, other than the sad tale of his childhood. How his mother died when he was ten and his father didn't want him, and one day they were moving, the father and the new girlfriend and Kev – or so Kev thought. So he *thought*, that is, until they left him behind to sweep out the empty apartment or trailer or whatever it was they'd been living in, promising to come back later, but nobody ever did. How Kev started out walking finally, thinking he had an idea of what part of town the two of them had moved to, but he never did find his father.

Eventually someone noticed him wandering around looking in garbage cans and sleeping in doorways. Just this ten-year-old little boy, an image that brought back Laura Ward's eyes, so lost and so hungry. The person delivered Kev to the Children's Aid, as it was called back then, and he spent the next eight years in and out of foster homes, managing to get himself raised somehow, and pick up a trade, and doing his best to leave numbers where he could be reached, in case. Once in a while his father would get drunk and call him up late at night, crying or blaming, but he always had an excuse – his worsening health, a new job he might be going to have, a problem with his car – why he couldn't meet Kev for a coffee somewhere.

On his days off, which was most days, Kev was committed to the soaps. Jen would come home late in the afternoon half-dead and starving and traumatized from the sad tales at work, and there he'd be, still in the sweats and T-shirt he'd slept in, curled up with Yellow, smoking weed and watching *Another World* with the curtains pulled. The question "What's for dinner?" would start him telling as serious as anything about how Lenore and Steve on the TV were having a baby and Iris was mad as hell, and suing for breach of trust. "Is that so," Jen would say, wanting to wring his sturdy neck. He had every one of those characters' problems and predicaments down pat, sitting there in that stuffy room – her living room! – craning his neck to see around her, in case she'd brought him home a six-pack. Jen tried to be patient, telling herself the soap characters must be a substitute for the family he'd never had. And maybe for the one Jen and Kev didn't seem to be having, either.

For the fact was, that despite all their carryings-on in the bedroom, not much in the way of damp-headed infants was shaking.

One day about four or five months in, Jen pried Kev away from the TV and dragged him out for a tune-up, it was high time. First, back to the dentist and the oral surgeon, then to the therapist, to help him deal with his past, finally to the fertility specialist, on behalf of the future.

The doctor, a shiny-haired person younger than Jen, took a tolerating look at their file. "You realize that at your age you have basically a four percent chance," she said, briefly glancing up.

"At what?" Jen asked, unable to look at it. The stark outline of it.

"Well, at conception, that's what you're here about, right?"

Jen looked at Kev. All that rutting for four percent. Kev shrugged his hairy shoulders.

"Yep," the doc went on, "you're getting close to forty, and by that time your eggs are tougher, you're ovulating less frequently, there's more radiation damage —"

Radiation damage?

"That's the world we live in."

The list kept on.

"And did you say you smoked, sir?"

Kev hadn't said so, but a fool could smell the stale nicotine seeping from his pores. Glumly, he nodded.

"'Kay, then there'd also be the reduced sperm count to consider." The doctor checked a box, looked bored.

Jen leaned back in her chair, weak with shock. All her life, or most of it, she'd been trying not to get pregnant, and now that she was finally ready, willing, and she'd blithely believed able, it was too late. She couldn't take it in.

The shiny-haired expert looked up. "For our purposes," she said, "you're *actually* forty, not almost. And after forty it's hard to getcha pregnant. Sure, we can give you the drugs and test your blood and do the in vitro and all the rest of it, but the reality is, it's rare as rump roast" — an appraising glance in the direction of Jen's posterior — "for anybody over forty on fertility treatments to take home a live baby." She smacked the file shut. "Just a biological fact."

Jen swallowed. "I see."

Nevertheless, the available treatments were outlined, their risks and benefits weighed, the staggering costs tallied. They could try an ovulation drug for a while and see if that worked; then, at two hundred dollars a pop, came artificial insemination, then in vitro at a thousand a round. They could fertilize Jen's aging eggs in petri dishes and then drill holes in them, to let Kev's asphyxiated sperm gasp their way in. (Probably the baby would get born jonesing for a light.) They could plant the eggs back in her, already fertilized and growing. They even had a drug that could trick her brain into thinking she was twenty, or some such craziness. There might be headaches, she and Kev were advised, mood swings. Financial stress. Murder and mayhem.

Instead of what she had always imagined would someday happen. That she would awaken one morning knowing a new, sweet thing.

They tried the drugs for a while, but nothing stirred, nor did any of the doctor's demoralizing predictions come true. Though Jen did think maybe she was more emotional on the drugs, and Kev agreed. "You're definitely bitchier. Plus" — he set about making himself a rollie — "talk, talk, talk." He gazed heavenward in supplication.

And you're such a beauty, she thought, on her way to the kitchen.

One day in the midst of all the dental and medical commotion came a message that Kev's father had died. Apparently, the man had choked on a chicken bone in some greasy spoon, and there'd been no one around who could Heimlich him out of it. Jen and Kev had been arguing about the smoking again when the phone rang, and it was the police, asking Kev to come and identify the remains.

"I'll come with you," said Jen, her heart contracting, "you shouldn't be doing this alone, after all you've —"

"No need for that," Kev responded. "Just as well the old bugger's gone." He drew a bent Players from behind his ear. "Far as that goes, maybe it's just as well *I* was gone."

"What's that supposed to mean?"

"Ain't gonna jump, if that's what you're thinking."

One of the last things the two of them did together was that awful trip after the father died, and before they split. Jen had thought Kev should at least find out where his mother was buried, since, with the father gone, he was going to be the only one left to remember her, and she bugged him about it until he finally agreed to drive out of the city with her to the parched little town where the cemetery was, a place with a name from a Warner Brothers' cartoon, pop. 582–581, with Kev's mother gone.

It was hot as hell, and they looked and looked. Finally, Jen went back and found the groundskeeper, a pleasant person with a copy of *Thus Spake Zarathustra* sticking out of his back pocket, and asked if it was certain Kev's mother was buried there, because maybe she wasn't. (After all, who in her right mind would choose to spend eternity in a place called Acme?)

Smiling gently upon Jen, the man explained that there were two parts to the cemetery, and that Kev's mother could be in the older part. "It'll be just through those trees over there, and across that same little grassy road you came in on."

They found it. There was no real marker, just this pathetic little half-hidden granite tablet with a name on it. Someone — the groundskeeper? — had set a vase of fading plastic roses on it.

Jen murmured, "It looks so sad, all sort of perfunctory and uncared-for, like that." Kev lit a cigarette and gave a grunt. Maybe he didn't know what perfunctory meant.

So, Jen got down and scraped and worked until finally she got the stone cleaned off so you could see it. She might as well have saved her strength. Kev stood there smoking the whole time she was digging, then took a look down and said, "That's that, then." As if he was glad she'd gotten it out of her system.

"You should have a real stone put up," she nagged him. "Otherwise in a few years there'll be no trace of her at all anymore." (Why was her throat swelling? She'd never once met the woman, and was pretty much over her son.)

Kev shrugged, took a last pull on his cigarette, and tossed the butt onto the head of a plastic swan.

They broke up for good soon after that, not unkindly, Kev was not an unkind person, and he was too lazy to complain or try to make things even, since he didn't really own much of anything to begin with.

Maybe that was why he helped himself to Yellow, who packed his figurative feline bags and left without so much as a baleful glance back.

Jen was not in a mood to be unkind, either; she gave Kev the kibble. Watching the pair head for the taxi, she had to smile.

Though for a while even after the breakup, Jen and Kev sometimes got together and played the let's-make-a-baby game, despite – or maybe because of – the fertility doctor's brisk damnation. Kev said it was the least he could do, and Jen corrected that in her head to: the only thing. But in the end what happened wasn't on the doctor's dire list at all. What happened was that Kev found himself someone younger and more cat-tolerant, whose house needed repairing, and moved himself and Yellow in with her.

Plus, something else not on the doctor's list. Though for once (why tell Kev anything at this point?), Jen had the sense to keep her mouth shut – except to start putting large doses of folic acid into it.

A time came, of course – once it was a sure thing, she couldn't keep it from him – when she did inform Kev of his successful, if unlikely paternity. By that time, he and Yellow (those two, at least, were a match made in heaven) had left, or more likely been punted, by the younger woman, and were shacked up in a Quonset in Canmore, where Kev, following a newfound mystical inclination, was growing weed and making mazes to sell to churches and rich people – "the more you charge the buggers, the more they want it" – and Yellow was now in the vole-hunting line.

They got married. Kev didn't know any better, and Jen thought that this time, thanks to all her life experience – she had just turned the unthinkable age of forty – this time, she'd get it right. "What should we call her?" Kev wondered in awe as they studied the infant's tiny pink postpartum face in the neonatal unit that first night. "After all, I contributed the sperm, so you get first dibs on the name."

Jen did not hesitate. "I'd like to name her after my little brother that died; I know it's been a lifetime, but I still think about him."

Sometimes Jen still thought about Kev's mother, too, whoever she was, or might have been, supposing she'd lived. What had she been like? Had she loved Kev? Would she have kept him with her, if her own life hadn't been cut short? Would she have cared for him, raised him, as Jen was intending to raise her own unstatistical and unscripted child, that sunny miracle or blatant irony or whatever it was going to be – on museum visits and libraries and *The Magic School Bus*, the chronicles of C.S. Lewis?

Or had the mother gone to her maker with rage and regrets, ruined teeth, and a nasty case of liver cirrhosis? Imagine, she thought out loud, if you could bring her back somehow, and ask her.

"You can't, though," said the groundskeeper – whose name, Jen could see by the stitching on his shirt, was Clive – one afternoon when, feeling like a drive, she came there with the baby, to put a flower on the grave.

Clive pulled his book, this time a well-worn Penguin edition of James Joyce's *Ulysses*, out of his back pocket. "Says it best right here. 'Can't bring back time. Like holding water in your hand.'"

Jen acknowledged that this was true, thinking for some reason, of Yellow, that wandering fellow, who not long ago had apparently gone to his ancestors too. "Guess it's the same with cats."

With a mischievous grin, Clive shoved his book back in his pocket. "Don't get me started on cats."

III

I LOVE YOU

It is no act of common passage, but a strain of rareness.

CYMBELINE

Jen stands in long grass at the side of a narrow overgrown road, alone. This must be back in the harbour where Dorie's life started, because there is the feeling that Jen has not been here for a very long time. An eternity. And because far off, through the vetch and wild roses and Timothy, she can sense the vast heave and glitter of the sea.

What she is standing on is more of a track, really, than any useable road. All around it and even down its centre, in the part unpressed by tires, can be seen Queen Anne's lace and daisies, black-eyed Susans, tiger lilies. Old-fashioned flowers, that must have been lugged here by someone once and ambitiously planted, but that now grow wild and leggy, mixed together every which way. Off to the side of the road in the midst of these rogue flowers stands a derelict house or shack, one skinny room off a slightly larger room, a pocked and crumpled tin chimney, a chipped sink with a rusted hand-pump at one end, a gaunt pantry. Grey and gaping, the building has sunk down on one corner of itself, so that its two narrow front windows tilt raffishly toward the sky. Broken glass grits under her feet as she peers through the yawning door, leans to see something, and is half-afraid to look: a sock? A washcloth? She cannot stop herself, she must lean further in: an arm. The dimpled half-cloth, half-porcelain limb of a doll. No head or body anywhere, just this arm . . .

And then she's hearing a voice. Brisk and well-modulated, nothing to do with a place like this, a sight like this. The voice is talking about the *Second Symphony*, by Gustav Mahler: "otherwise known as the *Resurrection Symphony*," it pleasantly adds, "written between 1888 and 1894." And as the clock radio pulls her further into her day in a city on the opposite end of the country, she has one of those after-dreams that can sometimes seem like a realization. What she "realizes" is that Dorie grew up in that house. Not in the slightly larger one down the steep old road Jen used to dread, from those long-ago Sundays at Grandma Elsie's. No, Dorie must have grown up in the one with the orphaned arm. The derelict one, in the dream.

Sunny is hollering: "Mom! *Mo-om!*"

What Jen thinks: For Chrissakes, can't you see I'm trying to sleep? What she says: "Hey, love, good morning, what is it?"

"I can't find my fedora, that's my *signature* hat, Mom, I can't go without it, have you seen it?"

Can't go without it. And it's seven o'clock on the morning, and their flight leaves at eleven, and she's bloody well still in bed. How the hell did she manage that? Now she remembers. Last night she took half a tablet, to make sure she'd get a good sleep before the trip. She got one, all right.

"What about the little plaid one," she calls as gaily as she can manage, "the one you had on yesterday, the little turquoise one with the silver thread in it, you look great in that one." Feeling around for her dressing gown, her glasses, her notebook, making a mental note to buy a proper alarm clock the minute she gets back; she doesn't trust her phone, God Almighty, she's getting fat, there's her glasses and she fumbles them on, adds placatingly, "Your grandma will love that one."

"I don't *care!* I don't even *like* my grandma! I don't even *know* her!" A door clunks shut, then splits open again. "And plus, I'm not a girl, if you'd ever pay attention. I can't wear that dumb plaid cap. That's a *girl's* cap!"

Jen thinks, *that* business again. Though ever-so-gently she calls out, "That's why we're going to spend a couple weeks with her. So you can get to know her better."

"No it *isn't,* it's so you guys can get divorced. My dad told me he's moving all his stuff out to the Quonset while we're away! He even *told* me!"

And Jen remembers the surprisingly legal-looking letter from Kev, that damn old maze-maker. "You mean, that's your actual job now?" she'd said, fascinated, when not long before Sunny was born, he'd shown her round the Quonset, which, married or not, he meant to keep. "Making things for people to get lost in?"

"To lose *themselves* in," he'd replied with a weedy smile, "there's a difference in those two concepts."

"But who buys them? I mean, what kind of demand is there for a — a maze?"

"You'd be surprised. Churches primarily, but also meditation spaces, yoga places, even some of the more touchy-feely dance studios, places like that. I'm pretty busy, actually."

These days, it seemed, he was busy hiring lawyers, with whose official-looking letters she will deal later. For now, she takes a deep breath, tells her daughter, "I know you're upset. But. That is not. The way. To talk to your mother."

And she realizes once again that she has no idea how to be one.

The WestJet lineup is long as labour.

Back into her mind comes that endless night, the hours of grinding contractions, the blinding delivery room light; the noise, the blood; the nurses slapping back and forth through her spent life. And after it was over: the empty hole sagging in her centre. As though a battering ram had gone in one end of her and out the other; the doctor between her knees at the end of the table stitching rhythmically, the thread tugging at Jen's bludgeoned flesh, his arms arcing wide as a sailmaker's.

"What is it?" Her voice so weak she could hardly get the words out.

Then someone calling from the other side of the room: "You have a beautiful little girl!"

A girl.

And it was two a.m. and she was howling like a baby herself, her daughter — her daughter! — swaddled in her arms, a Martian flower. The baby's long flaking fingers and searching mouth with its pale bubble in the top lip's centre, the astonishing splutter of her first red-faced cries, those inky eyes, her hunger. What would ever satisfy such hunger?

Two a.m. She'd imagined being instantly flooded with joy. Instead, she'd been bewildered by this wild new love that felt more like dismay. By the sheer fact, the presence, the fragrant weight, of the baby. Someone had lowered it into her arms, and she'd held onto it, hadn't had a clue what else to do, the words "bewildered by love" pulsing in her mind like a mantra.

Back in her hospital room, the attending nurse, showing her how to clean what was left of her sex, "You got to squat over da bidet, see, like *so*." Her stout varicose legs straddling. "And you staying there until the warm water get everyting. See? Every-*ting*. And you drying all veeery gentle and veeery good. At leas' five minute tree time a day. *So*." Shaking her head as though Jen had wilfully caused the carnage herself, her tongue clucking as she helped her patient to the bed: "JesusMary&Joseph!"

The strict bed with its board-like sheets and metal sides, its distance from the bidet. How was she ever going to get herself there once, let alone three times a day?

Sitting up in bed the next morning, gazing down at thc baby, its body no bigger than a hand puppet. Realizing, suddenly, that she hadn't even kissed her yet. The way the impossibly tiny human had opened and eased, its eyelids fluttering under the small assault of her kisses. The bottomless, unseeing gaze, the fragrant, downy, worried forehead.

The lactation consultant bustling in: "Does she have a name?"

And the sudden, almost-gone memory of the toad hole all those years ago — a lifetime, really — her little brother, on one of the rare occasions she'd ever seen him cry, begging through muddy tears to be let out, to be given mercy. "Her name is Sunny."

"Mom, there's a machine over there, can I get some juice?"

"Okay, but make sure it's juice, not pop."

"Mom!"

"Okay, here's a toonie. Here's two. But come right back."

"Mom, I'm not a little kid!"

(And you're not a confrontational little poop, either.)

The ticket agent: "And would you like a window or the aisle today?"

"Aisle, please."

"Mom, I told you I wanted a window seat."

"You might change your mind after you drink all that juice, it's a long flight."

"My dad would let me have a window, my *dad's* fun!"

Over Saskatchewan, the plane's steady roar morphs into a state half-memory, half-nightmare.

She's back in the little house down the dirt road and Dorie is hollering: "Jenny!"

But Jenny is trying to read. *Little Women*, *My Friend Flicka*, *Anne of Green Gables*. Green Gables is where she wants to be, reading is where she wants to be. "I'm busy right now," she grumps.

"I'll show you 'busy.' You get your little rear end in here and give the baby her wienersnbeans while I'm getting this supper on, I can't do for her and everybody else at once, I need you in here *now!*"

"When I finish this chapter," she stalls.

"There's more to this life than finishing chapters, little girl; one of these days you'll find that out, same as I did!"

"No, I won't," she hollers back, "I'm never going to find out what *you* found out! Anyway, she's not *my* baby, why do *I* always have to mind her? I'm *never* having a baby!"

"Yup, I heard that one before. Now you get in here! Else I'm calling your father, and *then* we'll see how many chapters you finish!"

That kitchen. The fogged windows crowded with unwatered money plants, the counters strewn with baby paraphernalia and cat-food cans, and spilled Jell-O powder, the Eaton's catalogue opened to that year's "car coats" and dribbled over with milk, the jolly jumper's inane swaying in the door, a rickety playpen squatting in the middle of the floor.

This is what the table looks like: Melmac plates of viscous Kraft Dinner. Chrome chairs re-covered by Dorie in orange MACtac. Matching placemats, also MACtac. Their brave gold fleck. A swan-shaped napkin holder beside a plastic container of margarine, a matching stack of Wonder Bread, a Tupperware Salt and Pepper. Dad's visiting ashtray and bottle of beer (in this scene, he's here). And of course, Sonny, who's also still here, and still tormenting their always colicky infant sister.

The living room is a shoebox, papered in fake wood paneling the pink-brown of cold instant coffee. Into it have been crammed: two couches and an antediluvian pump organ (in case it's valuable someday), a piano, a TV, a coffee table, a stereo and Dorie's stack of Book-of-the-Month-Club records of classical hits – Für Elise, Land of Hope and Glory, an Allegro by somebody or other – a crammed mini-freezer. Optimistically disguised by a picnic cloth: a Hoover Washer/Spin Dryer.

Her bedroom has no door.

But it has a ceiling. A calm white rectangle where the light is quiet and minus chaos, a secret room without a Rose the Baby or a giggling Sonny, where only Jenny can be. No Tupperware in that room. No baby stuff. No clutter, or money plants or Tupperware, no once-in-a-while father, and no beer. Only a chair. Just one chair, and it's hers. Her book on the arm of the chair, which she can position anywhere. A blue oval rug on the perfectly white floor. And if she happens to get up from the chair and go to the window of her room and come back, her book will still be there, right where she left it, untorn and unscribbled in. She can spend hours rearranging her room's cool stillness, owning its untouched floor. If Jenny had her way, she would never come down from there.

She's only nine. But even at nine, she can picture a future. On weekdays after rain, she likes to stand above the big puddle at the end of the school driveway looking down, seeing the rippling reflection of herself in a world far from here. In that world there won't be any wienersnbeans. But there'll be all the chapters she can read, and an always-calm room on whose ceiling she won't need to live, in order to read them. She doesn't know where that room is, not yet, but she's going to find it. If it takes her forever, she's going to find it.

—

The plane has started its descent. The captain's voice, requesting that seats be placed in the upright position, startles Sunny awake, the maple leaf pattern of the upholstery pressed pink into her cheek, her eyes large and blank as the first time Jen gazed into them.

"Are we there?"

"Look down."

"What is it?"

"It's Nova Scotia. See all that dark with the silver zigzags through it? It's trees and streams and then more trees."

"Mom! You know what it is?"

"What?"

"A maze!"

"Hey, you're amazed!"

"Just like my dad," she smiles.

Jen squeezes her daughter's hand. "Just like your dad."

—

Had she loved Kev? When she'd agreed to marry him? Or was the gesture, as a mortified Dorie had claimed, "your latest stunt?" He'd been Jen's latest stunt, and then she'd surprised herself by getting to work and loving him.

And she'd managed to keep it up, even when all the old habits started sneaking back in, the weed and the soaps and the perio-breath. It wasn't until he wandered off again that she invited him to stay put in his Canmore Quonset.

Kev liked to give his strange creations evocative handles: *Infinity. Forever. Amour.* (Which, over time and protracted frustration, Jen had taken to mentally renaming: *Nothing is (for example: Yellow). As if. Fuck you.*)

And still, she stubbornly loves the bugger, despite his bad breath and his Quonset and his nice new cat.

(Though, nobody needs to know that.)

She always forgets how small Halifax airport is. A teacup compared to Calgary. One grim room that seems to have escaped all the hearty smartening up that the rest of the world is awash in these days. Damp clumps of waiting relatives in zippered purple-and-teal nylon windbreakers and running shoes ("sneakers," they call them here, she suddenly remembers), one creaking carousel that looks like it came out of a barn. A lone taxicab – people here don't take cabs, the airport is in the middle of nowhere, nobody can do without a car – perched self-consciously outside the one set of sliding doors.

So small. Here comes the trapped feeling she always gets on arrival, that feeling she might not get out again, that some cosmic disaster will make the planes stop flying here, and she'll be stranded, swallowed up for good, by a maze of trees.

The pang of seeing Dorie huddled by a pillar, clutching her white purse and anxiously peering up at the descending passengers on the escalator – the swift wish to save her, take care of her, make it all better, mixed with the same shapeless old fury. What is there to be so nervous about in a pokey little airport? Why can't her mother stand up straighter? She is so much more stooped than the last time Jen saw her, and smaller, more pale. That look of slow concentration she gets when she's anxious, her head suspended from her extended neck, like a turtle's; a new slight tremor Jen hasn't seen before, that seems to affect her all over; the way her face hangs, powdery and old-ladyish now, under her pinkish fringe of tinted hair. None of it, as Dorie scans the arriving passengers, offset by her bad old vigour. Airports do something to her. It's that old thing of: other people go to airports, not us. Travelling is what outsiders do, smart, worldly people with fast lives and money to burn, *from-away* people, who have been to Mexico, whose clothes flaunt name brands, who can command the air to take them places. Fine for them. Dorie secretly dreads all that distance, blue-black and planetary, impassible, impossible. What if the pilot gets lost? What if the plane runs into something? What if there's a terrorist? Terrorists can be anywhere nowadays, what if . . .

If, in Dorie's world, you can't find where you're going by getting in the car and following trusted landmarks, the place you're trying to get to doesn't exist. And even then, there can be detours, accidents, weather, always and always weather. Going to "the Halifax airport" is harrowing for her.

Jen points Grandma Dorie out to Sunny, feels her daughter's slight body tighten as the relentless roll of the escalator delivers her, against her will, to a mythical place of trees and grandmothers. *The better to scare you with, my dear.*

Jen: "Let's surprise her."

Sunny: "Whatever."

Dorie — when did she get so small, so frail? — is watching so hard for them she doesn't see them descend right in front of her, sneak around behind a column: "Hey Mum."

And her hands are up on either side of her mouth, blue eyes round as a Kewpie doll's. Those porcelain-white hands and incongruous thirties-movie-star fingernails, long and red-enamelled and at the same time so terribly vulnerable. The infuriating lurch of protectiveness Jen feels, seeing her mother's hands again, and her toenails — she still has beautiful feet — as always, done to match.

Sunny's quick, untrusting glance up.

Jen: "It's okay."

And now, Jen sees Dorie seeing her own daughter for the first time as a woman going grey.

The horror show of hugging now. Bodies of strangers toppling together, embarrassed laughter, arms stiff as mannequin parts scattered on a showroom floor. And it's how-was-your-flight, and my-you-look-well, how-was-the-trip-down, my-oh-my-hasn't-she-grown. And the waiting. Standing, nodding, and talking about the weather — "oh, it was some foggy on the way down, you couldn't hardly see your hand in front of your face" — the nervous laughter, people looking all around at other people, looking at the floor. And nowhere to go but here.

A red light on the carousel starts leisurely to flash and buzz, and finally the luggage clunkety-clunks down the chute one forlorn piece at a time, everyone relieved to have something besides each other to pay attention to. Sunny's hand staunchly gripping Jen's.

Dorie, come back to life, now that the introductions are over, runs to find a trolley, struggles to pull their heavy bags off the carousel, get them piled on, arrange them cleverly, so that nothing will fall, the three of them starting for the sliding door.

Sunny: "Mom."

"What is it, what?" Suddenly Jen remembers how tired she is.

"I have to pee."

"What, now? Didn't you go when we got off the plane?"

Sunny darts Jen a wide-eyed look of outrage and mortification.

"Okay, just a minute, okay . . ."

Sunny yanks her mother's hand: "Where *is* it, Mom?"

"See that sign? It's right over there."

"But that's only for males and females, there's none for —"

"Sunny, do you have to pee, or not?"

"I wish my *dad* were here —"

Exeunt, pursued by a small, furious, full-bladdered bear.

Dorie hands Jen the keys to the car. "I'm sure you'd prefer to drive, dear."

"Fine," she sighs, too tired to protest, "I'll drive."

By the time they're out of the airport, dusk has started seeping down from the heavy sky, up from the pungent, mossy ground, out of those layers and layers of trees — another thing she'd forgotten, how early and how utterly night comes here. A bowl lowered and twisted tight over a tapestry of invisible owls and deer.

Sunny leans against the back window, her dainty face finally at peace in sleep, her mouth ajar.

Dorie's relieved to be out of the airport and on their way: "I hope you'll like your room."

"I'm sure we will," Jen replies, glancing in the rear-view. "Have you changed it since last time?"

"Oh," Dorie laughs amusedly, "I'm not talking about that one, I don't mean the one upstairs. I'm telling about the basement suite. It's brand new. It's got its own entrance, and a private bath, and everything. I had it put in after your father, remember? For the resale value."

If Dorie has an addiction, it is moving. A house will please her for four years, maybe five. Then she'll start condemning its low ceilings or the mildew in the basement, its proximity to neighbours with a yapping dog. It can be something as small as that. Next, she'll start finding it commonplace, she'll wonder how she could ever have looked at such an ordinary house, much less bought it, where was her head? Pretty soon, out will come the word "unique," Dorie's signal that she's either seen something more interesting, or that restlessness is setting in: "For me to really love a house," she will say, "it has to bc something very unique. Something truly . . . unique." There is no point in telling her that "very unique" is a tautology.

"Mum, don't tell me you're thinking of selling again –?"

"Well I just think . . ."

"I thought you liked this house. I thought you were done moving."

"I'm sure it's a foolish idea. I'm sure it is."

"It's not foolish, it's just. Do you really want another big disruption like that? I mean, at this time in your life? I'd have thought you'd be ready to take it a bit easy by now."

"And anyway. I could have other guests besides you." A cryptic smile. "There could be times. You never know . . ."

"My bad." (Jen swerves to avoid something huge and brown-black, and apparently floating above its four tiny feet: a skunk? A porcupine? A miniature bear?) "It's your house to do what you want with. None of my business."

"Thank goodness that fog's lifting," Dorie observes brightly.

"My oh my, I had to drive like cold molasses in the wintertime on the way down. My hands are still sore from how tight I held the wheel!"

Silence then, the trees streaming by in their mesmerizing layers.

Jen can feel her mother studying her hair.

"Dear?"

Now what? "Yeah, Mum."

"You look lovely, you really do."

A familiar prickle starting along her skin. "And?"

"Well, I was just wondering . . . have you ever thought of trying a little colour? They have all these wonderful shades out now, all of these really quite lovely shades of Natural Brown, I actually have a nice warm brown at home, by Clairol, it's the kind you can rinse out if you don't like it, you could try some while you're here, and no one would ever be the wiser."

"I'm not sure what's wrong," Jen says with more energy than she meant to show, "with my hair's actual colour."

"I didn't say there was anything wrong with your hair, dear. I didn't mean that, I just mean you're still very pretty, and you could look so much more . . . with a little colour —"

Jen tries to make her voice light, but it flicks out like a piece of ice. "And what about *your* hair, Mum? Aren't you a little on the senior side, to still be colouring yours? And as for natural —" Barely off the airport campus and it's starting, time beginning to collapse like the pillars of an antique empire, the world dissolving to reveal the ancient tug of war, the old, unsettled narrative of mother and daughter.

With a lifetime of well-honed skill, Dorie veers toward safer subjects. "Do you still have Emma?"

Emma. Jen wants to tell her, hell, no. She wants to pretend she doesn't remember Emma, the stuffed doll Dorie made for her fourth Christmas, worn now to a grey oblong, her yarn hair long gone, her simple smile faded past recognition, arms dangling by threads but still there, still in a box somewhere. Jen could never get rid of her.

"Yup," she says, her teeth on edge. Why does she so much want to lie? She checks the rear-view, calculates a pass. "I still have her. What's left of her."

"My oh my, I'd love to see her."

The Kia rolls to a stop in Dorie's dark yard, engine ticking over as it cools. One of Jen's feet is asleep. Sunny is stirring in the back seat, those blank, dreaming eyes clear as the first time she ever opened them. All the luggage to haul, and the getting-ready-for-bed stuff to do in a place they're not used to. Pajamas to find, and toothpaste, dear God, let her have remembered to pack dental floss, she can't believe she's dragged both of them all the way here.

But this is where she's always come when there's been trouble, nowhere but here.

Sunny yawns like a hippo, rubs her eyes. "Are we there?"

"'There' we are."

Jen shoves open her door and stands. The way it feels to stretch after endless hours in plane seats, car seats. Blood moving in stiff limbs. Tired joints realigning. The sweetness of moist oxygen, the earth of this driveway under her feet. The Atlantic air is thick as velvet, immense with starry quiet. And the trees. Maple and oak and sycamore. Elm. Grand old varieties she's almost forgotten, their great canopies slowly churning, high in the dreaming dark. Somewhere not far, the asynchronous ting of windchimes. Their sweet song of forgetting.

"Mom," Sunny cries, temporarily startled out of her sleepiness: "Mom, look! Look, there's fireflies – at school we read about those!"

And she's pointing and running toward the gazebo, its gracious shape ghostly among dark lilacs, soldierly sunflowers and hollyhocks. The fireflies wink and gleam along the gazebo's gingerbread trim, gauzy loops of them, their wings iridescent shades of pale purple and silver, apple green.

"Aren't they the dearest things," says Dorie coming up behind, "I found them at a yard sale out Berwick way once upon a time, and strung them up, I just love to sit out here on the swing in the evening now the weather's warm, and watch them."

Now she's telling Sunny that the lights are solar powered, that they don't use any electricity at all. During the day they soak up the sun and then glow all night, their glassy bodies pulsing with hoarded light.

Sunny looks up in awe. "Can I come out and sit? After I have on my pajamas?"

She stands in the soft darkness, watching the fireflies brighten and vanish and come again, brighten and vanish, and come again like waves, their chill signal blooming among dark leaves.

Dorie sighs: "Ah, 'the bewildering beauty of the night.'"

"What's that, Mum?" Jen gazes at Dorie's dark shape. "What's that from?"

Dorie is suddenly shy: "Oh it's just something I read in a book somewhere once. I've got so many of 'em in there, I'm always dragging them home, I can't just remember which book it was. Out here just reminds me of those lovely words, I guess."

Turning toward the kitchen window, Jen sees something besides fireflies glowing. "Holy, is that a computer? In there?"

Dorie flashes her old crafty smile: "I have to have *something* for amusement, now that your father's gone. It's only for fun." She does a big yawn. "Anyway, it's getting kinda late; what do you girls say we head inside?"

Sunny rolls her eyes extravagantly, whispers a warning, "Mom . . ."

"Sunny," Jen grabs all the bags she can haul on her own out of the car, "later."

"I thought you'd like to have the bed, Jenny dear, and I put the little cot in for Sunny." They've moved into the kitchen, everybody blinking in the harsh electric light. "Soon's you're ready I can show you the downstairs bathroom, there's a little bit of a trick to find it, you havc to go in through thc laundry room."

Warm natural wood walls like a ship's cabin line the new addition, built-in bookshelves crammed with paperbacks and *Reader's Digest*s, battered classics, *National Geographic*s. Knick-knacks and gimcracks of every sort crowd the shelves.

Sunny gasps, "Mummy," a forgotten name from childhood, "look at all the dolls!"

Emma. Emma. Emma everywhere. There must be twenty-five or thirty Emma doppelgangers displayed on metal stands and claiming every available surface in the room, all with the same wide-eyed smile and embroidered hair, the same ruffled dresses and buttoned slippers.

"Holy Hannah, Mom."

"Holy somebody, all right," murmurs Jen.

Dorie chuckles, a mournful sound. "I must have made hundreds of them before I got that old carpal tunnel. They always sold like hotcakes at the church bazaar . . ." She turns with that stiff, whole-body rotation old people have, lifts a strand of Jen's hair: "Dear, are you sure you wouldn't like to try a little colour? Just to warm it up. It'll do wonders . . . Oh, and by the way, I thought we might maybe take a little trip over to the shore one day while you're here, we could get an ice cream, Sunny'd like that, wouldn't she? There's always a breeze over there in the summer."

The way she just sticks it in, that little thing about the hair, then spins her web of distractions. While all those dolls, stuffed and ageless, stare down at Jen the faded human one, disappointing and real.

"Well, you must be tired, dears," Dorie sighs brightly. "Let me know if you need anything. See you in the morning." Her slow steps creaking up the stairs.

Beyond exhaustion, Jen turns out the light, the roar of WestJet still in her ears.

Nine o'clock Calgary time, noon in Nova Scotia. Jen excavates Dorie's kitchen for any kind of coffee, while Sunny explores drawers and cupboards and lazy Susans crammed with the contents and yard-sale acquisitions and the hand-me-downs of a long, anxious life. She's got three of everything. Three flour sifters. Three toasters. Three sets of dishes. Why? What for? Who needs that many sets of Salt and Pepper? And a gazillion boxes of tea, this is the land of the hardcore Red Rose drinkers. But no coffee. Not so much as a granule of the good stuff.

A sight Jen never imagined she'd see: Dorie in her coke-bottle glasses and Scarlet O'Hara dressing gown hunched over the computer, looking at a picture of some old guy. "God, Mum, tell me you're not doing what I think you're . . . doing."

"Do you think he's good-looking?" Dorie replies with a wily smile.

He looks like a mole blinking up out of its hole. "He looks okay, I guess." (For a hundred and twelve.)

"I don't like Bran Flakes," Sunny whispers. "Mom, is there any good cereal?"

She so needs that coffee.

Dorie scrolls. Dorie can scroll! "How about this one?"

"Mum, he's in Tucson. Tell me how you're going to date someone from Tucson. With the healthcare. And the way you hate airports."

"Mom," says Sunny, with more volume this time, "can we go to a coffee shop, I'd like to go to a coffee shop; at home, I always go to coffee shops with my dad."

If she just had a cup of fucking coffee she might not want, so badly, to shove Sunny's bonny head out the kitchen window, and say, "There! See that? Over there, across the road? *That* is a field of corn! That one over yonder is tobacco! And the one out back is alfalfa! Coffee shops do not grow around here, capiche?"

"Well, what about this one?" queries Dorie. "He's kinda cute, what do you think about him?"

"Ma, he's forty. See where it *says*. And he's looking for MILFS. Do you know what that is? God, Mum!"

Sunny's voice carries a warning tremor that is now loud and clear: "There's nothing to *do* here!"

And it's nine forty-two on day one.

Still desperately canvassing for coffee, she reassures her daughter, "After breakfast we'll borrow the car, how 'bout, and go pick up some of the things we need. We'll take a run over to Wolfville, just the two of us, and check out the farmers' market, how about that."

Dorie looks up from the screen, looks back down. Her fingers have stopped moving over the keys. "And there's the big yard sale on down the south shore all today and tomorrow, that might be —"

Sunny brightens: "Can I get a treat? At the farmers' market?"

"A healthy one, maybe. But you'll have to live with what's here for now."

Stashed behind a sausage maker she has never seen Dorie use, Jen finds a jar of gummy Nescafe, pries some blackened crystals out of the bottom, adds hot water. It tastes like a Band-Aid, but it has caffeine in it, or did once.

Dorie heaves a tremulous sigh and logs out of her Hotmail account, her frothy gown trailing forlornly behind her as she heads for the shower. Nine forty-four, and Jen has already managed to hurt her. Talk about a rock and a hard place.

Sunny, meanwhile, thanks to the promise of a treat, is down on her knees, rooting in a cupboard. "Didn't Dad give you a pair of kitchen shears before you guys split up? Like, the Christmas before?" She fishes out a hefty pair, slicing the air.

Jen looks out the kitchen window. The bird feeder in the clear air, the driveshed with its barely turning rooster-weathervane, the bright garden, swaying with flowers and reddening globes of tomatoes, their extravagant flare. "I think so," she says, "I think he did. Those ones with the blue handles, he gave me, I think. Why?"

"Because I was reading in my book of symbols that if someone gives you a pair of scissors, that means you're going to split."

"Okay." She brings the scalding Nescafe to her mouth, watches the jeweled blur of a hummingbird at the feeder. A streak of colour, a whir, then gone, the empty feeder still swaying slightly, from the force of its diminutive departure. What would a smart mother say? Her own housecoated one is suddenly in the doorway, her still generous bosom nestled in a fetching summer wrap, her tinted hair frowsy: "Whatcha lookin' at, Jenny Annie?"

The familiar knot starts to tighten in her gut. If she could get her hands on that hummingbird right now, she'd turn it into a feathered dot.

Dorie is holding something out toward her with the same coy smile she sews on her dolls, her red nails framing the label: "I thought you might want to try this. Just for fun."

Butternut Brown. A picture on it of a woman who could be Jen's grown-up daughter or a hooker, a glossy wave of auburn hair falling over one sultry eye.

Her hands tighten around her cup. "You might have gotten some proper coffee."

Dorie starts to back away, checking to make sure she doesn't fall. "I should mind my own —" She is fiddling with the computer, looking for her glasses, her hands moving restlessly. "I should just mind my own darn business."

"Mum, please, I'm tired from travelling, that's all, and — you know — the whole —"

"I'm always sticking my big nose in where it doesn't belong."

"Mum. Mum, listen." But Dorie's done listening, she has grabbed a rag and is furiously polishing the top of the stove, her hands describing tight, banging circles. "Dorie Longspell."

That's got her attention. "Am I in trouble?"

"Mum, it's just that —"

"Seems I'm always in trouble."

"Mom, when are we going to Wolfville?" interrupts Sunny. "I'm all ready to go to Wolfville."

"Just a —"

"I'm just an old busybody."

"Look, Mum, why don't you come with us. This afternoon. Come to the farmers' market. We'll all go together. It'll be fun."

And down smack the Bran Flakes as Sunny runs out of the room, the cereal box dancing a drunken totter on the table behind her. The slam of the door.

First the husband, now the mother and the daughter. She has come to the place, in her life, of the slamming of doors.

"You *said* it was going to be just us. You *said!*" (Sunny, sitting on her bed, flipping one of the dolls back and forth by the hair.)

Yes, I bloody said. She is also jetlagged and claustrophobic, and trying to eat a piece of ham with mustard while sorting their collective stuff, weeding the dirty things from the clean ones, trying to find a place amongst all the tchotchkes and *Reader's Digest*s, and the everlasting dolls with their stiff forest of parasols, for their toiletries, to organize the shoes and sunhats and colouring books and bathing suits and camera gear, to make, out of Dorie's sentimental haberdashery, something resembling order. Sooner or later on these visits, she always gets like this, the sheer pressure of *stuff* sending her snaky. She has to make space, whatever it takes.

Sunny picks up one of the dolls, fires it at the wall. "*You said* just the two of us were going to the farmers' market!"

Jen inhales a mouthful of ham, barks: "Sunny, that's—"

Another doll thwacks the wall, does a backward somersault mid-air, and lands beside her on her bed, grinning inanely up at her. One thing, just one thing, she knows. She is too tired for this. She really is. For all of this. She grabs the doll, just holds it, as if gauging its weight. Then she chucks it and starts grabbing more dolls and tossing them on the bed where the first one landed, heaping them on top of each other, foamy skirts piling up like snowdrifts, ceramic legs and arms sticking out all over, blue eyes staring above all those vapid grins, parasols like pink kindling. Sunny stares in amazement, she doesn't believe it. Then Jen's got a garbage bag from the laundry room, and she's stuffing the dolls in one after the other, stuffing them and grabbing more of them and using the grabbed ones to wipe the dust off the surfaces they stood on, and dumping her own stuff where they stood, making space, claiming territory.

"Leave them alone!" screams Sunny. "Leave them! They're not yours, they're mine, I'm taking them home!" Her hard little body hurtling toward Jen's, fists, knees, feet like bullets. "I'm taking them home to live with me at my dad's!"

"Oh, is that right," Jen says, grabbing, stuffing, the dust flying.

"I hate you, anyway!"

And there's Dorie in the door, a poor little old lady, saying: "I thought you'd like them, is all. I'd thought you'd want them for Sunny. That was why they were down here, I was meaning to give them to you, to take home."

"Well, I don't. She doesn't. I'm not. We can't. And I'm not a baby anymore. Even Sunny isn't one. And colouring my hair in and giving me a bunch of dolls isn't going to turn me back into the little girl you weren't afraid of."

"I'm not . . ."

"You *are*, Mum. Afraid."

"Why would I be scared of you? You're my —"

"Because I did what you didn't do. And ever since I left here a lifetime ago and, God forbid, got on an airplane and went to another part of the country and — all the rest of it — you've been scared silly of me."

"What do you want?" Dorie says, vaguely waving a veined hand around her. "I don't know what you want, I've never known."

"I want. Mum, I just — I want you to stop treating me like some long-gone little girl who all she needs is her hair coloured in, to be recognizable. I want us to be equals. That's all. It's all I've ever wanted, if you care to know the truth."

Out comes Dorie's this-never-happened smile. "I'm going pop upstairs to get ready for the market."

"Can you beat that?" Jen says. "One minute she's all tragedy, and the next she's off to stock up on organic veggies."

"Mom," says Sunny after Dorie has gone.

"What?"

"You've got mustard."

"Not now, Sunny."

"No, Mom! You seriously —"

"Oh, for — where?"

"In your eyebrows, Mom."

One of the dolls, dressed in a Victorian skating costume, stands on ice made from an octagonal mirror. Jen topples the doll, lifts the mirror, blows off the dust, and looks.

"Oh, God."

Sunny stifles a giggle.

Jen swallows one of her own.

And the two of them fall across the bed, dusty dolls and all, screaming with laughter, Sunny holding up the mirror, and Jen rubbing at her face, which serves only to smear the Heinz worse and further.

"Mom," Sunny gasps, "you look — you look like Santa Claus, only with yellow eyebrows!"

"Very funny! *Very* funny, ho, ho, ho!" And she's rolling over onto Sunny, tickling and poking, threatening to rub her eyebrows in her hair, leaning closer and dangerously closer, as Sunny shrieks and struggles with outraged joy in front of the dolls' ridiculously solemn stares. The yellow smell of hot dogs everywhere. Jen laughs until she's drained, until she's teary and gasping, until both of them are washed out and giddy, and lying chaste as light across Sunny's cot, gazing quietly at the toppled ranks of dolls.

"Mom?"

"Yeah."

"It was my fault, wasn't it?"

"What?"

"That my dad left us."

"Oh, my love." Jen turns to Sunny and takes her in her arms, her daughter born of war, and whispers all the ways it's not her fault, into her hair.

"It's okay, Mom, I guess it's okay if Grandma Dorie comes."

Jen always secretly imagines that country markets are going to change her life, as though by standing in the presence of all that homegrown broccoli and hillbilly music she is finally going to gain cntrancc into some lovely fecund alternate world where the men all have ponytails and striped overalls, and everybody goes home to candled antique farmhouses and makes babies. Predictably, the same old thrill rises in her as the stalls and tents and tables of the Wolfville market roll into view. By now Sunny, owing to the proximity of treats, is happy again, she is even easy with Dorie, who is seated beside her in her wrap-around shades and her sun visor.

"What kind of treats do they have?" Sunny wants to know. "Can I get two?"

"Okay, just as long—"

". . . as they're healthy," Sunny chimes in.

Jen strolls toward the stalls, Dorie trailing slightly behind, she doesn't want to be in the way. Nor, Jen can tell, does she have a particular interest in shopping here. She's a Maritimer, she prefers the cheaper canned vegetables you can get at the Sobeys in the mall on the way home. The way she stays just behind Jen and Sunny, that painful carefree thing she does with her arms held slightly out from her sides, as though she could be a young girl to whom something is about to happen. The completely private way her white hand, with its new tremor, lifts a pear. What is it that is so unbearable about seeing one's mother lift a pear?

Jen turns to Dorie. "You ready for lunch, Mum?"

"I'm ready to do whatever you want to do," says Dorie.

"Sun, you hungry?"

"Yeah!"

"You! You're always hungry!"

But Jen's hungry, too. She's so hungry. She wants thick bread and raspberries, and links of sausage with hot little peppers sliced thin, and heaps of warm, tangy sauerkraut tucked in around them. She craves the maple fudge the people make here, and good real coffee, and cigarettes even though she doesn't smoke, and sex, and movies. She lusts for the smell of roasting meat and bright fruit bubbling up through flakey pie crusts. And she wants broccoli, lots of it, dark green explosions of it in her throat. Sunshine glances off dusky bunches of wild grapes, and she would buy them just for their purple. To hold their purple in her hands.

She ends up buying fat German hot dogs and sitting with Dorie and Sunny in front of the hillbilly music, the three of them chowing down and tapping their toes, watching the people come and go. Dogs and babies are everywhere.

Dorie says, "He winked at you."

"Who?" Jen says.

"The guy on the ukulele."

"God, Mum, let it go."

"He did, though!"

Jen gives Dorie a companionable shoulder bump. "You old mischief, you."

Dorie pauses, looks away. "I always wanted to say." She stops, looks as though she might be going to cry. Her small cotton shoulders. Jen's hand on her knee.

"Hey, Mum. You can't not tell me now."

"Well. You know, back then. Back when you were about her age." Dorie takes a look at Sunny, who is happily sharing her lunch with a friendly rottweiler.

"Yeah, sure."

"Back when I was always after you to do stuff. You remember, look after the baby and mind Sonny, and all that. Your father wasn't around all that much, if you remember . . ."

Jen sighs. "I remember."

"Well, it's just – I always wanted to say."

Jen is waiting. Watching the music. Her half-eaten hot dog warming her hand.

"It's that, I'm sorry. Jenny. That's it. I'm just . . . sorry. And I have been all my life." Dorie's chin trembles.

"Why? About what?"

"For telling you." She swallows, crosses one ankle over the other, a gesture so forgotten and familiar, the posture of a chastened child. "For telling you there's more to life than finishing chapters."

"Oh, Mum, that's so long ago –"

"And I want you to know." Dorie looked the other way, where only she could see. "I always felt so bad about your piano."

It's bedtime, or soon will be. They're on the swing again, eased by its comfortable glide, its kindly creak, and by the night, which is always a kind of forgiveness. The cool light of the fireflies blooming and fading above their heads.

"Gramma," says Sunny drowsily. "Tell about when you were a little girl."

"Well," Dorie says, "my dad had to leave for a while too, you know."

Sunny sits up straighter. "What for?"

"For the war."

"Did he die?"

"No, he didn't die. But when he came back, he wasn't the same as when he went over. To the war. It was almost like we got back a different man altogether, he was that different."

"Different how?"

"Oh, I guess . . . he didn't seem to care, dear. About things. Anymore. And he had that darn old injury in his spine —"

"From a bullet?" Sunny demands sternly. "Was it from enemy fire?"

"No," Dorie's mournful chuckle. "Not from a bullet, he'd been into somebody's jug somewhere over there, they all did that, in the war, and he fell off the back of a truck onto some piece of equipment, and he hurt himself. Hurt his spine someway. And after he come home, he kept on with the drinking, and we never had enough money, never had very much of anything; I guess that's probably why I've got so darn much stuff around here now. But I tried to at least give my girls flowers. One thing I did have was a green thumb." Dorie wobbles up her hands, chortles. "I was always hauling home something green from somewhere, wasn't I, Jenny, and coaxing it to grow. Oh, I loved flowers." She smiles at her daughter. "Just like your mum does herself." A frown. "But you never knew what state things were going to be in back then, I guess you could say. We got by, but there wasn't a lot of fun in those days, not for anybody, after the war."

"But I hope you had some nice things to wear!" Sunny cries, her smooth small hand finding Dorie's freckled one. "I would have given you some clothes of mine!"

"I know you would have," Dorie smiles, patting Sunny's knee. "And it wasn't so bad, really." She waves away a moth. "I got pretty good with the old treadle sewing machine."

"And the knitting needles." Jen smiles. "You made all Rosie's and my outfits. Remember how you'd go to the church bazar and –"

"Sonny's too, I made his too, when he was – Oh, I'd buy up all those awful old lady suits, wouldn't I. But they were good wool, and a lot of them had real good labels in them –"

"And you'd take them all apart."

"And I'd wash the wool all up nice."

"And then you'd make me and Rose and Sonny –"

"That's right; I'd dream up the dearest little suits and skirts and –"

Sunny says, "Did you have some toys?"

"I remember one day I went home with somebody I went to school with . . . Bessie Irving, I think it was. Yes, Bessie. She's dead now, she had the epilepsy. And Bessie'd just gotten a Gibson Girl doll for her birthday, my oh my, that doll was a beautiful thing, I remember it was called an 'Emma' doll –".

"That's just like –"

"Same as your mum's doll, that's right."

"What did she look like?"

"She was made of real bisque, you wouldn't know what that was, but she had this beautiful white china skin with the dearest little roses painted in her cheeks, and a fancy little hat with pink daisies on the brim, and a genuine silk skirt and matching parasol – I thought I'd faint for wanting that doll! So, after a while I started making dolls, just out of any old thing that was around, you know, socks and worn-out pillowcases and whatever else I could get my hands on. I even think I used my own hair for a while, it was a lovely silky auburn then, same as yours, not like now!" Dorie runs an impatient hand through her white whisps. "I'd save it up and when I got it cut, I'd keep it to make braids for them –"

Sunny jumps up, almost stumbling on the swaying floor of the canopy swing. "That's why –"

"That's why I've still got so many of the darn things around, I guess, from never being able to have one when I was your age. And after a while I just got into the habit of making them. And then when I had a bit of money, I started buying them, too, and they piled up something terrible, 'specially after your grandpa was gone. Silly, really, an old girl like me with a house full of dolls, it's time I got rid of them." She stops, claps her hands on her lap, suddenly brisk. "Well, now. Is anybody chilly? I've got a nice afghan in there we could . . ."

Sunny grasps Dorie's hand, cups it in her small cold ones. "I think I'm hungry again, Grandma, maybe we should go in."

"Oh Mum," Jen murmurs. "I didn't realize."

"Don't trip in the dark, now you two," cautions Dorie, "that's just how life is."

Driving over to the shore on the last day, Sunny proudly wearing the new "poor boy" hat knit all in one night for her by her grandmother, Dorie and Jen in front, Dorie's hair frizzed out around her sun visor, a pink sea anemone. The narrow mountain roads, barely wide enough for two cars to pass. The falls hurtling down in the bright air. Asters and lupins, blackberries crowding close, their colours dulled with road dust. The crack of loose stones flying up under the car.

Jen parks near an abandoned shack off the main road. "Everybody out!" How could she have forgotten how pure the air is over here? As though designed for wings. As though she's just been issued a fresh set of lungs.

They descend the hill past the remains of the little house that was once Dorie's family home, then head on down to the shore. The gaunt old fish-houses leaning together, piled buoys on the crumbling wharf. Familiar smells of rotting fish and salt, sun-bleached kelp, softening tar. Down along the stony beach the tide is out, things can be found. Twists of driftwood. Nubs of beach glass, solid clouds of blue and green. Crystals of agate and amethyst. A once-fancy hairpin. Sunny is collecting odd-shaped stones, running from one spot to another, calling and calling, demanding to be noticed. "Over here, Mom! I need you here right this minute!" Her voice a triumphing clamour everywhere. Jen picks up a wedge of pottery from some long-ago plate or crock, traces its faint blue edge, wonders if it might have been a bowl. Dorie finds a devil's wheelbarrow, part of a creel, an intact crab shell. Sunny's got a small shark skull, its bone planes mean as needles, its intelligent spine whitened by the high chemistry of the sun. "Mom," she calls, "Gramma, hey, come over here!" Her words echoing over stone and water.

An overturned rowboat with peeling turquoise paint is a place to pool their treasures and set out the food they've brought, watch the tide slide in. The disembodied voices of the few other people on this beach ghost in and out of its echoing mist. The taste of things in this air. As though you'd never committed the act of eating before. Dorie's fresh-baked bread loaded with butter and pepper and cold chicken, warm tomato slices, this morning's leaf lettuce out of the garden. Four ripe little plums from Dorie's backyard tree. The tart sweetness of homemade raspberry jam. And a thermos of hot Red Rose tea.

Sunny finishes fast. "I'm still hungry, and I even ate my crusts, can we get a treat on the way home?"

Jen becomes mock-stern. "Only if it's unhealthy."

The three of them walk back toward the car together, stomachs full, pockets bulging with their scavenged haul. The afternoon sun warms the blackberries by the road, and Sunny pulls them hungrily off the bushes, devouring them dust and all.

—

Halfway up the hill, Jen stands with Dorie and Sunny in the long grass at the side of a narrow, overgrown road. In front of them tilts the derelict cottage Dorie grew up in, with its bent tin chimney and two skinny rooms, its ruined, skyward panes. Broken glass grits under Jen's feet as she creeps closer, some automatic part of her brain humming Mahler's symphony of Resurrection.

Sunny whispers: "Can we go in?"

A gust of wind sways the grass with its sudden sound of nothing, and is gone. Jen glances over at her mother; there is no reading her expression.

Dorie stands before the dismembered house, the wind stirring her thin hair. Her white hands cradle the husks and shells, the bits and pieces she has carried from the shore, a rough treasure, cold and familiar. "My oh my," she sighs to Jen, "look at how that garden's run wild, thank the Lord your grandmother can't be here to see that, she was some proud of her flowers."

She halts as though frozen, as though waiting for permission, her puzzlement reflected in the wonky old windows' remaining shards of broken glass. No sound, now, apart from the ocean's distant hiss, the wind's long discourse with the grass.

"I never told you," she begins, her back still to Jen. Tomorrow this place will slip once again into history, and Jen and Sunny will be back in the very present reality of Calgary. She wants so much to say those three infuriating little words to Dorie; why does it stay so hard?

"The way I was raised," Dorie whispers, shaking her head, "I just – never was able to tell you."

Jen reaches for Dorie's hand. "No need, Mum, I know."

BRIGHT JOURNEY

Never, never, never, Jen always said about ever getting married again. And yet, damned if she hasn't gone and done just that. Three times lucky? She'd argued to Dorie she'd done it so Sunny'd have more stability, but it wasn't such a bad deal for her, either. In some ways, Ian's easier than a husband; recognizing that he can also occasionally get on Jen's nerves, he likes to call himself "a pain with benefits."

All night, Jen and pain-with-benefits Ian (thanks to a positive COVID test, Sunny's sealed away in Canmore with their father and his new, fun partner) have been breathing stale lipstick (Jen) and staler pretzels (Ian) through too-tight facemasks on the Red Eye, and they're hungover as hagfish. At this age a person doesn't recover the way they used to, from things like all-nighters, whole bottles, surprise encounters with hard surfaces; it's been a long night. During which, having little else to do, Jen discovered, to Ian's dismay — "Leave that alone, you dufus!" — that her right kneecap wobbles drunkenly sideways and has gone spongy with accumulated fluid from a perfectly unremarkable stumble a month ago. It looks like a hurricane sky, turgid, snot-yellow, and threatening to let fly.

But she has her health, as the old folks say.

Old folks seem to be the order of this day, and of the ones to come. Jen's morphine-drugged stepfather, Blake, stopped eating and drinking three days ago, perchance to dream, and Jen and Ian are here on Death's dark business, hoping to see Blake at the hospice one last time before he checks out. But first, everybody else checks in: Ian and Jen today; Jen's fiddle-playing nephew and his pretty partner tonight; tomorrow comes Rose, a committed anti-masker, and her long-suffering wife. The funeral will be a family affair, with the nephew playing "Ashokan Farewell," the nephew's partner speaking about her memories of Blake — and Rose (no longer a minister, though still a good singer) delivering the eulogy and an unaccompanied "Amazing Grace" at graveside.

But for the rest of the day and tonight, it's just Jen, Ian, Dorie, and Billie the cat, who occasionally suspends her small murders to pay a hasty under-the-table visit, in case of treats. "She's an awful bad girl," observes Dorie, blowing on her tea. "Blake's the only one she'll listen to, isn't he, you bad Billie."

Jen looks sideways at Ian; Ian looks *shush* at Jen.

It's been two years since Jen was last in this kitchen. Not much has changed, and the world has. Since the last time, a vaccine "passport" is required in order to come here, Dorie can't do stairs, and Blake's gone to his ancestors or soon will have, though Dorie seems apt to forget her husband's impending journey. The gazebo where Sunny fell in love with the solar fireflies is stuffed with junk now, but the cluttered house is still loud with the relentless ka-tick-ka-tock of Blake's asynchronous clocks, making Jen think of the Old Folks Song, the one about the ticking clock on the wall, that "waits for us all." She shivers a little, thinking of Dorie here alone with the clocks, their heavy pendula echoing like slowing hearts in the dim rooms after all the foofaraw's over and everybody's gone.

Right now, though, Dorie's in high gear, jacked up on strong tea, family arrivals, and unspent grief – and therefore, indifferent to the clocks' mortal clatter. "Jenny, I put you two in our room, since it's got the bigger bed and the air conditioner –"

"But Mum, that's *your* room." What can't be said: Jen feels a bit queasy about sleeping in the bed Dorie and Blake until so recently shared. Will she catch something if she sleeps in that bed? False teeth, bunioned feet, widowhood?

But Dorie's as stubborn as ever. "I'm perfectly fine in the spare."

At eighty-seven, she's shorter and slower than last time, her hair, thanks to COVID's inconveniences, unshaped and too long for her face. "And there's towels on the counter in the bathroom, and some of that special Lily of the Valley soap you used to like by Avon, in the dish. And I'd love it if you could run down cellar and clean out the litter box sometime while you're here." With a brisk wave, she dismisses a cobweb from the corner of the door. "With all that's been – you know – I just haven't been able to get down there."

About to leave Jen and Ian to their own devices, she turns stiffly. "Is there anything else I can get for you, dears? Oh, and – just so you know, the door to your bedroom's a bit of a bitch, but if you jiggle it a little, it'll latch."

A bitch. Really? When did respectable Dorie go stevedore? Suddenly Jen sees her mother when she was probably about thirty – Jen would have been seven – leaping like a determined deer across a ditch and into somebody's orchard to snitch a couple apples to eat on the way home from tea at the neighbour's. As her foot hit the opposite bank, her ankle twisted and she had to limp the rest of the way, but she had her apples, and made neither complaint nor apology.

Jen's always found it startling when she's bumped into this earlier, strong-limbed version of Dorie. The whimsical thief, the secret smoker, the speaker of the very words she herself once reliably got in trouble for.

"That's okay, Mum," she smiles, briefly hugging her, "we're good. We are."

They're in the bedroom with the "bitch" door, organizing the deodorant, the makeup, the vaccine passports, the tooth gear. In the kitchen, the radio drones on about the Delta variant and the latest numbers. Above them hangs a framed Jesus, one of an identical pair. Okay: *who* buys two huge, identical, framed Jesuses? Dorie does. She's always been nuts about yard sales, and this gloomy image seemed to show up amongst the Tupperware and liquid embroidery and Corningware teapots and curled up boots at every event Jen got dragged to as a kid. It was one of those universal truths in this part of the world back then, that you could never be too well fed or have an excess of saviours. For a moment she wonders where the other one went. Probably she'll find Jesus 2.0 down behind the furnace with all the other things there's not enough room for, when she gets down there to change the cat litter.

The bedroom Jesus, like his absent twin, is backlit, absurdly white, and dressed in a bedsheet, the expression on his dreamily handsome face one either of deep concern for your mortal soul, or the will to steal. Ian glances up. "Christ, he looks like a frigging financial advisor. A suave but crooked one." He reaches up and adjusts the slightly off-kilter frame, releasing a whiff of stale underarm, while gazing earnestly into an invisible TV camera. "Your money is safe with us. Bank of Nazareth."

They fall on the bed, howling with stifled laughter until Jen observes, "Lord, you need a shower."

"I could say the same to you. Phooh!" He effects a Christlike expression. "Though I'm glad you recognize my title."

It's late afternoon when they surface, the fading light glowing green through a sea of leaves, so unlike Calgary's dried grid. Dorie's sitting at the kitchen table sipping Earl Grey tea — another thing that's changed since last time, the tea — and scribbling notes on a pad of lined paper, the big careful loops of her writing heart-catchingly familiar. "There was a call from the funeral home while you two were down."

Down. Nova Scotian for "taking a nap."

"Oh?" Jen is suddenly hungry and fourteen. "Can I have those blueberries?"

Ian, who didn't grow up here and is still his proper age, quietly helps himself to tea.

"We can only have twenty at the funeral. On account of the social distancing."

"Well, twenty seems plenty." Jen scoops up a handful of blue. "I mean, right?"

"Everybody in the Valley loved him. Plus, he's got more family than you can shake a stick at."

Jen grins to Ian. *How much family is that?*

The berries are astonishing. Dusky, fat, meaty and sour-sweet, just the way they should be. They make Jen want to go grizzly and eat nothing but them and the occasional slab of salmon. "I brought my laptop, Mum. We'll just have to email back and forth until we've got a list both sides are okay with." She inhales the last of the fruit and makes a mental note to get more from the farmers' market that didn't used to be next door. "Same as for a wedding."

The most recent wedding in the family was hers. Her third one, it was on New Year's Eve, Dorie's birthday, right here in her knick-knacked living room. Outside, on dark spruce trees and cold fields, a gentle snow was falling. In the still-Christmassy house, a few members of the family were gathered; Blake was still vigorous, goateed, and handsome; and dog collar and all, Rose was good-naturedly officiating. No one suspected Blake's cancer, which was already quietly at work under his double-breasted suit; COVID-19 had not been heard of yet; nothing so primitive as a pandemic had landed since well before any of the assembled guests was born; there was no such thing as lockdown or social distancing, self-isolation.

"How's that the same as a wedding?" Dorie wants to know. There's a shimmer of testiness in her voice that shows she disapproves of Jen's cavalier analogy. And just as she used to when she was annoyed with her daughter, she thinks of an uncompleted chore. "Did you clean the litter box down there?"

Yeah, Mum, thinks Jen uncharitably, I flew all night with my face in a sock, just to sort cat turds. Jesus.

"Anyway," calls Dorie as she departs the kitchen to get changed, "we're due over at the home in an hour; Blake'll be wondering where the heck we are."

Some thoughtful soul has hung one of the Jesuses on Blake's terminal wall, his limpid gaze promising spiritual, if not financial, salvation for all.

Meanwhile, it's hospice as usual, a place of order and goodwill, decent, gentle, and surprisingly beautiful. Large quiet, private rooms, swift and respectful caregivers, the main windows giving on avenues of pines, wildflowers, stepping deer.

When a person dies, as happens routinely here, a butterfly is placed on their door.

Blake's dying is underway when they arrive, and it's not pretty. He's drugged, dehydrated, and grunting out his last attempts to communicate with Dorie, who for some reason chooses the moment he lapses into a temporary torpor to tell him about the guy coming next week to fix the roof. Right away he's agitated again, clutching at air and trying to make words, his stricken legs struggling to spring him out of bed, man his post, get to work. Dorie's always after him to do stuff; does he think, in his delirium, that *he's* supposed to fix the roof? What goes through the head of a person in that state? *I'm late, I'm late for a very important date?* To judge from Blake's face: *I'm in bad trouble and I'm gonna catch hell.* Just in time, a smiling practitioner swims in with a shot of morphine and Blake gradually settles, only to have Dorie lean into him, stroke his hand, tell him in a wavering voice that "you can go now, it's all right for you to go, oh, oh."

Jen longs to hug her mother, smooth her hair, soundly smack her.

Meanwhile Ian, an EMT who's seen plenty of dying and knows there's nothing to be said or done, reclines calmly in the corner, one long leg slung over the other as, via his iPhone, he scores like the champion he is, in *Forge of Empires*. He's just switched to a new and more powerful guild in the arcane game, and thanks to the recent privations of Airplane Mode has a bit of catching up to do, so he's not paying much attention as the dark drama, whose every act he knows by heart, continues grimly to unfold centrestage.

Though, women don't get off as lightly as men in terminal scenes, any more than they do in other women's kitchens, and Jen, being a woman, doesn't have the luxury of burying her nose in a computer game. Instead, she seeks refuge in the contemplation of the weird sack that has impudently established itself on her knee, poking it here, provoking it there, watching its complexion change as she messes with it. It's like a nasty little pet or one of those canned amusements for kids, Slime or Snot, squishy and unsightly, grotesquely cute.

But snot won't do it. She has to get out of the butterfly room, and right this minute. For the God-minded, there's a little stained-glass chapel affair next door and she goes to sit there, observing through its big windows the sway of ornamental grass, the poise of irises, the quiet dignity of trees.

And as she breathes, she wonders an uncharitable thing. Is taste applicable to grieving? Can there be such a thing as style in its expression? Can pain be "put on"?

One thing is certain; Dorie adores Ian, son-in-law number three though he may be. The minute Jen and her knee-creature are back in the room, she turns to him, Mary at the Foot of the Cross, Greece on the Ruins of Missolonghi, Dorie, Dorie, Dorie. "Ian, tell me when."

When *what*, thinks Jen, when will COVID be over? When will my defrocked sis descend? When do I get to blow this apocryphal popsicle stand? Because right now there's nothing in this world she would rather do.

Is there a God after all? As if in answer to a prayer, in leans a slim young nurse in a crocus-purple dress. "Folks, it looks like Blake's not ready yet, and now that he's had his meds, he'll be needing a rest. We'll update you on developments as they happen." She smiles a gentle professional smile. "Take a break, and stay close to your phones."

As they leave the building, Dorie sighs under her breath. "I know that was hard for you."

"Mum, it wasn't—" But Dorie's got Jen over yet another

barrel in this life. If she tells her mother the real reason she had to keep leaving the room, she'll give her pain at a time when all her daughterly energy should go toward comforting her. So, she mans up for once, and squeezes Dorie's hand. "It wasn't that bad, Mum; I didn't sleep so well last night, is all."

And that much, at least, is true. If Dorie's good bed is that bad, she can't imagine what the spare one's like.

But she knows that if there's anybody around here who's going to catch hell, it ain't Blake; that if Jesus over there could talk, he'd be telling Jen her attitude sucks.

In case it might somehow humour the universe, the first thing she does when the three of them get back to the house is boot it downstairs and ream out the litter box.

Ian (he used to be a nurse, before) once said that hospital people, documenting patients' excretory output, will, depending on quantity, colour, and smell, use the shorthand "two brown foul." The obscenely succinct phrase comes squinting back when Jen sees the skin under her eyes in the mirror the next morning. Two sad pads of desiccated mud, echoing the ticking clocks' song of days used, life lapsed, time expired. But there's no time now to deal with her under-eye poverty. They've gotten the call. Blake has shuffled off his mortal coil, and Dorie and Ian are waiting for her in the car. She's coming. Give her a minute.

Something – is it our portable friend on the cross up there or was it last night's bedtime snack of smoked oysters? – gives her pause. She puts her purse on the terrible bed and, almost as though in prayer, slips to the floor.

It's just that she wishes Sunny were here.

That Sonny'd been here.

A butterfly is pinned to Blake's door when they get there. It's orange and black, a plastic monarch. The three of them look at each other, then gently tap and enter, only to encounter the ubiquitous Jesus. Not on the wall this time, but aimed instead, like a Civil War canon from between the sturdy legs of one of Blake's sons, who's crouched as silent and stark as the grim reaper himself on the far side of the room.

Other family members stand clumped like cold cattle, while Dorie claims her stricken place pieta-style beside the stiffening body, which is now still, a simulacrum of the gregarious, hypochondriac, talented man who until a day ago occupied it.

Probably Jen will go to hell; all she wants to do is yell, tear her hair, find a bar. Instead, they head directly from Jesus-as-ordnance to Gentle End Services, where a dapper masked man with studied deference and fluttering hands ushers them into a room full of plug-in candles and polished coffins. They're shown wooden ones, metal ones, fibreglass ones, biodegradable ones, even do-it-yourself ones, with names like Eternal Horizon, Peaceful Cave, Journey Done, Breath's Surcease.

Jen stares dazedly at Ian. *Breath's Surcease?* Jesus. Why not "See Ya'll Later"? or "Last Hi Five"?

Even better: "Outta Here." Which is once again where she desperately longs to be.

Dorie shows them a pre-purchased six-thousand-dollar number called Bright Journey, and finally they *are* outta there, only to learn, back in the thickly carpeted Welcome Room when Rose, for reasons that sound worrisomely Make America Great Again, calls the funeral home from her eyrie in Middleton to convey her nickel-spitting refusal to sing in, preach in, or give the time of day to *a mask*. "You don't know me, baby."

And Jen realizes that's not a word of a lie. Furthermore, she knows that not knowing her sister's on her. Rose was only nine, after all, when Jen vamoosed from here, all happy to be gone and onto her new, real life, "out there" where it mattered. After the first semester's nightmares about her little sister sliding silently over precipices, wandering into swamps, being devoured by monsters and so forth, she got busy with her own cliffs and beetling calamities, and let life be as it was going to be. After all, she wasn't Rose's mother, was she?

But still, she felt responsible, feels responsible. In the dark and private places of her heart, she will always feel responsible. She knew, for example, that Rose had got lost for a while. That there'd been a pregnancy, a runaway, troubles with men, obviously; that Rose had paid, and paid dearly for ills that Jen, her own sister, knew little of.

And that's on her too. That's the thing about life. You can think you're getting through it reasonably, even well (if you're lucky), for a while. You can think your suffering, dutifully borne, should give you, if not an A-plus, at least a pass; that you've done your time in the house of sorrow.

But what you can't know, while you're making all this touching sense of your experience, is the fact — tucked away like craziness or COVID somewhere in your blood — the fact that, in ways you never dreamed of, life can be counted upon to come back and bite you.

Rose's voice crackles through the phone. "Jenny? Are ya there? What —"

"I'm here, Rosie, sorry, I was just . . . anyway, it's a little bit late, isn't it, for you to be pulling out? I mean, we can't do anything about the masks; it's just provincial regulations."

But Rose couldn't care less about provincial regulations,

ditto for family expectations. Her choice, her life, her way or the highway.

Poor Dorie. If ever there was ever a time when Jesus might come in handy, it's now. *God almighty, do something.* But far from almighty, God remains propped against a potted plant where somebody stashed him for transport back to Dorie's, his gaze gently abstracted, dreamily otherworldly, no use to the dead, much less the quick.

Snidely, Jen thinks, He must be on His break.

Could it be that J.C. has heard her? It turns out that Blake had asked — and completely forgotten he ever did ask — three different ministers, including Rose the Baby, to speak at his funeral. Thus, in place of Rev. Rose and wife, two perfectly competent and compassionate dudes of the cloth have taken the service and ushered Blake satisfactorily into eternity. The day is late-summer sunny, with grand caravans of cumulus moving stately across the sky, and Blake's final resting place is a bosky greensward whispering with trees, brimming with a gracious view of the sea. Dorie, her more vigorous expressions of grief completed, stands at the graveside with weary dignity, as a cardinal, Blake's favourite bird, cheerily observes the proceedings from the safety of a nearby willow tree.

By now it's hot and getting late, and Death's dark work is finally done. The gleaming coffin awaits its portentous descent, and most of the mourners are ready to give their sober clothes the old heave-ho, scram to their cars, and find places to grab fish and chips washed down with a Keith's or three.

Jen being Jen, she can't stop wondering what Rose could be thinking, safe with her wife at home, and in what undiscovered country Blake might be, but at least she's quit bothering her knee.

As they move toward the car, Ian points to a flutter of black and orange colour that has momentarily, yet with odd determination, settled itself on the top of Jen's high-heeled foot. "Look, he whispers, "a butterfly."

WAR

It's about cause and effect, about how the past impinges on the present, and makes the future.

RICHARD FORD ON FICTION, 1987

"But they were right here. I put them *right* here." It's her hearing aids Dorie's after, though half the time she doesn't wear them anyway.

Jen sighs. "All that's up there is cobwebs; I'll get at those later."

"Are you sure you didn't—"

"Mum, I didn't take your hearing aids. Do you think I came all this way to—"

"I was *going* to say, did you *move* them. Anyway, what I was saying. About Blake's boys."

"How they came to the house, you mean."

"After the funeral, yes."

"You've got a good memory."

"Some things a person doesn't forget."

Changes have occurred since the last time Jen found herself in Dorie's kitchen, not least among them Blake's transition to the other world and Sunny's (these days, they go by Lake) to the other team. Though, the careful chaos of Dorie's house – all the little plaques and trivets and potholders with the cutesy slogans, and the gazillion sets of everything, and the damn clocks tick-tocking – all that's still the same; it's Dorie who's changed. Never a ballerina, she moves now like a sleepwalker, shuffling forward in her sweats and pink quilted vest and black boxy men's shoes, her hands, which are veined and thin skinned now, nothing like the swift spankers of old, held out as though in supplication or prayer in front of her. Blake's death left their affairs less than orderly, and she is still flinty about the way his sons behaved toward the end, insisting she be at the hospice to tend him 'round the clock, though she was herself barely recovered from a near-mortal surgery. "Where on earth did I get cancer? And not one, but *two* primary tumours!" (While she has no use for her dangerous invader, she loves the terrifying medical terminology that describes its opprobrious activities inside her). "And after all I did for their father, not one of them even bothered to come see me when it was my turn."

Her opinion of the miscreant sons was not much improved when, after the funeral, they presented themselves *en masse* at the house, though only to collect their father's valuables. "I gave them Hail Columbia, I can tell you!" As if in readiness for a fresh invasion, Dorie squints out the kitchen window, though nothing looks back except the rain that has been falling steadily since Jen's plane touched down in Halifax two endless days ago.

"Why do I have absolutely zero trouble believing that, Mum?"

"Parm' me?"

"Oh, nothing. Can I get you some more tea?"

Forty-eight hours ago, Jen schlepped her luggage — and her baggage — through Dorie's doors, having flown across the country through the pre-Christmas fog, sleet, and night, in her heart the warm thought of finally, after a lifetime, *really connecting*. No pissed-off kids or doddering old men around to complicate things. Just quiet hours of sorting and discarding, afternoon walks in the little wood across the road, dinner in front of the TV news, late-night tales of olden times reviewed. Just the two of them. This miracle to take place during the process of dealing with Dorie's lifetime troll's hoard of stuff, so that, in the spring, if things worked out, she could be moved to a nice manageable seniors' apartment in a pleasant stair-free building only half an hour away.

Forty-eight hours ago was Wednesday. Now it's Friday, the sleet and wind are still hurling themselves like the big bad wolf against the chinny-chin windows, and thanks to a sudden and impressive attack of back spasms, Jen has taken to walking like one attempting an absurd and undignified feat of athleticism better left to acrobats or young people. "I'll be right back. Gotta go get my support thingie."

"I can find you a couple Tylenol," Dorie offers when she recovers from the shock of Jen's anything-but-sudden reappearance in the kitchen. "I've got the Extra Strength."

Jen hollers, "That's okay, Mum, I didn't mean to scare you."

Another new development since last time: this exaggerated startling, a phenomenon surely brought on by the combination of Blake's death and Dorie's resulting solitude, not to mention her increasing hearing loss. They've been together barely two days, and already Dorie's terrorized leaps and grabs (the counter, the table, the doorframe, herself) are getting on Jen's nerves. Maybe she should take to calling the landline from her cell before emerging from her room, in order to give fair warning that she's heading Dorie's way and about to make landfall in the kitchen. It's either that, or get out the Naked Grape earlier than her usual time of day.

According to a recklessly purchased plane ticket, she's here for exactly eleven of them. And the forecast is for more of same.

"Holy," she mutters as she peers at the jumble of crumbs, cannisters, banana peels, leaking tea bags, and plastic containers littering the counters. "Dorie, do you have any kind of coffee?" Not the coffee nightmare again, please Jesus. Already, screw her grand intentions, she can feel the first stirrings of her historic panic at finding herself marooned in the loudly ticking quiet of Dorie's kitchen.

"I'm not much of a coffee person," Dorie observes, her habitual reserve — part apology, part challenge — colouring her voice. She's standing in her same Southern belle dressing gown in the spot she's occupied as far back as Jen can remember, in front of the sink, whichever sink, gazing out at the winter rain as though waiting for the imminent arrival of someone long departed and sorely missed (the Meals on Wheels lady). "But there might be some of that Folgers Instant you brought down last time you were here, in with the spices way up there." She raises a knobbed and wobbling finger.

Jen turns too sharply toward the spice cupboard, and her back torques like something cruel and medieval. "Fuckin' . . . *ow*." Putting off the punishment of reaching for coffee, she stares out Dorie's spotty porthole of a front window at the incongruously festive red and green holly shining like fairy lamps in the drenched garden, at the potholed and puddled driveway, at the nearly imperceptible movement of the sagging outbuilding's weathervane. Eleven days. And it's only ten in the morning on day two, and by her own rules, she can't have her first glass until four. "Would you want a coffee, Mum, if I made you one?"

"I would," Dorie affirms coyly after being asked a second, considerably louder time, "thank you, dear. And I can hear quite well; there's no need to shout."

"Sorry, my bad."

"Your what?"

Dorie loves a cup of coffee if someone else makes it for her. She savours its — to her — slightly forbidden bouquet, and adds the milk and sugar shyly, self-consciously, as though possibly caught trespassing. But it's tea that's her default fuel and remedy, good old Red Rose stewed black in the Pyrex pot all day. "Where there's tea there's hope," she used to say, keeping alive an old wartime line. So, tea, for her, is survival and sustenance in the midst of emergency, brutality, in other words: the muddled and frightening world of her childhood. Coffee, on the other hand, is laptops and wi-fi in cozy cafes offering arty greeting cards and tempting pastries: the inscrutable world of her daughter's nowadays.

"There's a little step stool there you can use," Dorie indicates, noting Jen's lumbar discomfort. "Just make sure you put it back under the sink when you're done with it, so I'm not tripping over it in the night."

"Okay, Mum," Jen sighs, annoyed in ways she can't fathom, could never fathom. "I'll put your stool back."

"What was that?"

The God of Instant has not forsaken Jen. There's the Folgers, right where she left it two years ago, stuck hard to the far corner of the spice cupboard, and smelling like tar. Doesn't matter; she needs coffee. She scrapes two cups' worth of black and gummy crystals out of the jar, rounds up milk and sugar — she'll find somewhere to buy cream and sweetener later — and hands a mug to her mother. "I have no idea if this is going to be drinkable or not."

Dorie goes shy again. "I'm afraid I haven't a *thing* to go with it, I don't eat sweets much anymore."

"Nobody eats sweets anymore," Jen grumbles, "it's all good."

And it could be worse, it could. Thanks to the fossilized chicory taste of the Folgers, the fog is beginning to clear, the headache to dissipate. Her body, worn with travel and two nights in Dorie's bronco of a spare bed, is starting to sense the proximity of caffeine.

Today she's tackling the kitchen, that sticky tsunami of habitual accretion. As she reopens the spice cupboard door, Dorie begins to wonder where, oh where, she put the smoked paprika. She pronounces the name with a lowered voice and solemn exaggeration, a little girl demonstrating her precocious mastery of an unwieldy, and possibly dangerous new word. Where did I put the *smoked pap-ree-ka?*

"Well, if there's smoked paprika up there, I'll find it."

Inwardly, she bridles, so much for her warm and fuzzy notions about mother-daughter connection. The only reason Dorie has such a thing as smoked paprika — *if* she does — is because she went out and hunted some down after Jen was here last time, in slavish emulation. Jen is not the world's best cook — there are no bragging slogans in her Calgary galley and no reasons for any — but she has a few comfort recipes, and when she's here, she makes them. Lemon chicken. Salmon with fennel pollen. Mac and cheese with smoked paprika. "When was the last time you used it, Mum?" Mean question.

Dorie shrugs, looks away off to the side somewhere like she used to when Jen was a kid, and she was mad at Dad. The wide

Betty Boop eyes. The tightened mouth. The barely audible but deeply disappointed sigh, and always that sorrowful voice.

"This is very good coffee." She slides her cup back and forth by the ceramic handle, making wet, beady circles on the plastic tablecloth as she stares out the rain-streaked sliding doors, the deserted bird feeder; it's not hard to tell there's something on her mind, there's always something on Dorie's mind. "I hope it won't offend you if I ask – what's happening with your separation?" Payback for the smoked-paprika jibe.

And Jen does mind if she asks. She *fucking* minds. "I'm looking, but I don't see any smoked paprika." Can Dorie hear the warning in her voice? "Anyway, I'm taking a run over to Sobeys later," she adds, to throw her mother off the scent. "I can pick you some up if you'd like."

"Eh?"

"I can buy you some SMOKED PAPRIKA. TODAY. When I go to SOBEYS."

"You'll do no such a thing." Dorie tips a little more sugar into her Folgers. "You came all the way down here" (she sees the map's depiction of the route from Alberta to Nova Scotia as a perilously steep, descending slalom, not for the faint-of-heart), "and you certainly don't need to be spending your money on me now that you're here." Like a merry old elf, she lays a finger to the side of her nose. "I don't know what you like for breakfast, there's some All-Bran there, and a nice poached egg I made earlier. I hope –"

"No worries, Mum, I don't really eat breakfast." All-Bran. Thank God this time, Sunny's where the deer and the antelope roam.

Dorie sighs. "I wish you'd eat more, you're not at the age anymore, where you can –"

"Mum."

"Jenny dear, I'm just . . ."

"Fine, Mum, it's all fine. We'll have a nice dinner tonight, and I'll eat 'til I'm twenty-five."

Meals when Jen was a kid growing up in Dorie's house were optional. They were also terrible. "Boiled dinner," a wartime specialty still popular in Dorie's kitchen, featured indistinguishable knobs of vegetable and fat-clotted meat, swimming in a greasy soup; Kraft Dinner with a side of wizened wieners; green-tinged boot soles of beef liver leather-fried with onions and served with what Dorie called "the traditional three vegetables": punky carrots and squishy grey peas out of a can, paired with disintegrating, overboiled potatoes, and followed with the reliable and relieving mug of strong tea. The Maritime way. You never knew until the last minute what was on the menu. Asked, Dorie would shrug and infuriatingly reply, "Oun't know."

What both of them do know: Dorie could care less about smoked paprika, then or now.

"I just think there has to be something very wrong, something truly wrong, for people who have perfectly good lives to end a marriage, that's all." It's day six. The clocks tick. The rain shows no sign of stopping. How do people stand to live here? How did Jen ever? Looking out the bleary kitchen window she feels like that Biblical character — was it Ruth? — who worked as a husbandless gleaner in fields not familiar: homesick. In the very place that once was home. "I guess it must have been my fault," Dorie adds darkly, "I must not have been a very good mother." She sips, yawns, follows the mailman's damp arrival. "I mean, once you take a step like that, it's very hard to take it back, is all. And I know you live in a big city and all that, dear, and that up there nobody cares, but divorce does . . . affect things."

She means reputations, bank accounts, children. Lives down the drain. Entirely unnecessary, self-induced folly. In other words: hers truly.

Jen shuts the cupboard door more firmly than she meant to. "I would've thought you'd be over that by now, Mum, after all, it's not as if it's the first . . ."

"Nor the second." Dorie sniffs, then stifles another yawn. "But you and Ian have a daughter together. Even if she's not his biological daughter, that's—"

"Yes, that's a huge commitment. And both of us have taken that commitment seriously. Come to that, so has their biological father, it's not like they're lacking in caring parents."

Dorie's expression suggests that caring parents is just what Sunny/Lake does lack. "I just can't help wondering . . ." She trails off, gazing out at the rain.

"What, Mum, spill it."

"Well, since you asked . . ."

"I didn't, but I guess you're going to tell. You can't help wondering what?"

"I mean, if Sunny hadn't had so much disruption, if maybe she—"

"It's 'Lake,' Mum, actually, their name is Lake, like we talked about, and their pronouns are they/them." (Cruel. Jen knows she's being cruel, but what is Dorie being? Herself, merely, is that so terrible?) "I'm sorry. I know it isn't easy, this whole thing, finish your sentence."

"Well, if she—if *they*—hadn't had so much commotion in the parent department, maybe she—maybe *they*—might not have to do what she did. Oh, Lord, what *they* did."

"The transition, I guess you mean."

"Yes, that. I mean, all your men were good people in their way, maybe if you'd stayed with one of them and tried to make it work —"

A surge of rage jumps like a bogey man in front of Jen's best effort at good sense, and she gives the cupboard door an unnecessarily firm shove. "Maybe if you *hadn't* stayed with Dad, I'd've been a little less 'disrupted' myself. If you ask me, no father's better than one that comes and goes just — when he feels like it, and doesn't give his family the time of day when he does show up." Not unlike his daughter, Jen hears her mind meanly quip. "Maybe if he'd stayed the heck away, I'd have figured out how to live in this —" Jen holds her head. "I shouldn't have said that, I'm such a lame brain, I know you did the best you could, there's no excuse —"

"Oh, here she comes," Dorie chirps, bright as a dental assistant as she fairly skips to the door for the Meals on Wheels lady. "Let's hope she's bringing more of that pretty red Jell-O with the raspberries in it that she had with her yesterday; that was some lovely. How I envy the children of today."

Dorie's own childhood began not long after Hitler was declared Chancellor, and not too much, either, before her parents managed to tie the knot. Her "illegitimate" arrival took place on New Year's Eve, while a bitter weather event was raging.

This was on the Mountain, a place (to Jen, as a child) of near-mythical horror, as opposed to the not far away — and supposedly more civilized — Valley, where she herself had been lucky enough to grow up. On the Mountain, grandmothers got burnt up in housefires; uncles were accidentally dropped off the wharf as babies, never to be the same; girls were fallen upon in fields, impregnated by family members, banished from school; husbands were rendered imbecile by alcohol; babies were delivered dead or afflicted with extra digits, cleft palates, wandering eyes, heart disease; babies were born — oh, and this was worse than all the rest of it put together — "out of wedlock."

Infants in those days were not the fashion item they are today. Even in enlightened places, you were unlikely to see them toted around to upscale cafes in cutie-pie sunglasses and designer teensy-jeans, by flamboyantly single wannabes. Infants, girl infants especially, in those days, were trouble, pure and simple. A little further along, the children they turned into, supposing they survived, were worse trouble. Far from brazenly sporting baby bumps, girls found to be unexpectedly expecting back then, especially on the Mountain, were said to be "in trouble." The best such girls could hope for would be a life of unpaid and unmarried drudgery, scorned by those more fortunate, their own children left to scratch through life as poor and dirty castaways, doomed to deaths both early and untimely.

Trouble enough, already.

"I'm taking all those old coats over to Value Village, today, okay, Mum? If I don't do it now, before I know it it'll be time to go, and they'll still all be hanging there." She sips her Folgers, which has been made considerably more appetizing by a good strong shot of Baileys. Only four more hours until she can have a glass of wine. "I can't believe I've been here eight days already; where has the time gone?"

"Time flies," Dorie hums. "Do you think you'll ever get married again?"

In the case of Dorie's mother, Elsie, a hasty marriage was arranged before Jen's grandfather went off to the war. Or—not quite a marriage, there was no time for that—but the next best thing in that age and place: a brief and expedient ritual called a "handfasting," in which the couple were ceremonially tied together with a bit of cord or, if they were lucky, ribbon, and said to be bound to each other for "a year and a day." If, after this period, the pair wished to enter into a legal union, full-on solemnization could follow. If not, they were free. It was enough to rescue the reputation of Elsie.

But it was not, and never would be, sufficiently lawyerly to save the self-esteem of Dorie, whose lifelong suffering at the discovery that she'd been born a "bastard" (another quaint but potent old-timer word) turned her to a fierce and early social—and occasionally spiritual—piety.

"Be sure your sins will find you out," she is as fond as ever of quoting in prim acknowledgement of others' misfortunes and mortifications, Jen's included, and in the Valley there was always a handy disaster—the two-timing wife next door, the United Church minister running off with the choir leader, that time Jen had two boyfriends at once and lost both as a consequence—to whom the damning Bible verse could be applied. Another thing Dorie used to like to say: "He never laid a hand on me." Meaning Blake. Never mind that Blake crammed their place with yard-sale junk; that until the day he died, he remained innocent of tax forms; that he let the house do what houses in hurricane climates are wont to do: flood and settle, run to mildew. But he did what husbands are meant to do, Dorie's always enjoyed saying with that infuriating little wink deployed, Jen is sure, to drive her crazy. "He made an honest woman of me." She can't understand how her own daughter, having three times been awarded the status of dignified legitimacy, could choose over and over to walk away from such an altar.

Telling her it's complicated doesn't seem to do a thing for her.

Dorie's cup clatters into its saucer. "All I can say is, it makes me sorry."

"Mum, do we need to keep these?" Three days to go, and she's barely made a dent in the kitchen's sixty years' worth of knick-knacks and recipe holders and multiple bowl sets and twice-used waffle irons and pristine meat grinders, and stacking whatevers, its junkety, junk, junk, junk. "Because if you don't, they're going."

"Well, dear, if you think so . . ."

"I know so. But I need to get out first. For a walk, since there's nowhere a person can run around here. I can't stand being cooped up any longer."

"You better take one of those umbrellas."

"And how about I take the rest of them to the dump."

Dorie startles, as when Jen makes her daily first appearance in the kitchen. "A lot of those umbrellas are still good."

"Mum, there's one of you and seventeen of them. How many umbrellas does one person need?"

A thing one can forget, about the Valley: no sidewalks. A thing Jen longs to forget: back spasms. A thing she can't forget, or make stop: the rain. Shoving open the least wonky item in Dorie's umbrella collection, she crabwalks down the road to the startled stares of people passing her in cars — nobody walks anywhere here — all but giving them the finger for their interest. What is the matter with her?

This place. This place is the matter with her. She stares through the blur at the poor houses along the road, with their rusting cars and rotting hay bales lolling in the yards, their sagging doorsteps on which huddle wet dogs and firewood. Massive trucks roar past as she stands in the thickening rain, covering her from head to foot in sleet and dirt. This place. Heart-catchingly beautiful, utterly impossible, redolent with everything she loves and hates; a person can't even walk on down the road without tempting fate. And now she does remember. All of it, all of why she left to begin with, never again, as things have worked out, to spend much time here. In pissed-off despair, she veers away, into a handy cemetery; at least for a few minutes the dead will give her umbrage from the splash and slop of hellbent, hurtling semis and cars. Squishing and squeaking on soaked feet, she wanders among the stones and vases and vacant-eyed angels until she comes upon Blake's grave, with its few fading plastic daffs, its ghoulish lichen, its stunning terminal line: *Dorie Longspell. 1933–*

Dorie. Annoying, impossible, infuriating, necessary Dorie. Her mother. *His wife.*

A new and unwelcome question drums suddenly louder than the rain in Jen's mind: where will such statistics be posted about her, and when?

"So tell me," Dorie says, staring, as usual, out the window. Two days before Jen's departure, the rain has finally begun to taper, and a band of watery light leaks along the ragged hem of cloud in the west, as night begins to ease its darkling net over the great trees in the yard. "I have to admit I'm curious what happened this time. I mean, marriage can be boring, but is that enough to tear your daughter's life apart over?"

"Son's, Mum. Sunny is not my daughter, remember."

"Well, I don't believe in that."

"Excuse me? You don't believe in what?"

"You know what. All that gender kaflooey the young ones are into nowadays."

"You mean, that they're being *allowed* into. By their godless parents." Jen accidentally cuts her thumb opening a fresh bottle of Cab Sauv, which makes her madder. "And wasn't it you who told me to 'set my face' to loving the Sunny I had, the same way you did with your – well, our – Sonny who died?"

"I was only –" Dorie looks down.

Jen knows she's hurt her. But right now, she's having trouble caring. Soon enough, she'll be gone, free to return to her lifelong stance of affectionate irritation and baffled regret concerning her mother. Though she knows that one of these days her damned attitude will catch up to her and find her unhouseled. When the time comes for that blank line in the graveyard to be filled. But right now, she can't think about that. "I'm going to the kitchen; can I get you anything?"

"Jenny, I never said –"

"Well, you did. Anyway, it's dinnertime; I gotta cook."

"You go right ahead and cook then, dear."

For once Dorie seems too bored or too hungry to argue, plus it's almost time for the news. The bad news. Racial intolerance and environmental disaster. People selling other people's homes out from under. COVID and starvation and depleted species, and war, war, war.

"What's on the menu tonight?"

On Jen's menu: more wine. "I think I'll do that salmon. You like salmon, right?"

"Oh, I love salmon. I surely can't afford it."

Who *can* afford it, Jen thinks irritably. Who can afford

anything? In this world, if you want salmon, you make salmon happen. "Okay, gimme half an hour."

You make salmon happen, she mimics her own mean-assed logic. A week and a half around here, and she's starting to sound just like herself.

The wine has started its mellowing work by the time she's serving dinner. That, and the fact that she'll be gone in a matter of hours. She's already thinking about that first G&T at thirty-thousand feet. "Mum, for a change, what about not watching the news tonight?"

"Eh?"

Does the "eh" mean Dorie's uncertain, or as usual, didn't hear, and is pretending she did? "How about we just have dinner," Jen yodels, "and you tell me a story."

Dorie goes still funeral statuary. She doesn't want these old doors creaked open, ached open. "Oh dear, I'm not much of a one for stories."

"Sure, you are. Tell me about the war."

"My, oh my, this salmon's lovely. What war?"

"Yours, Mum. I mean the one when you were a girl."

"Oh, you don't want to hear about all that old stuff."

"Tell me one story about when you were a girl living over on the Mountain, in the war. Just one."

"I'll take a glass of your wine, then."

"Seriously?"

Dorie does her naughty little girl look.

"Coming up." Jen wobbles out to the kitchen to her stash in the crisper, and comes back with a brand-new bottle of Frontera, her old standby, findable even here where the foxes say good night to each other, and a glass for Dorie.

"Thank you, dear. Well, there was this one night in the winter. I would've been around seven. Maybe eight. This was before the electricity come in, I remember that; I can still see those darn old shadows from the oil lamps climbing half-up the walls and ogling down at us like monsters. Phemie was maybe five at that time, and she was always scared to death of those shadows. Well, of pretty much everything, I guess."

"Poor Phemie. She had such a —"

"Your grandfather would've been away to the war a fair while by then, most of the men were gone, and the women with no one left to protect them." She sips her wine. "Ooh, that's good. And we were having one of those awful old storms we get in the fall."

"Like the one we've had the entire time I've been here."

"That's not a storm, that's just weather. You've gotten soft living up there. Anyway, trees were coming down all around and fish shacks going over, even some houses. Houses over there on that Mountain — they weren't much to begin with, if you remember."

"I remember."

"No insurance them days, either," Dorie adds, easing further into the Mountain dialect. "No social programs like today. And the boats getting destroyed where they rode at anchor, all down the bay. No night for anyone decent to be out, I can tell you."

A gust of wind rattles the windows and a chill dazzles Jen's spine. Once upon a winter's night. "Okay."

"Comes a knock on the door. A fumbling and a shoving, foolish laughter. Men, naturally." Dorie savours a bite of salmon. "My word, that's good. And the three of us holding onto each other. Our poor mother."

"Dear God. What —?"

"So, what it was, was three young fullers from around the harbour, boys we knew, been into somebody's still, and all liquored up. Took it into their heads they were going to come interfere with your grandmother and probably me and Phemie, while they were at. Imagine."

"Oh, God, did – I never –"

"No, you never knew." Dorie smiles. "There's plenty you never knew. Why would I want to tell you? A thing like that. I didn't ever want you to have to know about half of what went on over there. I'll have some more of that wine, though, just a splash." She sips, sits back in her La-Z-Boy. "But that was just how it was. If you were a woman or a girl over on that Mountain . . ."

"That's why –"

"That's why I always was after you and your sister to cover yourselves decent when you were girls, and stay the deuce out of the way." A small smile. "Though I guess it didn't work, did it. Anyway, I wasn't quite the old prude you always thought me. And I'm not now, either." She grins almost impishly. "D'I tell you I went on a date?"

"Oh my God, Mum, you didn't."

"Okay then, I didn't."

"You're impossible." Finally, the wine is starting to soften her, embolden her. "But what happened? What happened that night?"

"'Up the airy mountain.' Do you remember that little poem?"

"'Down the rushy glen.' You used to read it to me at bedtime when I was little. It kept me awake at night, thinking of –"

"The little men."

"'We daren't go a-hunting.'"

"That's right. 'For fear of little men.'"

"William Allingham."

"That's the one. Wouldn't it be something if a person could write like that."

The wine must be making further advances; Dorie's suddenly looking more bountiful than usual, more appeased, more at ease with her memories. "Well, you never saw a thing like your grandmother standing up to *them* little men. My, oh my. She drove the two of us into the bedroom, and then up she rose like a grizzly protecting her cubs, and let that bunch have it, all right. I was peeking round the curtain, I saw the whole thing, the bread knife in her hand and the look on her. I hardly could recognize my own mother."

"What happened, in the end? Did she – did they . . ."

"Oh, the silly things, they all hightailed it once they found out she knew where every darn one of them lived. But she wasn't done yet. Oh, no. Next day she takes me and Phemi, and away we went to all their houses and told their mothers on them. While they cringed in the background like the cowards they were. That was the last time they – or any more of their kind – ever come around our place, I'll tell you that." She enjoys another sip of her wine. "She was something, your grandmother was. Though I didn't know it then. Some things it takes a lifetime to know. And by the time you do know, the ones to be grateful to are gone." She yawns, stretches comfortably. "Dear me, look at the time; I usually don't stay up anywhere near this late, must be the wine. Have you seen my glasses anywhere? And you need your rest, for the plane and all."

By which Jen is to understand she won't be getting any more out of Dorie tonight. But she's not ready to quit. "So Mum, who'd you go on a date with?"

"No one you know."

"Be sure your sins'll find you out." Jen winks.

Dorie heaves herself out of her chair, with something that sounds almost like a chuckle. "That's just what I always used to say. Oh, and by the way" – she turns slowly, thoughtfully, one hand on her hip — "I had three small children back then, and one of them was Sonny, with all his problems, poor little . . . And there weren't the jobs or the services they have now, for women. I want you to know. I couldn't have gone on my own if I'd wanted to."

Thank God there's passable coffee in the house for the last morning. Also, fairly fresh raisin bran muffins, picked up at the new small variety store across from Dorie's mechanic's. Jen drove down there yesterday in the last of the bad weather, to get the car checked out for Rose, who will be driving her and Dorie to the airport tomorrow, and couldn't resist the urge to buy something; hence the muffins.

Dorie's not home, having gone off in the freshly tuned-up car, to see the woman who cuts her hair.

Without her mother in the cluttered kitchen, sadness finds Jen. The untidy counters and yard-sale knick-knacks and jolly slogans. *No bitchin' in my kitchen.* The absence of Dorie. Because she'll soon be back at her gym, she allows herself the indulgence of peanut butter on her muffin, but she pours the coffee into her travel mug and throws on one of Blake's old plaid hunting jackets, still hanging in their fuggy numbers beside the front door.

With mild annoyance, she notes that she never did manage to get around to the redundant umbrellas.

As she descends the wet steps, she notices that today her back is less tormented, that walking's not as bad. At least this time, the locals won't be wondering if they should stop and offer humanitarian aid. She walks fast, attempting to generate some warmth, her coffee breath clouding the wintery air, and soon finds herself across from the cemetery, though today she walks past it, seeing the changes in this place that once was the only place. An industrial-sized truck stop with a pizza parlour and a post office loom where she and Rose used to wait for the school bus on winter mornings; a Superstore outlet, of all things, rises like Jerusalem the Golden just down from that, and then comes an actual deli. Who knows, maybe it even carries smoked paprika. A John Deere sales centre, itself a kind of cemetery of grand, if spellbound monsters, brings up the rear.

And then it's just her, standing Ruth-like in the landscape she can remember, the small dells of evergreens, the occasional leaning barn, the sky's cold gold aslant the fields of alien corn.

POOR STORIES

FOR NORA

Now I no longer believe that people's secrets are defined and communicable, or their feelings full-blown and easy to recognize. I don't believe so.

ALICE MUNRO, "THE STONE IN THE FIELD"

Dorie never tires of telling the one about how she was born on New Year's Eve, in a real old-fashioned Maritime blizzard; Aunt Myrt, up from Halifax for the weekend, never tires of egging her on.

"Dorie, tell about how they got the doctor."

So, she launches once again into the memory, hers now by virtue of inheritance, of her father making the five-or-six-mile journey through the dark fields and woods – this was on the Mountain, just up the road from the dark churn of the Atlantic Ocean – with a horse and cutter that he would have had to borrow from someone.

By the time the doctor arrived, sometime during the bitter wee hours of the new year, Dorie was already born, but there were complications that threatened her mother's, Grandma

Elsie's, life. All of the doctor's, and everyone else's, attention had to be focused on the tear or hemorrhage or blockage that had accompanied Dorie's inopportune arrival in the world.

"They wrapped me up in a blanket and put me on the oven door that was open, to keep me warm, and forgot all about me!" proclaims Dorie, who tonight is uncommonly generous with her memories. "By the time anybody thought about me, I was blue. It's a wonder Mother and I didn't die, the pair of us!"

Jen cannot see her grandmother in this scene. The struggling infant with its long, peeling fingers and nascent nails and searching mouth she can imagine, forgotten, misplaced, and growing cold in the mortal commotion. She can see, or rather sense, the immensity of that storm waging war all around the tiny sea-battered house where the birth took place. And the patient horses, with their coats of thickened hair, standing outside in their clouds of breath. Her grandfather's long, straight movie-star nose and unruly hair, Popeye sleeves rolled to the elbows the way they are in all the pictures, sulking, smoking, over in the corner.

Other details, too: the unpleased doctor, taken from his New Year's Eve dinner to bend, instead, over the groaning, outrageous shape of Elsie, beached like a stranded whale on the kitchen table; the stolid, anxious forms of the neighbour women, called in before; the cloths and bandages, the pans of water. All of that, certainly. But the bloody details of the emergency remain hidden, shameful, a terrible mound. Jen somehow cannot bear to think of them with relation to her grandmother, with her freckled shoulders and sturdy legs, her stout and kindly, aproned belly; she needs to see something, anything, else.

"So, what about you," she asks Dorie, who any minute could catch on to what she is up to, and refuse to say another word, she's wary and unpredictable when it comes to family stuff, she will not be mocked. "What happened when they finally realized you were in trouble?"

"Well, I'm here, aren't I?"

Nobody died. Proof of this can be found in the small square sepia photos – Dorie and Jen and Aunt Myrt are looking through an old album of them, combing through them, and telling about them tonight – of Dorie and her three-years-younger sister, Euphemia.

Euphemia, Phemie. A cumbersome, unlikely, extravagant name, long as a wet Sunday, as Dorie would say, and dominated, no matter how it was said, by those drawn out, hysterical, ungovernable e's. A name always together in Jen's mind with truculence and poverty, with dimwitted undertakings, monstrous fecundity. Thanks to Phemie, Jen in her own puberty undertook a long, intermittent, and solidly unsuccessful campaign of dieting and self-mortification, with the fierce intention of avoiding breasts, hips, and all the other fleshy, smelly, hairy, dribbling, and otherwise betraying symptoms of femaleness. Casting about for ways to bring her strict plan to fruition, she hit on becoming a desert mystic (though Nova Scotia was not known for its deserts) or an emaciated intellectual. That, or dead.

In aid of her austere future, she read books by Nietzsche and Noam Chomsky, wrote bad and gloomy poetry, and made at least one earnest stab – hunkering on the roof outside her bedroom window on several rainy November nights in nothing but a raincoat – at getting pneumonia; for a while after that, she took to burning candles in her bedroom and imagining herself wimpled, devout, and possibly subject to some mysterious but tasteful wasting disease that would conveniently exempt her from the minefield of sex and its awful results, all her urges turned to prayers.

And all the while thinking: Phemie would never do this. Phemie could never be like this – and believing herself to have caused her own hardly started life, unlike Phemie's haplessly human one, to be focused, cerebral, under control.

"Where she ever got that darn name from," Myrt says good-naturedly, "I'll never know!" She means Grandma Elsie, she means *Euphemia*.

"I always thought it was because she never got to have anything fancy," muses Dorie, "so she made up for it with names."

"How does that explain yours, then?"

Dorie humps up her shoulders and looks pointedly away, lets out a so-familiar, sharp little burst of exasperated air. "You know's well as I do my name is Isadora. Same as the dancer. And long or short, it beats the pants off Myrt. Blurt. Fart."

What? Jen turns in amazement to Dorie, who darts her back a wide-eyed glare of surprise and alarm, and – lurking on her puckered lips – something else. Could it be . . . mischief?

"Dorie Carrie, *shame* on you!" crows Aunt Myrt with such outrage and delight that she comes very near to spilling the brimming teacup that is precariously balanced on her well-upholstered lap.

"*You* started it," Dorie giggles back: Dorie, who throughout Jen's entire childhood laughed little and giggled never in her hearing, and who waged holy war on all forms of impiety, especially the verbal kind, her most potent swear being the spelled-out letters – understood to stand for "shit" and to mean trouble – *S.H.Q.!*

"I'm not your garbage can," she was fond of threatening in response to any dirty verse or juicy joke brought home from a basketball game or the girls' washroom wall. "Don't you bring that stuff home *here*, to dump!"

And yet here she is, right in front of Aunt Myrt, a person of considerable dignity, saying, of all things: *fart*. A word whose cheerfully toilety connotations can no more be associated with either of these women – in disbelief Jen looks from one to the other of them – than the act itself, committed in church.

Never mind. Having betrayed herself once – the door that opened a tantalizing crack a few minutes ago has now clapped firmly shut again – Dorie is determined to make up for a moment's lost balance. "You're the one wanted to look at these old pictures, Jenny, now are we going to look at them, or aren't we?"

Girls in those old photos looked so different from the strenuous young women of today. Look at this one of Dorie and Phemie lounging – lolling – on the low, steep roof of some weathered little shed, very likely Elsie's chicken house, their generous curves arranged seductively, firm young bellies mounded under tight, side-buttoned shorts, their toes moist and rosy-looking despite the black-and-white background, trim, equine gams extending forward almost as far as the invisible photographer, whose long-gone shadow leans ghostly up the picture.

Dimpled knees. Winking cleavages. Flapper-style curls and come-hither smiles. "Those were the days," cries Myrt, "weren't they?"

And everywhere nodding and trembling and pressing all about the chicken house and the two posing girls: snapdragons, pale-green and orange, merry and startling. Of course, the photograph can't show them, but Jen knows they're there, from playing in and around that same shed so many years later, with Cal and the others. By this time Dorie was Jen's mother, Phemie was not mentioned, and on Sunday afternoons they were all – Dorie and Dad if he happened to be there, and Jen and Rose – driving up the Mountain to visit Elsie in her tiny, blue-shuttered house with its octagonal attic window, its chickens and kittens and shacky outbuildings, its car seats retired in the yard. Soon after they arrived, Jen and Rose would be sent outside with molasses sandwiches made of damp and heavy homemade bread, while the grown-ups got on with their dark conversations.

"Oh, it's some shame what's happened to the Brewster girl."

What shame? Which one? Jen and Rose leaning and listening, pressed up against the door, molasses yellow-brown and sticky on their hands.

"She's gone and got herself in trouble. Josie has. Four, five months gone already, and the father down in Dorchester for milking somebody's cow. Poor devil, he only did it to get a bit for his little brothers and sisters, they were so hungry with no money comin' in. And now he's locked up in there, and him with a little one of his own on the way. And *her* not married. That family'll never be able to hold up its head again, for the shame of it."

There it was, *shame*, that condition brought upon families by daughters and never long absent from any conversation. Pretty soon Dorie would start making ready-to-go-home noises – she hated mentions of unwanted babies, feared and deplored the fertile sabotage of women's bodies already let loose in her own family, thanks to Phemie. Likely she would be giving Dad "the look" by now.

"It don't make no odds," Elsie might say, summing up, with her mournful chuckle, everything from inconvenience to calamity. Sitting on a kitchen chair with her stout, freckled legs crossed at the ankles, her bare feet in a man's unlaced shoes, her anxious, consoling thumbs stroking her curled-in fingers: *It don't make no odds.*

"Now, where could we have been going to?" Dorie wonders aloud. She is showing Jen and Myrt a photo of herself and Phemie, this time as older girls, possibly old enough for high school, or jobs, maybe dates. They are wearing the open-toed pumps and cinched, full-skirted dresses of that time, wartime, rounded arms linked companionably behind, faces two white hearts set in clouds of dark pin-curled hair, mouths like black valentines. This time they are reclining against one of those voluptuous old cars – a Studebaker? a Roadster? (whose?) – all gleaming chrome and polished curves, grandly on display in some dirt driveway.

"I wouldn't know," says Aunt Myrt, "I wasn't spending so much time up home by then, remember?"

"Off gallivanting with the boys," Dorie says with a trace of some ancient amusement or malice.

"As if *you* weren't! What about Dougie Bennett? What about him?"

"Oh, that was just for the motorcycle, I only went with him for the ride!"

"Not how I remember it!"

"You go soak your head."

"I'll go invade your kitchen instead. I need some hot in this tea."

Dorie likes to say she's old as Methuselah. Myrt's getting up there too — and they might as well be sisters, though Myrt is actually Dorie's aunt, the sister of Jen's maternal grandfather, the one who came back ruined from the war. Because of their closeness in age, the two girls, the aunt and the niece, were constantly together as children — "we were always up to something, weren't we? My *word*, the things we did!" — until they grew up and got married, Myrt to a bad-tempered schoolteacher, Dorie to Dad, whose main claim to fame at that time was that he wasn't from the Mountain. Then came their own children and their not-similar lifestyles — Myrt had money, Dorie didn't; Myrt had boys, Dorie had Sonny who died and girls who didn't — and all the busy, distant years until the children and the husbands were gone, and they were themselves again. Nowadays Myrt's little red Omni, all the way up from city for the weekend or a holiday, is often parked in front of Dorie's porch, on which the two of them can be seen with their tea or a picking of peas to be shelled, or the photo album to be gone over, as it is with Jen, today.

"I know," says Dorie, her arthritic finger tapping the picture. "*I* know where we were going! That was that bolero Mum made Phemie for the Young People's social, the year she was fourteen and I was seventeen, up to the Baptist church! Remember that? Oh, that was that lovely grey-blue wool blend with a bit of a gold slub in it . . ."

"The one she made over from her wedding suit."

"Phemie looked like a dream in that, with her dark hair, she did so."

"Too bad she didn't stay looking that way."

"Well," says Dorie. Now it is her turn to get up and go out to the kitchen.

While she is out there, Myrt turns up a mournful, small photo of Phemie, her dress torn, hair a damp jumble, muddy tear tracks grinding down her round six-year-old cheeks. Myrt calls out to the kitchen.

"What's this one, Dorie? This one where Phemie's upset?"

Dorie comes back, takes a dark look. "Oh, that was that day she went up to the falls. The day she didn't come home for supper. I never did understand why Ma took that picture."

"Maybe to remind her."

Dinner on the Mountain was the midday meal, not the evening one (that was supper), and it might be potatoes and Swiss chard or fiddleheads, chicken or cod if they were lucky. Already plump at that age, Phemie was not one to miss her dinner, and Elsie declared she must be searched for.

This was one of those rare, clear days over on the Mountain — the trees, which were usually dim bluish shapes pressing through layers of mist were sharp as paper cutouts — and locusts were everywhere sawing the postcard-bright air, making it seem hotter. Elsie headed for the shore, hollering for Dorie to look in all the little buildings and ask the neighbours, and run to see if maybe Phemie was up in the raspberries where she sometimes went, for a snack.

Dorie did as she was told, not willingly, though dutifully poking her head into fish shacks and outhouses, asking any neighbours who were out, scratching her bare legs in the raspberry canes that grew wild along the road and up the bank.

But no Phemie.

No Phemie, and oh, the heat! Dorie had a white skin, and she burned easily; it was her habit and preference to keep to the shade at this time of day; she felt flattened, preyed upon, run to ground by the hard, hot sky.

And all for undeserving Phemie.

Now she comes out of the grabbing raspberries and down onto the road, whose cool white dust is refreshing as a birthday under the shade of the trees. Pushing her bare feet into its compact silk, Dorie gets an idea. The idea is that Phemie must surely be asleep somewhere, in her own bedroom undetected, or curled up in a beached rowboat down on the shore, or perhaps in the deep creosote-smelling hammock made out of a sail, where she has been found more than once before.

But because she is on the road to the falls, Dorie now gets a second idea. Why not go up there and lie in the grass and watch the water pound down? She does that often, though of course it is forbidden; the falls is her secret place, and she has had enough of looking for Phemie in the heat.

Along the road she goes, and over the fence and through the tall Timothy grass, now and then looking back in case anyone is out who might see, and tell on her. Twice she stops to dip her feet into the delicious trickle of water – fearsomely cold, fed by forest springs – that will soon widen and louden and join up with all the other streams and freshets that eventually thunder down into the bottomless pool far below.

Up one more hill now, careful not to step on any rocks or sharp sticks of last year's grass, and into the high, pale fields above the falls, which she can hear rushing and smashing, sending birds and gay rainbows of spray high into the air.

All this she is seeing in her mind as she makes her way to her secret place.

Then she sees something else. A pair of legs that, by their smallness and dirtiness and tender plump whiteness, she knows to be Phemie's; but where is the rest of her? Lying at a sickening tilt over the edge of the bank above the falls, her hand-me-down dress blown up over her bloomers, curly dark head dangling down.

Lulled, mesmerized, entranced by the rush, the dazzling spray, the sound.

Dorie stops dead in the hot air and the water's thunder, seeing her hypnotized sister — the bumps and bruises and little gold hairs on her familiar skin, the worn elastic around the legs of her underwear, the secret crease where her pale bottom begins — and knowing: this is forever. It's just me and Phemie and the water, and it's forever.

A negative whiteness blank as Javex is printed on the air all about Phemie, as though already she could be dead and in the past or under a wicked spell, forever now unreachable. At the same time, it is as though the spell is the only thing holding Phemie to the world; any movement or word might be all it takes to plunge her down.

Dorie remembers a family legend about a Mi'kmaq great grandfather who could approach grazing deer by crawling toward them on all fours, pretending to be an animal. She gets down on her hands and knees just like this grandfather must have done and begins to advance as slow as shade through the black-eyed Susans and wild strawberries and buttercups, until she is within reach of Phemie's sturdy ankle, on which an unfelt ant is brazenly crawling. Closer . . .

Closer . . .

Now! In one swoop, Dorie lunges, grabs, and hauls with both hands and all her body's nine-year-old strength, her heels digging in, stones and bits of moss and grass flying, sweat breaking out on her neck, the hot tree-rimmed sky spinning above her thrown-back eyes, never for one second letting go until she has wrestled her stunned and astounded sister back into this world.

For some minutes the two of them lie panting in the grass at the edge of the cliff, all the words thumped out of them.

Then, Dorie remembers herself. "Get up," she says, not trusting that some fresh calamity – a dislodged boulder sailing down from further up the rock face, or some bird of prey (eagles lived around there) or even possibly the falls itself, sending a watery claw after what it missed out on the first time – won't suddenly rise up and scoop or flatten, devour them. "Get *up*, I said!"

Phemie, beginning to divine the trouble she is in, is whimpering now, hiking up her bloomers with one hand and fondling her sunburned ear with the other as she makes her aggrieved progress through the grass and gravel back toward the road.

"Shut up!" hisses Dorie. "Just *shut* your mouth!"

Which only sets her little sister off on a genuine, spitty, open-mouthed wail.

"That's enough! It's enough I said, you button up, you *quit* that!" Dorie is grabbing grass now, ripping and firing fistfuls of grass and dirt and sticks, and anything else she can get her hands on at Phemie, who is howling and choking and threatening, despite her own uncertain moral position, to *tell*, her long black lashes matted together, snot running in two greenish streams down her pretty lip, her crying made half-comical by a wicked case of hiccups.

"You could've died," yells Dorie, "you could've died, it's a wonder you're *not* died and turned into a *stupid dumb ghost!*" She has no idea why she is carrying on like this, when mostly all she is feeling is a ferocious relief and the beginning of a lively appetite for her dinner, which she has reason to hope will be stewed chicken – the bantam went on the chopping block this morning – and a nice mess of dandelion greens with lots of vinegar, to go with.

(Phemie's actual death would not take place until decades later, and not at the edge of a cliff, but on the flat white sheets of a hospital bed following a massive heart attack, the result, no doubt, of a lifetime of stress, bad diet, childbearing, and related wear and tear. By then Jen would be addictions counselling as her marriage wobbled (again), and all the rest of it; plus, she had barely known Phemie, and Dorie said there was no need to spend the money to come all that way. These were the reasonable excuses — all true and useless — that Jen rigged up and believed in, concerning her failure to attend Phemie's commemoration.)

Just around the time of that photograph of the two of them leaning against the fancy car, Phemie would do the worst possible thing. Nine months later she would be married to Archie (no scarcity of ribald jokes about the long form of his name around this time); married also to his bad back, which steadfastly prevented him from doing any kind of serious or sustained work, and, whether she liked it or not, to his great fondness for homebrew. Plus, she would have gotten a solid start on the large family of skinny, runty, terminally unwashed children whose names, after the first two or three, Jen was never able to keep straight, and of whose rampaging, rickety visits Dorie would live, for many years, in mortal dread.

"I hope to high heaven they don't all land in here today," she would sigh half to herself back then on a Saturday morning, worriedly scanning the horizon as though watching for enemy drones. Saturday was when they would all pile into whatever borrowed or found vehicle Archie managed to get on the road and come down off the Mountain — Dorie and Rose and Jen and occasionally Dad lived in the Valley, where there were reasonable things like stores and businesses, streetlights and monuments – to do their grocery shopping, get their abscessed teeth pulled, walk around looking at things, and eventually end up at their house, by which time Archie could be counted upon to be cordially drunk and Phemie ready to put her swelling feet up in the coolness of Dorie's kitchen.

Dorie would close her eyes. This was exactly what she had tried so hard, worked so furiously, got herself married, to escape.

Too bad.

"Bo-, Su-, Lu-, Ol-," Phemie would holler cheerfully as one by one the kids (their names went all the way to Zach) piled out of the back seat of the car, "here now, you put yer shoes on, leave them roses alone, who said they belonged to you, that dog's liable to bite if you keep on runnin' at it that way, I hear you talk to your sister like that one more time, you'll get the back of my han'," all the while rocking and heaving and merrily grunting in an attempt to release her pale bulk in its faded print dress from the front seat. "Wouldja look at *that*," she would cry with the gratified gaze of a tourist returned, as her feet in their open shoes or man's bedroom slippers finally found solid ground, "they still got the same ol' cat!"

She might bring the raspberries she'd sent some of the kids out to pick that morning, or a harvesting of dulse, and always the Mountain news that Dorie had gladly missed out on.

"Barney killed he's rooster, we was up there the day he did it. Cooked it up with some them onions he's got growin' out the back there, and was it ever good!"

Joy. Real joy on her wide flushed face as she recalled the gift of the meal, its texture and its taste.

"You should see Gertie Bennett, she must be havin' twins, my Lord, she's swol' up bigger'n a blood-poisoned cat, she can't get off the bed, poor thing, Wylie's 'fraid he's going to have to take the door off when her time comes." Shaking her head sorrowfully, while enjoying Dorie's tea and watching out for misbehaving children.

"You know them clothes you brought me over the other week, the big box the church give, for the kids? I set 'em out in the room there to take a look at 'em, and the kids was so excited my hands went out *four times*, I couldn't get a grab at any of it!"

She admired the house. "Dorie, I wisht I had your talent for makin' things nice, that's the prettiest curtains I ever seen, and my oh my, don't you just keep everything some clean! Course you've got a well man and everything to do with. My poor Archie, he can't hardly lift a finger with that back of his, he got a chance at some roadwork there the other week and he wasn't no more'n started when his back give out and he had to come straight home to bed! He's a good man though, Archie, he's never laid a hand on me, no, he wouldn't hurt a fly."

"Remember how she used to always say that," groans Dorie to Myrt, "how he never laid a hand, wouldn't hurt a fly? As if *that* made everything okay." (Forgetting that she herself had on more than one occasion summarized her mostly-absent husband similarly.)

Myrt chuckles. "Oh, I remember, all right. The bar wasn't set very high, I guess you could say, over there on that Mountain."

Once, when Phemie was about to have one of her babies, Dorie magnanimously offered to take one of the older ones for a couple weeks, "to give her a break." On the assumption that Jen and Rose could keep her company and show her some Valley ways, Lilly, a girl Jen's age, as white as her name, and with long dusty brown bangs falling across her face, was the child elected. Far from appearing delighted – had Dorie expected her to be? – Lilly, that first night, had stood dumb as a deer just inside the door, her grimy face averted, as though in this way she might cause herself not to be seen, might somehow find herself returned to the safe and smelly mayhem of home.

"We'll have to get you all shined up first," said Dorie with missionary zeal, ushering the girl unceremoniously into the bathroom, from which the sound of running water – a thing unknown in Lilly's Mountain home – could soon be heard.

"Jenneee," she now sang out gaily, tossing a bundle of small grey clothes out the door, "go and find a nice outfit of yours, how about the blue pop-top and pedal-pusher set, the one with the cute little anchors embroidered on it, for Lilly to wear. Look sharp now!"

Look sharp? Jen had never before heard her mother use such a jaunty term. Dorie seemed galvanized by her staunch generosity, into some sort of jolly Reverend Mother or bustling Girl Guide leader, determined to cause, if not a miracle, at the very least a stunning transformation of Lilly from soiled, silent waif into a clean and grateful, bright, and braided girl. Was she planning to shine up Lilly's vocabulary, supposing that could be coaxed out of her in the two weeks ahead, to replace her Mountain expressions with civilized discourse, to introduce her to piano lessons – Jen was taking them, ungratefully, from an ancient lady Dorie paid in eggs – take her to church teas (another puzzling part of Jen's own preparation for life) and Sunday school in a cute little bonnet and fresh white gloves? Would Lilly gain a familiarity with the children's classics, be delighted by *The Cat in the Hat*? And suppose Dorie did accomplish all that, and Lilly bloomed and brightened, took to reading *Anne of Green Gables*, liking baths, and saying please and thank you, what then?

Jen need not have worried. Lilly made it through precisely one night in her alarmingly clean and foreign bed.

The next morning, when Dorie enquired cheerfully, what would she like for breakfast? Lilly said nothing. Her eyes were rimmed with red. Anyone could see there was a problem, but Dorie pressed on, earnestly itemizing the terrorizing bonanza of eggs and bacon and fruit and flakes and juices of various kinds and description, that were on offer in her kitchen.

Still nothing.

"Well then," said Dorie with the elaborate kindness and excellent diction that might be accorded a foreign delegation or a visitor strayed from outer space, "what do you usually like to have, at home, for breakfast?"

"Potatoes."

The word, a mere croak, was all it took to undo Lilly, who, freshly scrubbed and stricken with homesickness, looked wilder and whiter than ever in Jen's tame cotton nightie. A feral howl came out of her now, so hard and real, so unearthly and authoritative that the cat left the room, and even Dorie was subdued. That night when Dad came home from his hangout behind the butcher shop, Lilly was packed up – there was precious little to pack – and taken back up the Mountain.

"She never should've come off it in the first place,"

grunts Myrt, "but you meant well, Dorie," she adds in a hurry, "that's the main thing. And it was a help to Phemie. Or it would've been, if she'd stayed."

Dorie is unpersuaded. "It wouldn't've helped much, the state things were in up there."

Around the time of the funeral, Jen did find out, on the phone with Dorie, that Phemie had not spent her entire life, as you might have expected, in that staggering shack with no running water or electricity, up there on the Mountain. In fact, she and Archie had moved to the Valley after most of the kids had grown up and left—had, in fact, for years lived in a tidy little house not three miles away from Dorie.

Not three miles.

Did Dorie visit her, Jen wanted to know, did she and Phemie get together, now that they lived so near each other, did they have tea, exchange neighbourhood gossip, talk about old times?

No, answered Dorie in the particularly solemn way that was her sign of impending clam-up. No, they didn't.

Not ever?

Dorie made a stab at changing the subject, but Jen kept on. Showing off her city ways, her social ease and worldly superiority, she demonstrated mystification at such outworn and unnecessary shame. And she didn't stop there. She demanded to know why Dorie wouldn't want to visit her own sister from time to time, especially now that the untidy old days of babies and welfare and trips up and down the Mountain were long over?

"I just don't think she ever really liked me," Dorie mused, her gaze locked on a nearby corn field, "no, I don't believe she ever did."

Usually back then — for there could at any time be hand-me-downs to deliver, food to contribute, a new baby to visit — Jen's family were the ones who did the driving, paid the visits, their great, finned, gas-guzzling green and silver Buick lolloping over those dusty Mountain roads, Dad muttering about wear and tear, Dorie keeping an eye on Rose and Jen (and *not caring* who started it) in the rear-view mirror.

Rattling protest, the car climbed through woods and partly wooded fields, past houses painted turquoise and yellow and chocolate and pink — a child's paintbox colours, Licorice Allsorts colours (or not painted at all) with loaf-shaped metal mailboxes leaning drunkenly at the ends of lanes, and yapping mongrels, and old heaps of cars rusting in the yards.

Finally, the last rutty dirt road, *their* road, through thick bush and past cow pastures and swamps and gullies. No more houses, colourful or otherwise, along here. Plenty of trees, though, and rickety fences, and the occasional abandoned car, rusting comfortably among weeds. Then faces. Sallow, hollow, grey-white ovals hurrying forward like a bouquet of pale balloons, a band of shy ghosts. And a great many bare-footed white and dusty pale-haired versions of Lilly, frayed undershirts flapping, noses sturdily running, their mouths wide with wonderment at the size and colour and make of the car. Some of them waved and raced about, others hung upside down from trees; a couple hid behind the woodpile. Still others (how many were there? Jen could never remember) brought things — a bee in a bottle, a robin's egg, an eyeless doll — to press upon Rose, or demonstrate to Jenny.

Binny. Nancy. Lucy. Holly. As their car rolled down the final hill into the dire yard, Jen would go over all the names she could recall, as though by telling them to herself she could somehow contain, restrain their bearers, make some safe distance in which to spend the next couple of hours.

(Or — how easy it is to be satisfied, seduced by one's own phrases and cadences and tricks of comforting summary — possibly it wasn't a bit like that. Why couldn't Jen just as well, sometimes, have been pleased and eased by the bountiful greenery and the smell of woodsmoke and pine gum, taken courage from the caperings and yelps and brandishings, the splendid, ungoverned savagery of her fierce and skinny, dirty, uncountable cousins? Maybe she was secretly glad to get over there and cut loose in the bushes and up in the trees and amongst the old car engines with Danny and Bonnie and whoever, while Dad disappeared behind the woodpile with Archie, and Dorie occupied herself with Phemie and the babies and the staggering need inside that house.

Jen thinks, she does want to think, that there could have been times like that.)

—

Euphemia "Phemie" Carrie, 62, of the community of Pereaux, died Saturday, January 7, 1998, in the Annapolis Regional Hospital, Wolfville. Born in Cotter's Harbour, King's County, she was a daughter of Elsie Carrie now residing in the Evergreen Home for Extended Care, and the late Burnell Carrie. She enjoyed country and western music — who knew? — *playing darts, reading, knitting, and crocheting. She loved life and spending time with her family. She is survived by her husband of forty-eight years, Archibald; six daughters, eight sons, twenty-three grandchildren, eleven step-grandchildren, and twenty-six great grandchildren. Rest in peace, Phemie.*

The memorial service was held at the little United Church on the hill overlooking the bay, on one of those winter days when you can't tell the sky from the sea.

—

Dorie on the phone later could not say enough good things about this funeral, which apparently was acceptable, unremarkable, and well attended – "Who would ever have thought she had so many people that knew her?" – and which drew people from as far away as Halifax, all of them speaking fondly of Phemie's kindness and her generosity to her family, her way with a good joke or story, her willingness to be happy. Wealthy people were there, and respectable people, even some leaders of the community, people from away. The hymns, the flowers, the reception – "everything was done by the United Church ladies" – were all above reproach. "I don't know when I ever went to a funeral that was so . . ." Dorie paused, searching for the right word. "So . . . tasteful."

What about Phemie's children? Did she see any of them?

From Annie to Zach, the whole alphabet was there, and every one of them, despite their inauspicious beginnings, had turned into ordinary citizens with mortgages and jobs – Dorie had spoken with several bank tellers and a plumber; "and there was even some person claimed they were a writer!" – and not enough time in the day, like anybody else you might bump into at the post office, or in the lineup to pay for groceries.

"I went right up to Lilly at the reception," she beamed, "and I said, '*I* know *you!*'"

Myrt leans sideways as Dorie gets up to let the cat out. "Bet *that* made her day."

When Jen had called to discuss her non-attendance at Phemie's funeral, Dorie was cheerful, brisk, reassuring. "It's an awful long way for you to come, and you never can tell what the weather is likely to be, down around that Halifax airport at this time of year. Nobody's expecting you to be here."

What else, besides cheerfulness and good order, was Jen hearing in her mother's voice? It couldn't be. Could it? Was the new, and lighter, more confident tone she was picking up across the miles, relief? A sense, possibly felt by Dorie, that the world could accommodate her better without Phemie in it?

With the pressure off, she was free to consider the reasons she had given for staying away. To some extent, of course, they came out of that crippling old diffidence in the family – part inertia, part shame, part pure bafflement – that held all of them back from imagining that anything to do with them could be worthy of commemoration; the other thing, though, and possibly the real thing that detained her, was that she was not ready, yet, to face what Phemie's death meant, for her.

Was it regret that she had never known Phemie, never taken it upon herself, despite Dorie's disapproval, to know her? That she had never sent Phemie a birthday greeting or a Christmas card, had never dropped in to sit at her kitchen table, heard her aunt's voice on the telephone? That she didn't have the faintest clue what pleased or bored or moved or appalled her, that for most of her life, if she had met Phemie on the street, she would not have recognized her, her own blood, her mother's sister? Oh, certainly. But that was not all. Now there was the preposterous, brand-new surprise that she wasn't going to be able to know her mother through the light of Phemie. That she would never, now, get the glance of Phemie's particular, strange and familiar light shed upon the durable mystery of Dorie.

She had let herself not open that door. And now, it was closed for good.

"So," Jen asks Aunt Myrt, "what kinds of things did the two of you get up to, back then, when you were girls?" It's Myrt's last night with Dorie, Jen's last chance to get some of these stories while her mother is beguiled, by the amnesty of her old friend's ease and unorthodoxy, into telling them. The two of them are still sipping their tea, which has long since cooled, but Jen has snuck into her secret stash of Appletons. The sun is almost gone; barn swallows, swift and soundless, have come out to stitch the apricot sky, the boldest ones dipping to touch the pale water in the birdbath. A sweetness of mown grass rises from the darkening earth, where only the occasional chirp of a cricket, the distant whoosh of a car out on the highway, breaks the stillness.

"Dear oh dear," Myrt chuckles, looking over at Dorie, "remember Grammie Carrie? That time with the Holy Ghost?"

"Don't forget Oral."

Myrt shot a look at Jen. "Oral Roberts. And the hankie? Poor old Grammie, do you recall her house at all, Jenny? Were you ever in there? Were you ever in that tiny little living room of hers, with that awful old pump organ she had?"

"She loved to play her hymns," Dorie confirms.

"That's right. And don't forget the RCA."

"Oh, yes, that radio!" Myrt's bent over, laughing.

"It was half the size, again, of the room."

"Well, she had to be able to hear Oral."

"She did so. Oh, she was some sweet on him, wasn't she?"

"Remember how she used to sit there giggling and making eyes, and waving her hankie whenever he was doing his prayers'n all the rest of it?"

"Thought he was right there in the room with her!"

"He was always going on about the Holy Ghost, Oral was, telling you to open your heart and invite it into your life today, and all that rigamarole. And the choir in the background, 'Something *good* is going to hap-pen to you, hap-pen to you, this very day . . .'"

"Je-e-sus of Na-zareth . . ." chimes in Dorie surprisingly, "is pa-asing your way!"

"Oh, I'd forgot that part! Well, this one time, us girls got the idea —"

"From all that Holy Ghost nonsense, likely."

"Yes, and her not being able to see all that well."

The rum is starting to warm Jen's gut, loosen her limbs. She eggs Myrt on. "Do tell."

"Well, we decided we were going to give her a bit of a start, didn't we, Dorie."

Dorie snorts. "We should've been horsewhipped, the pair of us."

"So, Jenny, what we did, we got a couple sheets off the line this one day. Grammie'd just done a wash that morning, and all the white things flapping, that's what gave us the idea. Who thought that up, Dorie, was it you?"

"I believe so."

"And we snuck up under her living-room window, and we waited till the radio come on. Pretty soon, we could hear him loud and clear."

"Oral."

"Oral, yes, on comes Oral, with his whole business about how 'the important thing isn't the size of your faith, it's the one *behind* your faith,' and the choir singing away in the background, and us down there in the nettles under the window."

"Didn't we itch!" Dorie's giggling.

"Oh, terrible. We could hardly keep from hollering, remember? And there was nothing wrong with her ears, either."

"No, not a thing."

Myrt grins at Jen. "And we wait 'til Oral starts in with the Holy Ghost."

The two of them are laughing helplessly now, patting the

tears at the corners of their eyes, the teacups clattering in their laps.

"Then in we go, in we snuck through that awful little kitchen of hers, and we crawled along behind the furniture 'til we were right in the living room."

"We'll go to hell, the pair of us."

"You'll go first. Anyway, we kept on until we got right in behind her chair, that moldy old wingback she liked to sit in."

"Pretending to be 'the one behind' her faith, like Oral said; only, I guess we were the *two* behind her faith. Shame on us!"

"Dear me, yes. Then Jenny, what we did? We got under those sheets, and we stood ourselves in behind Grammie Carrie's chair."

"Oh, and then — weren't we the very devil? — then we started just moving back and forth real slow, toward each other and then away, thinking we must look just like a real ghost with her bad eyes, all blurry."

Dorie taps her cheek. "I don't think we even made a plan to do that part, did we? Didn't we both just get the same idea at the same time?"

"I believe we did; 'great minds.'"

"And all of a sudden she whips around and spies us."

"It's a wonder we didn't give the poor old thing heart failure!"

"And up she flies, faster than hell can scorch a feather, and takes off to the bedroom!"

"Had to get her teeth, had to put her teeth in, so she could smile real pretty for the Holy Ghost!"

"Well, when we saw that we nearly peed ourselves."

"Shame on us."

"That house was no bigger than a strawberry box, Jenny, and right up to ninety, she was spry. Back she trots with her teeth in, we barely had time to get ourselves out of there."

"I can remember like it was yesterday, the two of us running and tripping and falling in those darn old sheets, trying to get away!"

"And killing ourselves with laughing!"

"And her after us with the fly swatter when she figured out what was going on, hollering Hail Columbia."

"And the choir singing, 'Something go-od is going to happen'!"

"Dorie, you were a devil to think that one up!"

Dorie sighs. "Now she's a ghost herself, poor old Grammie. What was it she always used to say? 'Them times are gone, and the people, too.'"

"So she did," smiles Myrt, and then, "Oh Dorie, remember before Phemie took up with Archie, what a pair of beauties you two were?

"I s'pose so," says Dorie, sounding suddenly tired, possibly cross.

"She was such a picture back in those days," Myrt, continues, cheerfully ignoring the warning in Dorie's voice, "that lovely dark hair and white skin, my, oh my, didn't she have a lovely skin? And funny! I tell you, that girl could make a cat laugh."

(News, all news to Jen.)

Add this to the bulletin that, along with the poverty and the muddle and the shame, there had been fun and foolishness, beauty and shenanigans, in Dorie's childhood. That tricks had been played, memories made. That Phemie had once been funny and Dorie young, that being poor had not been altogether dire.)

"But that Archie was the death of her. Archie and his damn old back, pardon my French. And all those kids. It wasn't just once or twice I went in there and found her nursing a toddler *and* a newborn, both. Dear heavens, Dorie, what in the *world* did they have all those kids for?"

Dorie's up now collecting dishes, stretching and yawning, making going-to-bed noises. "She always used to say babies were the one thing she could have that was new."

"That's right, and soon as the littlest one could peel its own potatoes, 'member we always said, she'd start in on the next one. She never was one to complain, though, Phemie wasn't," Myrt reminds Dorie's retreating form. "She was always as pleased as punch with anything you did for her. And she'd give you the shirt off her back. Oh, she was a lovely soul."

—

Once Dad was gone for good, Rose and her wife bought Dorie one of those backyard kits you can make a little fishpond with, in your garden. Dorie added flagstones that she lugged from somewhere, to put her patio chairs on; she dug up and planted irises and lilies and other water plants that took over and thrived, almost as if the pond was real; she went on Kijiji and found ceramic statues of fantastic fish with bulging eyes and cunning smiles, such as you might see coiled at the corners of old maps, or lounging in the gardens of Versailles. The pretend pond is a sweet place to sit and have your coffee in the morning, or to watch the Mountain brooding over its dark old secrets, as the light leaves the sky.

Dorie and Jen — Myrt likes to get an early start — have just waved goodbye. They're sitting by the fishpond drinking coffee and watching the water skippers doubling themselves on the water's taut film, their slight weight a feat of suspension. In the night, rain fell as usual, at times heavily, though now the sun is out, all the world a-glitter in the soft ocean air.

"I could use a refill, Mum," yawns Jen. "Do you need anything from the house while I'm in there?"

"I'll have a little more," Dorie decides, and forgetting that her daughter isn't ten anymore, "but don't forget to watch out for that big puddle in front of the step there, you don't want to spoil your nice going-away outfit."

Jen grins, to master a rogue wave of love. "I won't forget, Mum."

In fact, standing over the puddle for old times' sake, she remembers. The trembling shape she sees in its brown far-down sky isn't the face of that little girl who was going to be remarkable. It belongs to a woman who is no longer young, and who in so many ways has done – and been – wrong. Wrong about herself and her big ideas. Wrong, times without number, about the people who have loved her. In one way or another, wrong to all the men including Ian, who nevertheless insisted by the grace of God-knows-what on returning, mayhem notwithstanding, to her life again.

(Though she carries the calm room of her childhood imagination inside her now; she's done the work, you have to. And she has survived. All things considered, maybe that's remarkable enough.)

She considers it one of her more pleasing achievements that she's never bought a wiener in her life.

Fresh Nescafe in hand, Dorie remembers something too. "Once on a winter's night when I was a very small girl, a knock came on the door."

The two regard each other.

"I believe it was around the time of my birthday, and there was a *towering* storm."

A distant coldness nudges Jen, a paranormal tingle down her arm.

"Another knock. Maybe someone in trouble." Dorie's eyes widen to show suspense. "Such things can happen, on a night like that."

Jen sips her Nescafe, offers a teasing smile. "Mum, is this another ghost story?"

Dorie ignores this effrontery, she's used to it. "Well finally, your grandfather opens the door, and in come three of the loveliest ladies you could ever imagine, asking if we were the Carries, and saying that they were members of the local branch of the I.O.D.E. I thought that must stand for some kind of elves or fairy godmothers, by the look of them."

"Oh, Mum."

"Soon as they were satisfied who we were, out they went again, how they got there to begin with on a night like that, I'll never know, and when they come back in, they were pulling on this enormous big box that it took all three of them to drag into the room."

Dorie waits for Jen to absorb this detail.

Jen watches the water skippers. "Okay . . ."

"Well, we sat and watched, we couldn't for the life of us imagine what they were up to 'til they got it open, and started reaching in. And it turned out that that box was chock-full of clothes and linens and pots and pans . . ." she smiles up at the lilac leaves, remembering, "just like Christmas! Right in the middle of that awful gale, in the dead of winter in that god-forsaken harbour.

"And there were two of the most beautiful dresses in that box, one for Phemie, and one for me. And when they lifted out those two little fairy gowns, all trimmed in lace and ribbons, and held them up in the lamplight, it was like something mysterious – oh, I can't describe it."

Jen nods; if only she had a cigarette. She hasn't smoked

since paisley Pat (whatever happened to her?) and the smoking lessons way back before grade ten, but right now, she could use one. In case Dorie's caught her woolgathering, she nods again.

"Well, we wore those dresses right to rags, Phemie and I did, but it wasn't until years later that I found out the meaning of I.O.D.E." Her gaze becomes solemn as she sets about pronouncing the unwieldy name. Slowly now, hesitantly, as though she were once again, or still, that small girl in the dark room in the "towering storm," she sounds out the expensive syllables:

"International. Order. Of the Daughters. Of the Empire."

She shakes her head, smiling to herself.

"And that was when I realized. The reason those ladies came to us that night with that box of things was because we were poor. The I.O.D.E. is a *service* organization, and that box was a donation." Her eyes widen with a kind of wonder, a tender amazement, shy triumph. As though she were offering something of great value, she adds in a voice that is almost a prayer, "We were the poor."

Jen is not sure how to answer Dorie's unusual candor, and so she is silent, imagining, instead, the enchanted garments rising and opening like some gracious species of moth, Nudoria Mundana, Acentria Euphemerella, rising and floating up into the shadowed cold to settle their alien sheen over the two amazed little girls.

Owing to Jen's slowness to respond, Dorie has recovered her customary pragmatism. "I just thought that was the kind of silly old story you'd be interested in, that's all." Her chin tipped low, she lets out a small chuckle. "Kind of like how you used to try to trick me into yours, about that awful old 'shit pile' the Van der Eckes had over there all those years; my, oh my, that thing was an eyesore."

Late as this surprising conversation came in the lives of Dorie and Jen, it was still a while before real senescence set in. The last time Jen could be with her, Dorie thought she was Phemie, and she scolded her resoundingly for going so near the falls. Jen didn't want to embarrass her mother, or to confuse her further. "I wasn't at the falls, Dorie," she said, trying to muster something that could pass for sibling irritability. "I was only down the bank, getting some gooseberries for a pie, that's all I was doin'."

"Oh well," said Dorie, for the moment satisfied. "that's where you were, then."

ACKNOWLEDGEMENTS

The following stories were previously published:

- "Armdale," in the *Maple Tree Literary Supplement*, as "Going Forward"
- "Accident," in *The Fiddlehead*
- "Pictures," in *Prism International*
- "Here and Now," in *Scarlet Leaf Review*, as "Lessons and Carols"
- "Remains," in *The New Quarterly*
- "Bright Journey," in *Queen's Quarterly*

I would like to thank my editor, Naomi Lewis, for her canny guidance and cheerful support in the making of this book.

Thank you to Kelsey Attard, for her always respectful, insightful editorial support and quick responses to all my conundrums.

Thank you also to my first and best readers, Ali Bryan and Paulo da Costa, for their great patience, fun, and insight.

Thank you, Esme, for putting up with your word maniac of a mother.

And to Jerry, there are "no words" for my gratitude every day.

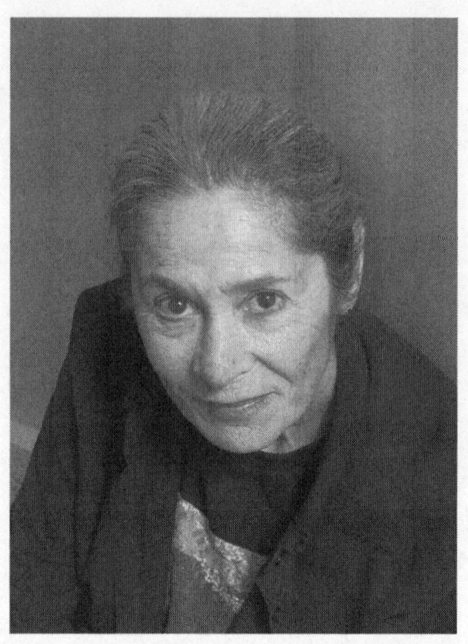

JUDITH POND was born and raised in Nova Scotia's Annapolis Valley, and currently lives in Calgary. She holds an MA in German Literature from Queen's University and an MFA in Creative Writing from the University of British Columbia. She has published both literary fiction and poetry in a wide range of Canadian literary magazines, including *Prism International, Queen's Quarterly, Scarlet Leaf Review, Maple Tree Literary Supplement, The New Quarterly, Antigonish Review, Existere, Fiddlehead Magazine, Marathon Literary Review, Prairie Fire, Event, Ryga, A Journal of Provocations, the Malahat Review*, and *Grain Magazine*. She is the author of four collections of poetry with Oberon Press and her first novel, *The Signs of No*, appeared as part of the University of Calgary Press's Brave and Brilliant literary fiction series. *That's Where You Were, Then* is her latest book.